"No, please! What can I do to appease you?
To make things right?
Just say the word and I'll do it!"

The tree-being opened its arms wide. "There is only one way. Become one with me."

Although fear seized Doc, he managed to stand up and face the glowing monstrocity. "What will happen to me?" he asked. "Will I burn up like the Chosen?"

The forest god roared. It was a horrible, anguished sound that echoed through the trees. "I consumate and consume—then I give again. That is my nature. You understand, for it's your nature, too. But I tell you this: the Chosen will be a corrupt woman, unfit and unworthy. Do you not think my trees have ears? They hear and know everything! This is the only way now. Come to me. Let us become one and set the wrong to right."

Doc shook his head. "But I'll die if you touch me."

"You don't believe you deserve death," the being bellowed, "but I say you do! I know what you did twenty years ago. You stole the Chosen from me. Have you forgotten? I never forget. Never. But she was mine in the end."

Doc hung his head. "We were in love and planned to get married. It wasn't fair—"

"I decide what's fair! You are barely fit for priesthood. Choose your fate, little man. My brothers can smell you and they are ravenous…"

THE RAVENOUS

T. M. GRAY

Black Death Books
an imprint of
KHP Industries
www.khpindustries.com

Also by T. M. Gray:
Mr. Crisper
Ghosts of Eden

THE RAVENOUS
by
T. M. Gray

Black Death Books
is an imprint of
KHP Industries
http://www.khpindustries.com

This is a work of fiction. Names, characters, places and incidents are either products of the author's imagination or are used fictitiously. Any resemblance to actual events or locales or persons, living or dead, save those clearly in the public domain, is purely coincidental.

The Ravenous Copyright © 2004 T. M. Gray

All rights reserved. No part of this work may be reproduced or transmitted in any form or by any electronic or mechanical means, including photocopying, recording or by any information storage and retrieval system, without the prior written permission of the Publisher, except for short quotes used for review or promotion. For information address the Publisher.

ISBN: 0-9747680-5-7

Cover art by KHP Studios

10 9 8 7 6 5 4 3 2 1

*For Gard Gray
Love you Dad*

Author's Note:

Grateful acknowledgement and thanks is made to Karen and Rob at Black Death Books; British author, Mark West, my partner-in-crime who graciously gave The Ravenous a second read and offered sage advice. I also want to thank my husband, Bob, my ever-faithful first reader, whose practical comments are always a great help.

While the towns surrounding Gotham Creek do indeed exist, Gotham Creek itself will not be found on any Maine map. Character names have been changed to protect the innocent.

T. M. Gray

*hide from me, this place i see
where trees cry out for blood*

"The Ravenous"
Lyrics by Edward Speers,
Performed by Skullz-N-Speers,
©2004, LostTown Records USA

1

Henry Jenkins leaned near the window as he shifted position on the yoke, initiating a graceful left bank. A thousand feet above the earth, he circled the sky over Gotham Creek, a Rockwell-picture-perfect town of tidy streets and well-groomed lawns with pretty houses in neat rows, but the woods to the northeast caught the pilot's eye, causing him to blink in disbelief.

"Holy cow, looks like the Redwood Forest down there," he murmured as he peered out the window. "They're not Sequoias, though. No...looks more like oak. The mothers of all oaks." Glancing back at the control panel, he shifted altitude to make a low sweeping pass over Gotham Creek.

Below, Route 1 cut a grey line straight by the south end of town, flanked by a string of telephone poles to the right. Main Street, narrower and lighter in hue, ran perpendicular, across Route 1, south to Addison and north to Route 9. Along the upper part of Main Street, Gotham Creek had sprung up over the years, born first around the old silver mine, then branching out to form businesses that developed from the mine's prosperity. Several side roads shot off Main Street, all at nearly right angles. Henry knew stern-hearted Yankees like himself preferred right angles to gentle curves and that most folks detested traffic circles and four-lane highways. None of the latter were found east of Augusta. Not in 1996, anyway.

He gave a toss of his shaggy grey head, his gold ball earring glinting in the sun, and flew over the forest that caught his eye.

Here great bull oaks grasped for the sky in an expanse of green covering one hundred acres or more. Henry guessed the height of the forest canopy to be in excess of 200 feet. He could barely see the trunks of those giant trees through the leaves, but to be that tall, he knew their bases would have to be immense. He figured he was probably looking at trees that had sprouted at about the same time Christ was born.

Was that even possible?

He reached down, fumbled for his map and spread it open over the instrument panel. He studied it with a trained eye and again, mumbled to himself. "Why isn't this forest part of the National Park Service? The size of those trees, man! They really ought to be protected." He refolded his map, none too delicately, and turned to look out the window again. But a spinning motion caught the corner of his eye and his glance turned forward to become a disquieted stare.

The instrument panel, in particular—the compass needle—was turning in 360-degree rotations, counterclockwise.

"What the—?" He flicked the compass with his finger, hoping to stop it from spinning. His tan brow creased as thoughts of the Bermuda Triangle came to mind.

"Flight 19," he muttered under his breath. "1945. Three more in 1967. Don't let me go down like them, please God, don't let me go down!"

The plane's left engine began to sputter as he maneuvered a right bank away from the forest but then it coughed and resumed its normal pace. Henry wiped the sweat from his brow and swerved eastward toward Lubec and the airstrip that awaited his arrival.

With one slender hand cupped over her brow, Kate Speers watched the plane soar overhead. The plane was a single-engine, probably a Cessna, a pretty red bird in a cloudless sky. *Might be sightseers,* she surmised. *Or surveyors, maybe from that map company up in Old Town. The plane's too civilian to be NARC.*

For one fleeting moment, she wished she were up there in that plane, gliding over town. To her the great wide open looked like the ultimate freedom. Then she heard the engine sputter. She watched the plane, wondering if it was going to come crashing down. Seemed there had been a lot of plane crashes in the news lately. But the small plane soon recovered and she breathed a sigh of relief as it soared away, becoming a speck in the sky. The close call reminded her that she really didn't like to fly after all.

Of course, the *only* time she'd ever been in a plane was when she was six and her family flew down to Aunt Aggie's funeral in Miami. Back then, Bangor International Airport's planes belonged to Delta Airlines, which utilized Boeing 747s and 767s. Those

Jumbo jets were more like being seated in a crowded room than in an airplane. She didn't even get a window seat. Aunt Aggie's death cast such a gloom over the excitement of travel—within five minutes after take-off, the trip had all the charm of a long Greyhound Bus ride—and Kate got so sick that she threw up in her father's lap. Her mother was holding baby Eddie, who decided that he *also* hated flying, and he began to bawl, spitting up soured milk.

Once in the sunny state of Florida, she learned that there wasn't time to go to Disney World or Universal Studios or Busch Gardens. There was only the funeral—a long procession of solemn grownups, most of them elderly—and Aunt Aggie lying in her satin-lined coffin. She remembered the horror, after her mother gently urged her to "say goodbye to Aunt Aggie." Upon intense scrutiny, she'd noticed her aunt's lips had been sewn shut. Two of the stitches, done in white floss, showed through the makeup. She was quick to point that fact out to her mother.

"Why'd they sew up her mouth, Mama? Were they afraid she might talk?"

Her mother whispered that funeral workers sew up the dead person's mouth to keep the jaw from sagging open during the funeral. "Nobody wants to see their loved ones actually *look* dead, Katie," she'd explained. "It's hard enough dealing with the grief." Kate noted the sadness in her mother's brown eyes and nodded in silence.

At ten, she'd learned that makeup hides lies.

At 19, she refused to wear it, except for a sheen of lip gloss when her mother insisted she look *special*, like at the festivals when she was proudly shown off as the first member in her family to go to college.

Not that the Speers weren't an intelligent lot—Kate came from a long line of thrifty, hard working people. Her father was a mechanic; her mother ran a nursery in the greenhouse beside the garage. Kate knew how much they scrimped and saved to pay her tuition and she was determined to make them proud—she planned for a career of working with handicapped children. She was two years away from a degree in Physical Therapy, but her grades were high; she maintained a perfect 4.0 average.

Kate watched the speck of the plane veer to the east, probably headed to Lubec or Calais. As the low hum of its engines faded out of earshot, she lowered her hand and pushed the loose sleeves of her sweatshirt back up onto her arms.

She glanced at her wristwatch; it read Sunday, October 1, 1996, 12:04 p.m. How long had she been standing there beside the road watching the plane? Too long. There were things she needed to do before returning to school Monday morning—she had to buy a new notebook for Physics 202 and copy some notes into it.

She smiled as she walked to Gotham Creek Convenience, pausing to wave at the only car which passed by, a blue sedan owned by Hettie Brown, her mother's best friend. She crossed the paved parking lot and the maypole, grimacing at the faded tatters of ribbons that waved in the breeze. *Why can't someone take them down?* she wondered. *Probably for the same reason people keep Yule wreaths hanging on their doors until they turn brown and fall apart. Too busy to bother putting away the old before bringing in the new.* With that thought in mind, she pushed open the screen door and entered the dim coolness of Gotham Creek's only store, a four-aisle mom-and-pops, which sported a large beer and soda cooler in the rear. She quickly realized that she was the only customer. Sundays were always slow here. Dead. It hadn't been very long ago that the store wasn't open on weekends. Just this year, they began selling beer on Sundays, despite the protests of many Gotham Creek residents. Behind the counter, Missy Sands gave her a friendly wave.

"Hey, Kate. How's it going?"

She waved back, making her way to the shelf where notebooks were on display, along with Scotch Tape, PaperMate Pens and dusty, plastic bottles of brown mucilage. *Who uses mucilage these days?* she wondered absently, then looked up at Missy with a smile. "I'm fine. How are things with you?"

Missy threw her hands up in disgust. "B-o-r-i-n-g. You're the second customer today. I tell you, Sundays are so dried up around here. I don't know why I can't have the day off."

Kate gave a compassionate nod and rummaged through the stack of notebooks. She preferred college to wide-lined because she could cram more notes onto college-bound pages. She selected a five-section Mead with a red plastic cover and as she pulled it from the shelf, the door opened.

Just my luck, she thought dismally as she glanced up. The third customer that day would *have* to be Norris Randolph Hymes. Norris was the same age as Kate—but that and the fact that they both were born and raised in Gotham Creek were the only similarities they shared. She instantly ducked, pretending to take great interest in the dusty stacks of typing paper on the bottom shelf, praying he wouldn't notice her.

Not that he was a bad person; rather, Norris was just plain repulsive. Kate recalled that he'd always been that way—even back in grammar school; their educations parted ways when he was held back in sixth grade and again in seventh, more for his social problems than academic failure.

He never attended high school, but turned to drugs and drinking, a wastrel. She shuddered at the memory of his pustule-pocked face, green teeth and long greasy hair. How his mother allowed him to run around looking like that astonished her; for Edith Hymes, although stern and humorless, was an impeccably well-groomed woman. Kate supposed that if she'd spawned something as awful as Norris, she just might be a colossal bitch, too. She listened to his Frankenstein boots clump toward the back of the store as he headed straight for the beer cooler.

Quickly, she stood up and darted for the counter with her notebook, laying it face down, and turning it so Missy could read the price tag on the back. "Ring me up quick; I've got a ton of stuff to do this afternoon."

Missy bit her lower lip and nodded, her hot-pink polished nails flashing over the register buttons. "$5.96," she told Kate.

She pulled six dollars out of her purse and pushed the money into Missy's hand. "Thanks. Don't bother with the change." She grabbed her notebook and had only taken one step when Norris Hymes turned the corner of the aisle and nearly knocked her over.

"Geez, Katie. Sorry about that. How's college treating you?"

She noticed his eyes zoning in on the front of her shirt and hugged her notebook, shielding her breasts. "College is great, thanks." She glanced over at Missy and gave her a helpless look. "See ya later."

Pushing past Norris, she wrinkled her nose at the way he smelled, so stale and mildewed. Downright foul. As she hurried out the door, she heard him whistle at her as he clunked his six-pack onto the counter. Outside, she broke into a power walk across the parking lot, hoping for a fast getaway.

Too late. Behind her, Norris Hymes called out, "Hey, Katie. Wait up."

Kate sighed and slowed to a stop, turning to watch him jog toward her, clutching his brown paper bag. "I'm really in a hurry, Norris."

"Want a beer? I got me a six pack. Ice cold."

She shook her head and glanced up the road. "No thanks, I really have to get going."

He gave her an injured look. "No time for an old friend?"

"Sorry, not today." She hugged her notebook to her chest again, resisting the urge to shudder at what twisted circus acts were playing behind those close-set brown eyes of his.

"But I don't hardly see you around anymore." He managed to look crestfallen.

Kate sighed again. "Look, Norris, I don't want to offend you, but I don't want to drink with you. Not today. Not ever."

He didn't appear very shocked by this revelation. With one hand, he reached into his pocket and fished out a wrinkled pack of Luckys. As he poked a bent cigarette into his mouth, his eyes lifted from her notebook to her face. "You can't mean that, Katie."

"My name's Kate. Not Katie. I'd appreciate it if you'd remember that." She saw his stare falter, his gaze dropping to the scuffed toes of his work boots. She hated being so mean to him; but he could be stubborn.

"Maybe next time, huh, Katie—I mean, uh, Kate?"

She shrugged and turned away, hoping he wasn't going to follow her like a lost puppy. After a while, she dared to give a quick glance over her shoulder. Good, he was walking away in the opposite direction, beer bag swinging in one hand and a cigarette in the other.

She might have chosen a gentler reproach, had she seen the look on his face.

The phone on the table was ringing, a high-pitched series of pulses. Sheridan picked up the receiver and placed it between his shoulder and head as he rifled through the papers in his briefcase.

"Hi—oh?" He had a Kermit-the-Frog voice and more than once had been told that he sounded like that friendly green Muppet. Sometimes, he answered the phone with 'hi—oh, Kermit here', but not today. He half expected the caller to be Emily Godfrey, calling back from the D.A.'s office.

"Sheridan? This is Billy Harris from the National Forest Service." The voice on the other end was definitely not female, but very sexy, at least to Phillips.

With elation, he set down the papers and grabbed the receiver with one hand. "Billy! How are you, champ? What's up?"

"I've got a scoop for you; I think it's a hot one."

Sheridan raised an eyebrow. "What is it?"

The man on the other end cleared his throat. "Well, it's going to sound strange, but a pilot just called us. Was going on and on about a forest. I really think you should look into it. This one might be worth fighting for."

"Why do you say that? Where is it?"

The caller paused, taking an audible breath. "North of Gotham Creek, up in Washington County, Maine. According to the pilot, they're the tallest damn trees you ever saw. Oaks big as Redwoods—"

Sheridan took the phone to the bed and sat down. "What are you saying, Billy? Oaks that size? You've got to be joking."

"I'm dead serious."

"Where's Gotham Creek?"

"Are you familiar with Washington County?"

Sheridan yawned. "Vaguely."

"Well, Gotham Creek's between Columbia Falls and Jonesboro. Take a left off Route 1 onto Main Street, the Old Creek Road. You can't miss it." The voice paused again. "You'll check into this, won't you?"

"I'll see what I can do. Hey, thanks for the tip." Sheridan hung up the phone and shook his head. "Giant oaks, my ass. Why hasn't anyone said anything about them before?"

Nevertheless, he pulled a notepad from his shirt pocket and jotted down the directions he'd been given. He chuckled to himself as he tucked the pad back into his pocket. He'd come such a long way since the mid-seventies. Now, instead of seeking out causes, causes were finding *him*.

His whole life had been a series of arguments.

Sheridan Phillips considered himself a self-invented eco-warrior. He'd spent over twenty years calling for a statewide ban of the clear-cutting of Maine's forests by paper companies. At the start of his career, there had been demonstrations, violence and jail time. Even now, people still called him "that tree-hugging granola" even though he no longer looked like a hippie. But he had a voice that people found easy to listen to (even if it did sound like a Muppet) and some of those people were lobbyists in Washington.

He was no longer an embarrassment to his parents. It took ten years for them to forgive him for dropping out of college and another five for them to back him financially. Since then, he penned two books, both conservational and controversial. *Death by Industry* had been his first, followed by *When Trees Bleed*. The right people read these books and by 1991, Sheridan was manipulating legislature.

Still, calls like the one he'd just received from Billy Harris were what made his life an adventure, firing his blood. That's why agencies like the National Forest Service hated him; he was, after all, an infiltrator and an imposter. A rebel for the cause.

He stood up and crossed the room to the table to close his briefcase. A sticker blazed across the side facing him: HAVE YOU HUGGED A TREE TODAY?

He wondered what it might be like to embrace and protect an oak as big as a redwood. Just the thought of it made him swoon.

Norris Hymes shuffled across Main Street to the parking lot of Cuffy's Restaurant. Cuffy's was a saltbox-style establishment of weathered cedar shingles and a long row of windows facing the parking lot. At lunchtime on Sunday, this was the only place in town that seemed to have any life; in fact, the parking lot was too full to warrant him going inside. It was too crowded and he'd have to sit *near* people.

Cuffy never minded him coming in; but since his death the restaurant was under the management of Mike Elwin, and it was clear to Norris that he was no longer welcome. Especially when the place was full.

Mike always treated him like shit, telling him to make friendly with soap and water. Asking him when he was going to change his duds or comb his hair. One day, he said, "Gorry, Norris, you smell just like those corpses you bury!"

That remark was just another of Elwin's little digs, Norris thought to himself, excusing the pun. Everyone knew he worked as the caretaker of Gotham Creek's Eternal Rest Cemetery. And Mike Elwin knew very well that he ran a bulldozer—the days of shoveling out every grave by hand were long buried in the past.

"Damn but I'm hungry," he remarked as he plunked down on the bumper of a pickup truck, staring at the restaurant with the same measure of longing that he'd had when he'd examined the front of Kate Speer's shirt. It wasn't his fault she was built that way, no sir. He pulled another Colt 45 from the bag between his legs and popped the top. It hissed, a most pleasant sound on this Indian Summer day.

His thoughts turned to liver smothered in onions. Cuffy always gave him liver and onions...and over time, it became his favorite meal. Cuffy fried his onions in *real* butter, not that artificial yellow crap that didn't even melt on toast. Liver and onions never tasted the same since.

So Norris treated Cuffy Sample's gravesite with special care, scrubbing away the first signs of moss on his stone. How could everyone, especially Mike Elwin, expect him to keep neat and clean all the time when he had such a dirty job? *Didn't see Elwin volunteering to help on the cemetery committee or any other committee where he might dirty his hands,* he added, wryly.

Elwin would have fainted dead away in that fancy white polyester suit of his, had he been called to do what Norris did yesterday. Moving graves was morbid work...and yet, secretly fascinating. The graves he'd moved were old, too close to the eroded edge of the creek and in danger of sliding into the water. Moving them had been tricky work, sometimes requiring a shovel.

It amazed him that corpses turn to dirt—the richest, blackest soil—after so many years. Occasionally, while shoveling, he'd come across a ring, a necklace, eyeglasses or dentures. It crossed his mind as he worked that he could take these items as booty and pawn them in Machias for a good amount of money. But that would be stealing from the dead and that just wasn't proper.

Besides, Ma would have disapproved. She made sure he had a hot supper every night and while he ate, she always exhorted the virtues of righteous living, cursing those who failed to follow the straight and narrow path, which included most of their neighbors. No, Ma would have a cow if he'd taken things from graves, of that he was certain.

He was on his third can of Colt when the door of the restaurant opened and out stepped a leggy blonde waitress. Norris couldn't remember her name, but he hadn't forgotten those legs. Or that cleavage. He watched her pause on the steps to rummage through her clutch purse. She pulled out a cigarette and sandwiched it between her glossy red lips, grimacing a bit as she flicked her lighter. Repeatedly.

Ah, a damsel in distress. He stood up and felt for his lighter in his pocket as he approached the waitress. She was the only person at Cuffy's who ever bothered to smile at him or refill his coffee without being asked. He always left her a tip, even if it was just a dime.

"Hey, you need a light?" he called out.

The waitress looked up and nodded, stepping down onto the pavement. Her hair shone like new brass in the sunlight and he couldn't help but notice the dark roots near her scalp. *Out of a bottle,* he thought, *that color came out of a bottle, sure as hell. Ma would have a heyday with that, yes sir. Any woman vain enough to dye her hair ought to be snatched bald-headed, that's what she'd say. But hair or no hair, this waitress would still be a looker.*

"Yeah, I could use a light, thanks," she said, dropping her dead lighter into her purse. She leaned forward as Norris flicked his Bic. He could smell her perfume—a mixture of baby powder and roses. Sweetly heady.

He watched her chest as she inhaled; there was a mole just over her right breast and instantly, he wanted to touch her, to bend down and kiss that mole. She straightened up and stepped back, exhaling a plume of smoke through her nose. Sexy.

"What you doing out here, Norris?" she asked, holding her cigarette between two fingers.

"I'm hungry...but the place looks full. Thought I'd wait until the lunch crowd clears out."

Little frown lines creased the waitress's brow. "It's Mike, isn't it? He treats you like crap. No, don't answer, I know what I've seen. Tell you what, working for him is no picnic, either." Her blue eyes lit up. "Look, my shift's over and I'm headed home. I could cook you up something quick. Would you like that?"

Norris blushed. "Well yes, ma'am, I guess I would.

Deidre glanced back at the restaurant, hoping she'd be seen leaving work with Norris Hymes. In the third booth, back by the window facing the parking lot, a salesman was seated—a traveler who should be quite unhappy by now at having passed up her none-too-subtle offer of companionship. And of course, Hap Kingsley was there, too, enjoying his third cup of coffee. Hap was Gotham Creek's constable and the most handsome guy in town. Pity, he was chained to Felicity—a snooty bitch who'd tried to run her out of town five years earlier and who made her existence in Gotham Creek a living hell.

How dare she call me a strumpet, Deidre thought as she squeezed the steering wheel. *What are wives really but legalized whores?*

She hoped *all* the men in the restaurant saw the desperation they'd driven her to...Norris Hymes, of all guys. The bottom of the barrel. Not that he was a bad person; he was a town employee, after all. But he wasn't very bright or clean.

She planned on changing all that.

She'd come to Gotham Creek on the arm of her third husband, a naval Petty Officer stationed in Lubec. Jerry divorced her shortly after acquiring the trailer out on Old Woods Road and got himself re-stationed in Norfolk, Virginia. She hadn't the means to leave Gotham Creek and after that first public scene with Felicity Kingsley, Mike Elwin hired her out of pity—and his undying belief that most people are genuinely good at heart. She worked at Cuffy's Restaurant ever since. Although Mike was first to admit she was a hard worker, he also dubbed her an incurable slut. 'A *nymph-O-maniac*,' he'd called her to her face.

Norris had retrieved his paper bag from the pavement beside the pickup truck and jogged over to her car—an old red Mustang. As he slid into the passenger seat, she'd turned the key in the ignition. At that moment, the radio came on. Patsy Cline's "Crazy" sounded tinny in the dashboard speakers, but she felt it suited both her situation and her life.

She flashed him a winning smile and turned up the volume as she pulled out of the parking lot.

Mike Elwin peered out the kitchen window over the fryer and shook his head, watching his waitress leave with Norris Hymes. "What can she want with him?" he asked Hap Kingsley, who was busy pouring his fourth cup of java.

Hap shrugged. "Who knows? Maybe she's just lonely." He slid the coffeepot back into its slot in the maker and tore open a pink packet of Sweet-n-Low, stirring it into his mug with a swizzle stick.

"Hard up's more like it," Mike said in a brittle tone. "I kind of hoped she'd settle down, make an honest woman of herself."

Hap shot him a grin. "You never know. She and Norris could be a match made in Heaven."

Mike shot him a humorless stare. "Yeah. Or hell."

While Deidre Garnet drove away with Norris Hymes, Kate Speer's younger brother was home, playing Tetris on the Playstation in his room. His best friend, Jess Brown, sat on the carpet beside him, watching in silent awe. Eddie was a real pinball wizard—not deaf, dumb or blind—but boasting lightning reflexes and the uncanny ability to solve most video games within hours of first trying them.

His full concentration was on the television screen as colorful blocks tumbled downward in rapid succession. He was at level 22, but didn't dare glance away to look at his score, which had to be his best yet.

Just as he reached level 23, something squeezed inside his head. It felt like a bony fist with cold steely fingers, making his sinuses pop against the vacuum it created and his ears began to ring. Over the ringing, he heard a low familiar hum.

Jess didn't realize anything was wrong until Eddie dropped the controller and leaned forward, rocking, grabbing his head with both hands. At that moment, blood trickled from his ears, spilling down onto his neck in thin watery streams.

"Eddie!" Jess grabbed his friend's arm. "Eddie, are you okay?"

He continued to rock back and forth, holding his head. "Get a towel! And hurry. You know the routine."

Jess nodded, rising to his feet, and rushed for the bathroom. He knew *the routine* all right. Eddie had such attacks often and he always tried to hide them from his parents. Jess didn't know what caused them, but they never lasted very long so he didn't think they could be all that serious. Last year, Eddie's parents took him to Bangor for an M.R.I., against the advice of old Doc Putnam. Nothing abnormal turned up on the test. No hemorrhaging, no tumors, no diseases, infections or birth defects.

Jess opened the linen closet beside the tub and pulled out a towel, which he hurried back to Eddie. Jess asked again, "You're going to be okay, right?"

He nodded, taking the towel and hanging it around his neck. "Yeah, the pain's going away. I just wish the frigging humming would stop. It drives me nuts." He dabbed the towel at the sides of his neck. "Did I get it all the blood off?"

Jess reached over and touched the towel to Eddie's right lobe. "Yeah, I think so. You'll want to clean your ears with a Q-Tip, though."

"I will." Eddie looked up at the screen and grimaced. "Just figures, this had to happen now. I think I could've beat the game."

"I know you were so close." Jess glanced at the screen, which was flashing bold-lettered words: GAME OVER.

2

Sheridan Phillips parked his dark green Volvo in the small lot in front of the Gotham Creek Town Hall. He pulled the keys from the switch and pocketed them, then opened the door and stepped from his vehicle. He gazed at his surroundings with a bit of trepidation, a nervous rabbit of a man, jingling his keys in the right front pocket of his chinos—a habit his mother had always scolded him for, but one he couldn't resist, especially when confronting something, someone or some place new.

So this was Gotham Creek.

Hardly different than any other small rural town in America. One Main Street, one store, one school. Peopled with folks who had roots going back several generations, who'd developed words and dialects only they could claim as their own. If they were fortunate, they had enough new blood moving in to keep them from becoming inbred, but Sheridan doubted it. In his opinion, Washington County was a kissing cousin to the back hills of Kentucky.

And in this place, strangers like him stood out like florescent paint.

He locked his driver's side door and turned toward the Town Hall, a one-story brick building with white clapboard trim. He crossed the lot and opened the door. The smell of over-brewed coffee and dust greeted him, indicating a pace of life slower and different from that which he was accustomed. A long counter of walnut paneling, overlaid with Formica, commanded the room. Seeing no one there, he released the door, letting it close behind him and at the noise, a head poked up from behind the counter.

"Hi—oh," he said, as he pushed his wire-framed glasses higher up the bridge of his nose.

A big red-haired man stood up and leaned a beefy elbow on the counter. "Hey there, stranger. How can I help you?"

Sheridan raised an eyebrow. "I need to do a bit of research. I assume your town maps are here."

"Of course." The man bent down, reached under the counter and pulled out a thin map book. He pushed it across to the newcomer. "You a surveyor or a realtor?"

Sheridan smiled thinly. The man had large freckles dotting his arms and hands and he'd never cared much for freckled people. "Neither." He'd pronounced his reply with a long î sound, hoping it indicated a breeding better than surveyor or realtor. He approached the counter and flipped the map book open, hardly giving another glance at the man behind the counter.

But the man behind the counter wanted to talk. "I'm Jim Digby, town manager. Been here forever, so if there's something you need to know, all you have to do is ask. Anyhow, there's some coffee in the pot, if you're interested."

Sheridan didn't look up but wrinkled his nose. "No thanks."

"You looking to buy land here?"

"I hardly think so."

Jim stepped back, rubbing at the reddish stubble on his chin. "You know, you look awfully familiar, if you don't mind my saying so. I *swear* I've seen you before, but I just can't place you."

Sheridan granted him only a hint of a smile. "I don't doubt that. I'm field agent Sheridan Phillips, National Forest Service." He pointed to the map, placing a slender index finger on the largest parcel of land in town, the northeastern woods, clearly marked as 'Tree Growth', therefore warranting a lower tax status.

"Who owns this lot?"

Jim leaned forward, eyes narrowed. "Well now, that's Doc Putnam's land."

"I need to get in touch with him immediately. Is he here in town?"

Jim nodded. "Last house on Old Woods Road. Can't miss it. Just past the trailer park. He's semi-retired so he's usually home."

Trailer park? Sheridan scratched his ear, barely hearing the rest of the sentence. *Great. Seemed every town in Maine had at least one sprawl of cheap metal homes—the rural equivalent of inner city ghettos.* He closed the map book and glanced at his Rolex. "Thank you. I'll go there right now."

"Well, nice to meet you. Hope you enjoy our little town. Say, there's a restaurant up the road, if you're hungry. Best clam fritters this side of Boston."

"I'm a strict vegetarian," Sheridan replied in a clipped tone. "Thank you for your help. I might be back later to go over the deeds."

"Well, see you later then." Jim watched Sheridan leave the building, then turned to the window to study him walking back to his car. "Sheridan Phillips, now where have I seen you before?" he asked himself aloud. As he put away the map book, an image formed in Jim's mind…television…the nightly news…not last night, nor the night before, but recently. Something about a paper mill being sued by local landowners, somewhere down near Portland. And leading the fight was a man whose name struck fear into the heart of logging corporations everywhere. A tree hugger. A granola.

"Sheridan Phillips!" Gotham Creek's town manager declared as the Volvo pulled out of the lot. "Damn! Wonder what he wants with Doc's land?"

Doc Putnam stood on his porch, stroking his beard, eyeing the approaching stranger with suspicion. "Yes, I hold the deed to these woods, clear and legal. You don't have a dispute with that, I hope. Ownership can be easily proven."

Sheridan shook his head as he looked up at the porch, a shaded monstrosity matching the rambling farmhouse of canary yellow. "No. I've come about the trees. I can see the tops of them from here. They're huge."

Doc followed his gaze. "You're right, they are. And they're listed as tree growth, just so you know. I won't give anyone permission to cut them."

At this, the stranger gave a sigh of relief. "Well, I'm glad about that. My name's Sheridan Phillips. Perhaps you've heard of me?"

Doc Putnam nodded. "Oh, I've heard of you all right. Recognized you as soon as you got out of your car. You're the one they call 'the tree hugger'."

Sheridan grimaced. "The National Forest Service sent me to examine these woods. Make sure the growth is healthy, you know, that sort of thing. Mind if I have a look around?"

Doc shrugged. The government could be a bitch if it wanted to be. "No, go ahead," he said at last, "so long as you leave those woods just as you found them. And keep an eye out for mine shafts. The ground is riddled with them."

"Of course, I'll be careful." Sheridan didn't bother to hide his offended expression.

"You'll be needing a compass," Doc added. "There's over a hundred acres out there and some of it's mighty thick. Easy to get lost in if you're not careful."

He glanced toward his car. "I'll be careful. Do you mind if I leave my Volvo in your dooryard?"

Doc smirked at the thought of that fancy little foreign car barreling over the ruts through the woods. He'd never make it out with his muffler intact—and maybe not his transmission, either. Could cost city boy a pretty penny in repairs at Speer's Garage.

But Doc was kind. "No, go ahead and leave her here." He pointed a gnarled finger at Sheridan. "I wasn't kidding about taking a compass, either. Now if it starts doing strange things, like spinning, you'd do well to high tail it right out of those woods before you get lost. The old mine left a lot of magnetized debris behind when they shut it down almost seventy years ago, and the forest is thick, easy to get lost in."

Lost! Sheridan huffed and went back to his car. After opening the trunk, he pulled out a toolbox while Doc folded his arms, watching him shut the trunk and head off into the forest without so much as another glance in his direction.

"Damned fool," Doc said, shaking his head.

An hour later, Doc looked up from his brunch of tea and scones at the first rap on his front door. "Hold on, I'm coming," he called out, rising from his chair, his joints creaking. It wasn't getting easier, moving about—his arthritis was kicking up again. Ironic, how everyone thought country doctors were supposed to be healthy. Physician, heal thyself. *Yeah, right.* He tottered to the door, trying to ignore the rusty pain screaming in his knees.

Glancing out the window, he saw Hap Kingsley's blue and white cruiser in the yard, and raised an eyebrow as he opened the door.

"Good morning, Doc," Hap said with a smile. "Felicity sent me over. She's out of tea and wondered if she could have some more. If you don't have any, there'll be hell to pay, if you know what I mean."

Doc nodded, knowing *exactly* what Hap meant. Felicity Kingsley could be meaner than cat piss, especially at her time of the month. She had one of the worst cases of PMS he'd ever treated...a hormone imbalance that turned her from a basic bitch to a murderous shrew. Believing firmly in the holistic nature of herbs rather than synthetic drugs, Doc had concocted a special tea for her, enjoyed by many of Gotham Creek's womenfolk. The tea consisted of Valerian, St. John's Wort, Kava Kava, Catnip, Spearmint and a liberal sprinkle of dried oak leaves. This mixture kept the hormones mellow, no doubt saving more than a few marriages and probably several lives.

"I always have tea for the ladies," he said, stepping aside. "Come on in and I'll get it for you."

Hap followed him into the kitchen, a high-ceilinged room with lofty cabinets and walnut-stained wainscoting dating back to the earlier part of the century. "Would you care for some brunch?" he asked, motioning toward the table at the plate of scones.

Hap shook his head. "No, I'm really in a bit of a hurry. I'm falling behind in my reports and I'll be as busy as a one-armed wallpaper hanger trying to get caught up."

Doc chuckled as he went to a cabinet over the sink and opened its door. He peered inside for a moment, then poked around its contents. "Ah, here it is." He pulled out a large tin canister marked TEA—Ladies' Special Blend. He set it on the cupboard beside the soapstone sink and pulled open a drawer below. After retrieving a Zip-lock bag, he opened the canister and filled the baggy with tea, which he zipped up and handed to Hap.

Hap held up the bag and grinned. "You know this looks illegal as hell."

Doc nodded, humorlessly. "Yep, but the Devil's Weed, it ain't. Now remind Felicity to store this in an airtight container. Otherwise, it'll lose its punch."

Hap turned to leave. "I'll tell her." Spying the Volvo out the window, he motioned with his thumb. "Say, who's your visitor?"

Doc stiffened. "He's not *my* visitor. That car belongs to Sheridan Phillips. He's doing god-knows-what out in the forest."

Hap turned to Doc, his eyes alarmed. "Sheridan Phillips? The tree-hugger?"

"Yep."

"What's he doing here in Gotham Creek?"

Doc shrugged. "I haven't the foggiest. Said he was checking something out for the National Forest Service. Might be something about the tree growth tax break, I don't know but I figured it best to let him go about his business. With any luck, he'll be on his way soon."

"Hope he doesn't get lost," Hap said, opening the door and stepping outside. He started down the porch steps, then stopped and turned back to Doc, who'd followed him as far as the front door. "Give me a call if he's not out of the woods by five."

Doc nodded. "Will do," he said, giving Hap a wave of his hand.

Old Woods. Hap thought about them as he drove back home to drop the tea off to his wife. He remembered in 1975, when his father went out there searching for a couple of lost deer hunters from Massachusetts. Nine men formed the search party, complete with police whistles, flashlights and dogs. Of those nine searchers, only two ever returned home. The deer hunters were never found and neither were Hap's father or the other missing men.

Some claimed the Old Woods were haunted.

Hap had been weaned on tales of the tree spirits that supposedly inhabited that forest. According to local legend, a band of Wabanaki hunters were camping in those woods, not long after the first arrival of European settlers. Something terrible happened there, for only one survivor made it back to what is now Old Town with a gruesome tale of vicious tree spirits that killed his party and claims that the trees themselves had *eaten* his friends.

Eaten them up alive! It was a crazy story, but still, Hap wondered what really happened to his father and the others. The only explanation that rang true involved the old silver mine, long since abandoned, at the north end of town out behind Doc Putnam's house. In its heyday, in the 1930s, workers boasted that the mine went a quarter mile underground and stretched for miles, directly under Old Woods.

He assumed that most of the mineshafts were concealed by now, with tree roots and a thick mulch of rotten leaves and twigs. It was quite possible that someone could fall down through one of these holes and die in the darkness of a long-neglected shaft.

To his knowledge, no one had ever gone into those woods alone until today.

Why Doc never posted that land was beyond his comprehension. Why he allowed anyone—especially a government man—to venture into those woods without a guide remained a mystery.

He pulled into his driveway and parked the cruiser but left the engine running. "Tree spirits," he said, shaking his head as he reached for the baggy of tea.

Norris Hymes laid back on Deidre's bed, puffing on a Lucky, filling the air with a filmy blue haze that filtered the sunshine dappling through the curtains into dusty beams of light. Over the steady sound of running water in the bathroom, he could hear her singing. Singing in the shower, the same song that had played on the radio in her car. 'Crazy' by that woman who died in a plane crash. *Who is she singing it for,* he wondered? Surely, she wasn't thinking about *him* or the physical pleasure they'd just shared. Or was she?

She hadn't been hard to please; in fact, she seemed to enjoy the things he did to her. She asked for more, even after he did her twice within the hour. That she'd insisted on wearing a blindfold didn't bother him in the least, nor did her use of velvet handcuffs.

So, the girl has a few kinks, he thought, flicking his ash into a nearly empty can of Colt. *It didn't bother her that I'm a virgin. She said next time I'll last longer. I wonder if she really came?*

He took another puff off his smoke and dropped the hot butt into the beer can, where it sizzled as it hit bottom. *A woman like her can make a man like me change his ways, that's for sure. Shower and shave once a day. Stuff like that,* he decided as he swung his hairy legs over the side of the bed. *I showered for her once; I can do it again.*

He stood up, naked, and padded down the dark narrow hall to the bathroom. "Make room, Dee," he called out at the steamy shower curtain, "I'm coming in."

Sheridan picked his way over what remained of Old Woods Road, two deep ruts twisting through the forest glade. Three-foot high seedlings sprouted between the ruts, indicating that the road hadn't been used for some time.

For the first few hundred yards, the tree growth appeared normal. More deciduous than he was used to seeing this far north, but ordinary in its development. The huge oaks, looming up in the distance, were the only indicators that all was not normal. He pushed onward, still marveling at their magnificent size.

The earth felt spongy beneath his L. L. Bean loafers as he approached the giant trees. He stopped to set his toolbox on the ground, opened it and removed a Polaroid camera. Although the forest was thick and dark, due to the canopy of leaves overhead, he trusted the auto-focus on his camera. He took several shots, after which he set the camera back in the box, along with the photos.

Approaching the thick base of the nearest oak, he pulled out his caliper. Before measuring, he carefully examined the trunk bark for signs of disease, fungus and insects.

There were none. This was the most perfect tree bark he'd ever seen but instead of being beautiful, it struck him as eerie.

Strange, there aren't any bugs, he thought with a frown. *Every tree harbors some type of insect.* He looked up, following the branches with his eyes. *Funny, I don't see or hear any birds, either. No birds, no insects. Come to think of it, I haven't seen any signs of animals of any kind. No droppings, no tracks. What's going on here? Has some sort of poison contaminated these woods? Maybe acting as steroids on the trees?*

He scratched his head, puzzled. *Why aren't fungi growing on the bark? Obviously, these trees are ancient. There should be mushrooms. And moss. Lots of it.*

He drew his caliper around the base of the tree. With a 45-foot circumference, he estimated the height to be at least 150-feet. And this was one of the *smaller* oaks. He put the caliper back into his toolbox and took out his compass.

Shaking his head, he carried the compass to the base of the oak he'd just measured, and flipped it open as he leaned back against the bark, facing the path he'd just walked. His eyes narrowed as he gazed down at the instrument in his hands.

The needle began to spin, turning counter-clockwise slowly at first, then picking up speed. "What the hell?" He tapped the face of the compass, but the needle didn't stop turning. "Must be that mine debris the old doctor mentioned." He was looking over at the place where he'd left the path, judging he could find his way back just fine, when something grabbed him from behind.

He could feel what felt like sharp fingers digging into his sides, wrapping around his arms. When he looked down, he saw these were branches, moving like snakes all around him. He struggled to free himself but in an instant he was lifted off his feet, tree limbs digging painfully into his arms and torso.

In all his work for environmental causes, Sheridan had yet to experience anything like this. A brief and vivid memory shot through his brain—the angry apple trees in The Wizard of Oz. He'd seen that movie when he was five and it scared the piss out of him.

He screamed, but no one heard him. *If a tree falls in the forest,* he thought madly, *and there's no one around to hear it, does it make a sound? What about a tree-hugger? Please, someone, please hear me! Oh, no. Oh, God, no.*

The compass tumbled from his hand to the dead leaves at the base of the tree. Blood began to fall like fat raindrops, one splatter landing on the face of the compass, streaking crimson across the glass.

The pain became worse than unbearable, squeezing, pinching his arms, legs and chest. He fought no longer to free himself; he was struggling only for air. Slowly, his movements ceased; his screams died to a whimper. There were no other sounds in the forest, except the wet snapping of his bones and the low-pitched hum of an ancient tree devouring its meal.

Kate Speers stopped brushing her teeth as soon as she spied the bloodied towel lying on top of the hamper. She opened the bathroom door and yelled with foamy lips: "Eddie! Eddie, come here. Right now." As she waited by the sink, holding the towel, she heard Eddie's footsteps in the hall.

"What's up?" he asked, then seeing the foam on his sister's lips he added, "Hey, your rabies is acting up again."

She frowned, looking every bit the mad dog, and held out the damning evidence at arm's length. "Does Mom know about this?"

He paled as soon as he saw the towel. "Oh shit, I forgot to rinse out the blood. Geez, Kate, it's no big deal."

"You didn't tell her, did you?"

Eddie shrugged, knowing he was caught. "It only lasted a minute or two. Jess was with me."

She turned away from him and ran water into the sink to rinse out her mouth and toothbrush, then washed the toothpaste from the sink. She put the stopper in and filled the basin with warm water. With a warning glance at Eddie, she plunged his towel into it and scrubbed the bloodstains with a bar of Ivory soap. "Mom *has* to know about this. Either you tell her—or I will."

He crossed his arms, looking belligerent. "Why? She'll just make a fuss and haul me off to Doc Putnam. Besides, it's just allergies. I really don't want to have to take any more of that pukey syrup-stuff he gives me."

She looked up at his reflection in the mirror over the sink. "It's for your own good, Egghead. You know that."

He nodded, rolling his eyes, trying to ignore being called Egghead, her pet name for him. "Easy for you to say. *You* don't have to take it."

"I'm just afraid for your eardrums. Promise you'll tell Mom, okay."

He unfolded his arms and held a hand behind his back, fingers crossed. "I'll tell her tonight during supper."

She smiled. "Good. Now get out of the bathroom. My first class is at ten and I have to finish getting ready."

He held out both hands, backing away with a laugh. "Hope there's a big fat spider waiting for you in the tub, Kate."

She groaned and shut the bathroom door. Eddie could be such a pain.

The ringing of the phone on the wall jarred Edith Hymes from her mid-morning tea. She got up from her chair at the table and hurried to answer it, not necessarily wanting to talk to somebody, but more to stop the damned ringing.

She picked up the phone, a yellow Slimline, and held it to her ear. Her voice was tense, unfriendly.

"Yes?"

"Hello, Edith. This is Una Potts."

"Oh, hello, Una."

There was a pause on the other end of the line. "Edith…do you know where Norris is?"

Edith frowned, wrinkles creasing across her brow. "Working, I suspect. What do you want with my boy?"

"Nothing. It's just that, well, I saw him this morning, and I was wondering: what's he doing with that Garnet woman?"

Edith's frown deepened as she tapped the countertop with her fingertips. The only Garnet woman she knew was that slut, Deidre. *Norris knows better than to associate with girls like that. Doesn't he?* "Una, what are you saying?"

Another pause. "Well, I saw him yesterday morning. Right next door. Going into her trailer. And now he's back. *Inside with her.* She's got her hillbilly music turned up so loud its rattling my teeth. Now you and I both know there's only two things people do when the music's loud—and one of them ain't dancing."

At this, Edith gasped and clutched the countertop. "Oh, no! Not my Norris! Not *my* boy. Not with that tramp."

"Sorry if it upsets you. I just thought you should know."

She muttered a thank you and set the phone back on the wall. For several minutes, she paced about her kitchen, gazing upward, holding a hand to her ample chest. "Oh, Norris, what am I going to do with you?"

3

"Do you know what I really want?" Deidre gave Norris a warm smile as she rolled over to face him. Her hair was still damp from the shower, wet gold molding to her forehead. Fool's gold.

He groaned. "No, I'm too tired to do it again. You've drained me, girl."

Her smile dropped into an instant pout. "I'm not talking about sex, Norris. Not right now, anyway. No, I mean—do you know what I really want out of life?"

He clasped his hands behind his head and gazed up at the brownish water stain on the ceiling. "I don't know. I ain't no mind reader, so why don't you tell me?"

Her hand crept up under the blanket and she played with the curly dark hair on his chest, rolling it like fleece between her fingers. "I want to be loved. Really loved. Like Romeo and Juliet. Like Anthony and Cleopatra. Napoleon and Josephine, King Edward and Wallis Simpson..."

"Who?"

Deidre rolled her eyes. "Never mind, it's not important. They were all couples very much in love. Can we be like that, do you think?"

He put an arm around her, relishing the silky smoothness of her back under his palm. "Yeah, I think we're lovers."

She raised up on her elbow and gazed into his eyes. "Getting laid and being in love are two different things. Do you love me? Really love me?"

He nodded slowly. "Yeah, Dee. I guess I do. You're the only woman in town that ever gave me the time of day. And you're real pretty, too."

"I want to be the *only* woman in your life," she told him, drawing a circle with a red-lacquered fingernail over his heart.

"Well, you are. Except for Ma, of course."

Her fingernail dug into his flesh causing him to wince. "What do you mean *except for Ma?*"

He reached out and grabbed her wrist to stop her from drawing blood. "She's my mother. I'm supposed to love her. Don't you love your mom?"

Frowning, she pulled her wrist free. "What a stupid question! I never knew my mother. She left me on a bus when I was three months old."

He looked shocked. "Geez, Dee. Who raised you?"

She blinked back the tears that threatened to spill over her lashes. "No one. Everyone. I was bounced around in foster homes until I turned seventeen. Then I ran off and married a sailor."

"Ah, that guy you first came to town with. I remember him."

"No, not him. Jerry was my *third* husband. I have a bad habit of picking guys who treat me like shit." Her lower lip trembled. "But you'll be different, won't you, Norris? You'll treat me good? And really love me?"

He reached up and stroked the side of her face. "I'll treat you good, that's a promise."

Settling down onto the bed, she lay her head on his chest and closed her eyes, smiling contentedly as she drifted off to sleep.

Norris watched her for a long time, marveling at this beauty in his arms. It wasn't everyday that a guy like him found a doll like her.

Indeed.

"Is that you, Hap?"

Hap Kingsley frowned and looked out his office window as he held the phone receiver to his ear. "Speaking. How can I help you, ma'am?" The voice on the other end was obviously female and quite upset.

"Well, this is Edith. Edith Hymes." There was a pause and Hap thought he could hear her stifle what sounded like a sob.

"What's wrong, Edith?"

"I—I need you to arrest Norris."

His eyes widened at her request. "Why? Has he hurt you?"

There was a pause again, followed by sniffles. "Well, not physically, no. But he's just about broken my heart."

"What happened?" He pulled a notepad from the top of his desk and positioned it in front of him, then waited for her reply, pencil ready just in case.

"He's sleeping with that Garnet woman!"

Hap dropped his pencil and would have laughed out loud, had it not been for the fact that laughing would have been unprofessional as well as rude. "I can't arrest your son on those charges, Edith. I can only take him into custody if the law's been broken."

The sniffles stopped. "Well, the law *has* been broken. That woman's an adulteress. Everyone in town knows it. And now she's corrupting my Norris. Besides, he doesn't have permission from the Elders."

Hap shut his eyes and reached up to pinch the bridge of his nose. He sighed, then rubbed his forehead with his fingers. "Look, Edith, I can't police morality. The situation between Norris and Deidre Garnet is beyond my control, being that they're both consenting adults. The only way I'll arrest Norris is if he breaks the law. There's really nothing anyone can do about who he's seeing. And as far as the Elders go, you know that men don't need their permission. That rule is only for the womenfolk."

She paused, then maintained, "Hap, you've known Norris all his life. Won't you please just talk some sense into him? Perhaps he'll listen to you."

He wanted to groan out loud. "Sure. Next time I see him, I'll speak to him. But I can't promise you that he'll take my advice."

"Just do your best. What with all those dreadful sex diseases out there, I'm in fear for his life."

"I understand." He opened his eyes. "Meanwhile, I'd like you to do me one favor, Edith. You really need to calm down and relax. You've been fairly lucky with Norris until now. He's never been in any real trouble. One slip won't mark him as a bad man. Maybe right now he just needs your love and understanding? Okay?"

There was no reply, except for the buzzing of a disconnected line.

Evidently, she'd hung up.

He shook his head and set the receiver into its cradle. Edith Hymes was a strange woman. She'd never been married and while there was some speculation about Norris Hymes's paternity, she'd never given any hint to the man's identity.

So what if he's sewing a few wild oats, Hap thought to himself. *Deidre Garnet isn't evil. She's just lonely. Maybe they both are.*

Still, he'd made a promise to talk to Norris and Hap Kingsley always kept his promises.

Doc glanced nervously out the window and began to fidget with the stethoscope around his neck, a nervous habit of which he was barely aware.

Phillips hadn't come out yet and the sun was beginning to set below the tree line. He looked up at the clock on the wall. It was now 4:55 p.m. Frowning, he reached for the telephone and dialed the emergency number.

"Hap? Yeah, this is Doc. Uh huh, he's still out there. Sure, I'll be here. Yep, bye." He hung up the phone and peered out the window again. The Volvo still sat out in the driveway and as he looked at it, an unexpected sadness filled his heart. *That's one car that will never be driven by its owner again.*

Moments later, he turned at the sound of gravel crunching beneath the tires of an approaching vehicle, and he hurried to open the door. Stepping out onto the porch, he waved at the cruiser pulling into the yard.

"Well, I suppose it's time to get worried now, isn't it?"

Hap poked his head out the open window of his car. "Have you yelled for him?"

Doc looked shocked. "Why no. Not yet."

"Well, that's my first suggestion." Hap turned off the engine and opened the car door. After stepping out, he reached in the back seat for his megaphone. Doc was already walking toward the woods.

"Phillips," he yelled. "Sheridan Phillips, can you hear me?"

Hap shook his head at the sound of Doc's hoarse voice. He came to stand beside Doc and raised the megaphone to his mouth.

"Sheridan Phillips—if you can hear me, come out of the woods immediately. This is an order from the Constabulary of Gotham Creek."

Together they walked around the edge of Doc's lawn, yelling for Phillips, but no one came out of the woods or shouted back a reply. Finally, Hap lowered his megaphone in defeat.

"I guess I'd better notify the National Forest Service," he told Doc. "Can't file a missing person's report—it hasn't been 24 hours yet—but it's probably best they know what's going on."

"It *will* be 24 hours tomorrow morning at 8:30," Doc told him. "That's when Phillips went into the woods. Maybe you should wait until then before making the call. Who knows? He might come out before morning."

Hap shook his head. More than anything he wanted to believe the possibility that Sheridan Phillips would emerge from the woods, but his guts told him the odds were slim to none. "I think it's best to play it straight with them," he told Doc.

"Do whatever you think best. Just bear in mind there could be consequences for getting the government involved."

Hap frowned. "It's too late. They're already involved whether we like it or not."

Doc pointed his finger at him. "Well, I don't like it one bit."

Neither did Hap, but there was little either of them could do now that the ball was rolling. All they could hope for was to maintain damage control as best they could.

"Mom, Dad, there's something I have to tell you." Eddie looked up from his plate of macaroni and cheese, and drove his fork into his green beans. Kate watched expectantly from across the table. He'd waited until his father finished griping about a camshaft on order from Portland, which hadn't yet arrived.

Silence followed and he swallowed nervously. "It happened again. My ears. The headache. I meant to tell you yesterday…but I kind of forgot. Jess was here."

His father pointed his fork at Eddie, still chewing. *Leave it to Eddie to drop a bomb at the dinner table*, he thought as he swallowed. "You mean to tell us that Jess was here and your ears started bleeding and neither of you boys could remember to tell us?"

Eddie blushed and dropped his fork. "Hey, it was no big deal. I didn't have a brain hemorrhage, so it's nothing to worry about, right?"

His mother shook her head adamantly. Her brows were knit the way they did whenever she was about to fret (or what Eddie secretly dubbed 'pitching a cow'). "We're *all* very worried about you. Doc Putnam said it might not stop, but it won't have a prayer of healing unless you take your medicine everyday." She unfolded her napkin with a wave and dabbed at the corners of her mouth with it. "Aunt Aggie had terrible allergies. Remember, Ned?" She glanced over at her husband. "But *she* took her medicine faithfully." Her gaze returned to Eddie. "That's exactly what you have to do."

He gave his mother a stricken look. "But Mom, it tastes like shit."

Immediately, the color rose to Maisie Speers's cheeks as she covered her mouth in shock, but Ned took direct action, reaching out and cuffing Eddie upside the head.

"You watch your mouth, boy! I won't have you speaking to your mother that way. Not in *my* house and not at *my* table."

Eddie looked genuinely embarrassed. "Sorry, Mom. It just tastes real bad and I don't want to take it anymore. I know *you* think it works, but all it does is make me want to hurl."

Ned turned to Maisie, who was still obviously stunned that her son had used the S-word at the dinner table. "He might have a point. I don't think he's got allergies. I know Aggie *claimed* she had them, but if you remember, she also thought she had angina, diabetes and anemia. Her doctor said she was the epitome of good health, before she walked out in front of that delivery truck. Tell you what I think. It's those damned video games. They give me a headache just hearing them. All those beeps and buzzes, they're enough to drive anyone nuts."

This stunned Eddie. "It ain't the video games, Dad."

His mother blinked, still in S-word shock but not stunned to silence. "Ain't *ain't* a word."

His father leaned back in his chair and peered at Eddie over the top of his horn-rimmed glasses. "Well, I read in the paper that some of those video games are giving kids epileptic fits. Why don't you lay off them for a while and see if you have another…well, another attack?"

He stared at his father in disbelief. "I think I'd rather take the medicine."

Ned threw his hands in the air. "Fine. Take your medicine, but you won't be playing any video games for over an hour a day. Keep it up and I'll toss the whole works right out the window, just see if I don't."

Eddie groaned and shot his sister a miserable look that said it all: *it's your fault for making me tell them. Why can't you just mind your own business?*

Kate caught the accusatory look in her brother's eyes and lowered her gaze to her plate, poking at the disks of smoked sausage, mixing them in with the macaroni and cheese.

"Well, I'm taking you back to Doc Putnam tomorrow after school," Maisie declared, breaking the silence.

Eddie groaned. "May I be excused? I'm not very hungry right now."

Ned nodded. "But no video games. If I catch you playing tonight, Jess won't be coming over for a week. Understand?"

He mumbled as he pushed away from the table. "I understand." But it was a lie. He didn't think he'd ever understand his parents. They were old, out of touch with his generation. He bolted upstairs and into his room where he slammed the door and threw himself across his bed, burying his head in his arms.

Even though he didn't think it right that a guy should cry, he released his anguish into his pillow. Below, in the dining room, he could still hear his parents' voices, but couldn't quite make out the words. Not that he really cared. He didn't want to hear them talk about him, anyway.

Kate sat back and took a sip of water, staring across the table at her father, trying to decide what to say to him. She set her glass carefully on the place mat and looked him straight in the eyes. "You were awful hard on Eddie. Suppose it's not the video games? What if it's something else?"

Ned raised a dark and bushy brow. "What else can it be? The M.R.I. found nothing. I can't afford to keep shelling money out to specialists who can't tell me what's wrong with my son. Not if you want to stay in school."

She picked up her napkin and wiped her mouth with it. "I just don't think smacking Eddie's the answer."

Her father bristled at this advice. "Look," he said in a voice that warned her that his patience had worn thin, "if *I'd* said that word at the dinner table when *I* was a kid, my father would've knocked me into next week. More than once, I've woken up in a corner. You think I'm hard on your brother, but I'm easy. Easy as pie."

She pushed away from the table and stood up. The trials and tribulations of Ned's childhood were no secret, but why couldn't he see how hard he was being on Eddie? There was little use in arguing the issue with him; she knew he was stubborn. "Excuse me, please," she said. "I've got some homework to do."

Maisie gave her a silent nod and Kate hurried upstairs to Eddie's room. She knew how sensitive he was, even if their father didn't see it. He hadn't smacked Eddie hard enough to really hurt him, but the look on his face when he'd left the table had cut Kate to the bone.

It was her fault, after all, for making Eddie tell them about his ears.

October twilight glittered with the promise of cold to come. The moon rose above the horizon, round and lemon yellow. A breeze, cool enough to raise goose bumps on the skin, rattled through the trees outside.

In his bed, Eddie Speers drifted off to sleep, recalling how Kate had come to his room to comfort him—and that had been sweet of her—but there wasn't much she could do to remedy his situation.

"Just plug your nose and think of your favorite food when you swallow the medicine," she'd suggested.

"It might turn me off from tacos forever."

She'd smiled. "Well, try it with your second favorite food first. It might work for you. I still do that every time I have to take cough syrup."

His thoughts turned strange as his mind entered the R.E.M. stage of deep slumber. In his dream, Eddie found himself surrounded by trees. Big oaks, like the ones in Old Woods, where neither he nor Jess were allowed to go.

He heard footsteps, twigs snapping and dead leaves crackling underfoot. The sounds were getting closer. He looked around, but all he saw were thick tree trunks. He crept around the nearest tree to get a better view, hoping it wasn't his father.

No, it wasn't and Eddie sighed with relief. It was a stranger with grey hair and a short bushy beard. He wore light-colored chinos and a darker shirt with a Mormon collar, buttoned at the neck. He carried a red toolbox, which he set down when he stopped walking.

The man pulled a camera from his toolbox and took some photographs. Eddie thought it strange that he took pictures of the trees. Then he put the camera away and took some kind of tool out of the box. Something disk-shaped. As soon as he began using it, Eddie knew it was a measuring device.

Why is he measuring the trees? he wondered. Didn't the man know these woods were off-limits? No one was supposed to be there.

That moment, he discovered the reason why.

The oak the man had just measured came *alive*. Animated, it grabbed the stranger with its branches, using them like hands and arms. Many arms, like the tentacles of an octopus, but with long twiggy fingers instead of suction cups. The tree lifted the man off his feet by the neck. Eddie watched in silent horror as the man kicked against the trunk of the tree, his face turning red, then purple, eyes bugging out becoming bloodshot. Then his feet hung still and a blackened tongue protruded from his open mouth.

The humming began and through the reverberations of it, Eddie heard strange words: *Héinne! An féidir le héinne cuidiú liom?*

Blood was falling on the forest floor beneath the hanging man. Just then, the oak opened up its trunk, revealing a widening gap, like a horrible elongated mouth. The branches pulled him inside that mouth and it closed around him.

Héinne! Héinne! Héinne!

Eddie crept up to the trunk of the tree, wondering how it had done that, trying to fathom the meaning of the words he'd just heard. He flinched as he saw the stranger's face, molded perfectly beneath the bark and he felt himself jump when the man opened his eyes.

Startling eyes that were the color of blood with luminous pupils glowing bright green.

The face in the bark grinned. "GAME'S OVER, EDDIE!" it screamed with shrill laughter.

At that moment, Eddie Speers woke up, startled from his nightmare and drenched in cold sweat.

It was a long time before he could get back to sleep.

A half a mile away, someone else wasn't sleeping, either.

At the edge of Old Woods, a cloaked form knelt upon a bed of dead leaves. The full moon bathed him in its cold white light. His face was painted blue and he wore an antlered hat.

And then he spoke, uttering his words with reverent care: "Sacred Forest, accept this offering. If possible for this bitter cup to pass from our community, accept the outsider as the Chosen instead of one of us. We have served you faithfully all our lives, as done by our fathers. All we have you have given us and we remain ever thankful. Please accept this sacrifice as you've accepted all others, I beseech you. It may be early for the festival, but consider those of us who guard your woods. Don't command us to drink of your bitter cup this year. May your will be ours as well. Grant me a sign of your decision and know that your will shall prevail as always..."

The cloaked figure set a sprig of mistletoe down before him and bowed his antlered head, clutching the talisman worn about his neck on a cord; a strangely shaped piece of copper, engraved with ancient symbols. He released the talisman as he stood up, and it fell back against his stethoscope.

4

Hap Kingsley tapped the eraser end of a pencil on his desk calendar. He sighed into the phone receiver, hating being put on hold, hating the generic elevator music being pumped over the line and into his ear—a musical rendition of "Honey".

He hummed along with the melody. On the second chorus, the music stopped and a voice asked, "May I help you?"

"Are you a real person or a machine?" he asked and with good reason.

Moments before, he'd been instructed to press 2, 4, 6, or 9, according to whatever he needed. Or, if he didn't have touch-tone, to wait. Figures, all he had was rotary dial, so he'd waited, listening to Bobby Goldsboro's "Honey" without the vocals.

"Oh, I'm a real person all right. Name's Ginger Curlass. How may I help you?" Her voice sounded perky, friendly. Undoubtedly, a "people-person". Strangely, Hap pictured her wearing a cheerleader's uniform, a tall, blue-eyed blonde with a picture-perfect smile. It would have surprised him to know she was short, dark-haired and Oriental.

"This is Constable Hap Kingsley from Gotham Creek," he told her, still tapping his pencil eraser. "I need to talk to someone from the Forest Service. It's important."

"Sure, I'll connect you with Janis. She's their head secretary. Hold on, this should only take a moment."

"Skip the music, okay?" he asked, but it was already too late. "Honey" was playing again. Hap tapped his pencil against his forehead, unaware that he was doing so. Then he heard the phone clicking out a ring over the line. It rung twice and was picked up.

"National Forest Service."

"Yes," Hap said, stopping his pencil mid-air. "This is Constable Hap Kingsley at Gotham Creek. One of your field agents came here the day before yesterday. We have reason to believe he's missing. I'm calling to let you know that I've released a missing person's report and a search will be conducted today."

"Who's missing?"

"Sheridan Phillips."

"Oh my God." The voice paused. "I'd better patch you through to my boss, Gerald Leighton."

"Thanks."

This time there was no generic elevator music. After a brief moment, the phone came alive again—answered by a very agitated man.

A voice full of gravel barked into Hap's ear. "Sheridan Phillips is *not* one of our field agents. In fact, he's in no way connected to the National Forest Service. That's one of his tactics, posing as an agent."

"Well, whether he is or not, we have reason to believe he's missing." Hap turned his pencil around and began to doodle on his calendar. Harsh lines, thick, dark and angular.

"Who cares? Now there's just one less nut to crack, if you ask me."

"Okay," Hap said with a sigh. "Do you know whom I should contact concerning his disappearance?"

"No, I don't. He doesn't belong to any legitimate outfit that I'm aware of."

"All right, well, thank you for your time."

The voice paused. "Wait—if you do find him, he should be arrested on the spot. Impersonating a National Forest Service field agent is breaking the law."

"I'll look into that, thanks," Hap told him, but in his guts he wasn't half as confident as he made it sound.

"Oh, and be sure to keep me updated. Not that I personally care about Phillips but I'd love to nail him on several charges. Here, I'll give you my personal number: 207-587-3479, Extension 2. If someone else answers just ask for Gerald Leighton and tell them it's an emergency."

"Will do." Hap set the receiver back in its cradle. As he did, his doodling on the calendar's upper right-hand corner caught his eye.

He didn't know it at the time, but he'd drawn trees. Huge trees.

Three men made up the search party: Hap Kingsley, Bruce Kelwick and Pat Nevels. Doc wanted to join them but he had an appointment scheduled for a patient. The search didn't begin, though, until he described the man they were looking for as being rail-thin and grey-haired, wearing a dark shirt and light-colored chinos. Then he presented each man with a large acorn strung onto a leather thong. 'Talismans,' Doc called them. The three exchanged wary glances as he insisted that they wear these as protection.

"Protection from what? I don't feel good about this," Bruce said, once they were far enough away so Doc couldn't hear them.

"Same here," Pat agreed.

Hap ignored them and pointed out the bent grass, footsteps trod between the tire ruts of the wood's road. "Looks like he stuck to the path," he said.

Bruce nodded. "But I'm willing to wager he probably left it at some point further on. Let's keep our eyes peeled."

The woods were silent and dark as the men ventured deeper into the forest.

"You can't move in with that woman." Edith crossed her arms and glared at her son with indignation; the tight set of her chin and jaw, the hard thin line of her lips told him in no uncertain terms that she was pissed.

Norris stiffened and crossed his own arms. "Well, you can't tell me what to do anymore, Ma. I'm moving out and that's that." He turned and balled up the contents of his middle drawer, dumping the whole works into a heavy-duty garbage bag with a yellow drawstring top.

"Well, I won't stand for this. I've talked to the Constable, you know. There's a warrant out for your arrest." Her lie escaped her mouth before she could stop it. Instantly, she felt the heat rise to her cheeks.

Norris stopped and turned to face her, arms extended. "What's he charging me with? I ain't done nothing wrong."

She tapped her foot impatiently. "Public indecency, I believe it's called. It's down right shameful—you shacking up with *her*. Why, oh, why couldn't you choose a *nice* girl?"

"Dee *is* a nice girl." Norris resumed packing, which pissed her off even more. She knew she had to try a new tactic. Morality, obviously, wasn't getting through to him.

Tears formed in her eyes and threatened to spill over her thin blonde lashes. "I'll be left all alone," she said in a tiny choking voice.

He looked up, his back stiff. "No, you won't, Ma. Old Woods Road ain't but five minutes away. I'll check in on you everyday."

She pointed a shaking finger at him. "You walk out that door, Norris Randolph Hymes, and you needn't be coming back. I'll disown you—I swear I will!"

He bent down and opened another drawer. "Fine, whatever."

She spun on her heel and left the room. Her fists were clenched, her mouth white with rage. Norris wasn't a little boy anymore. She'd lost control over him, but it had come on slowly, like a consuming disease. It might have started when he stopped keeping himself clean, or when he came of legal drinking age, or when he began buying those filthy nudie magazines he kept stashed under his mattress.

"I've lost him for good," she muttered to herself as she hurried to the dining room hutch; a monstrous, free-standing wooden cabinet where she kept her fine silverware, linen napkins, Irish lace tablecloth—and handgun.

She opened the middle drawer and reached for the gun. It felt cold against her palm and fingers, a nasty little snub-nosed revolver loaded and ready for intruders. Not that she'd ever been robbed, but she read the papers and listened to the news. Nowadays, she couldn't go to bed without locking all the doors…and she couldn't rely on Norris to protect her, especially with that slut taking up his time and energy.

Wordlessly, she carried the gun to his bedroom and standing in the doorway, she lifted it with both hands, aiming it squarely at his back. Her arms trembled as she cocked back the hammer. At its metallic click, he turned, saw the gun in his mother's grip, and the color bleached out of him.

"Good god, Ma! What you doing with that gun?" He dropped his clothes at his feet.

"I won't let you leave me. Not for that hussy."

He let his jaw fall in disbelief. "You'd shoot me? Jesus, Ma."

She nodded, tears streaming down her cheeks. "Don't you 'Jesus, Ma' me! You've left me no choice. I can't lose my son, my only child, to that man-eater slut. Oh, Norris, please reconsider. I *need* you. I love you. Don't make me do this."

He looked at his mother's face, then at the wavering handgun and searched for the right words to say. "I know you need me. I need you, too. You're not going to lose me. Just give me the gun. Come on, Ma." He approached her cautiously, hand extended.

She blinked and swallowed. "You won't go?"

He grasped her wrist and pried the gun from her hands. "Now I didn't say that. What I mean is—you're not going lose me. I'll always be your son. You'll always be my Ma." Quickly, he unloaded the gun and pocketed the bullets. He couldn't help but notice that the gun was locked on safety.

Her eyes narrowed. "You *tricked* me! I thought you were going to stay here." She pushed him away from her. "I meant what I said. If you leave, don't bother coming back."

Shaking his head, he wiped his brow with the back of his hand. "I'll be by tomorrow to check on you, Ma."

At this, she groaned and sank to the floor. Hugging her knees, she began to sing as he pocketed the gun and resumed packing.

He tried to ignore her. She'd pulled some weird stunts over the last few years, but nothing quite as strange and terrible as aiming a gun at him. And the song she began to sing—the same one he'd heard above his crib as an infant—now struck a disconcerting chord deep within.

"Rock-a-bye, baby…in the treetop, when the wind blows…"

He cleared off the top of his bureau into another bag. His change dish, his baseball and the lucky rabbit's foot—which hadn't been so lucky for the rabbit.

"…the cradle will rock…" He tried not to listen to her croaking voice as he reached into his closet for his jacket and sneakers.

"…When the bough breaks, the cradle will fall…" At that moment, the sack containing his marble collection fell from the top shelf of his closet, raining its contents to the floor. Norris tried to back away and lost his footing. He fell on his ass in front of the closet with marbles bouncing around him, reflecting glints of the afternoon sun from the window.

He shot a dark glance at his mother, who was curled up in a fetal position beside his bed. "There, I hope you're happy now."

She gave no response that she'd heard him or even seen him fall. She just continued to sing in her froggy voice "…and down will come baby, cradle and all".

"This is nuts," he remarked, managing to stand up. He snatched up the garbage bags containing his earthly belongings and went to his mother. "Goodbye, Ma. I'll stop in to see you tomorrow." He started to bend over to kiss her, then stopped himself. "See you later, okay?"

She appeared not to hear him.

After he left, she stopped singing and sat up, rubbing her elbows. "You dirty bastard," she whispered. "You're just like your father, wanting only one thing." She put her finger to her mouth and blew, "Shh. Don't tell a soul. People will talk. The bough will break and the cradle will fall. Don't tell a soul what we did in the woods…" Louder, she added, "You dirty bastard! I thought you were trying to save me. Why did you do it to me? Was it worth it?" At that, she laughed with the harsh irony of it.

Death would have been kinder than this.

"Sure, I'm serious about him." Deidre put on her apron, a short ruffled red thing that showed off her lean thighs. She gave Mike Elwin a hot glance. "You didn't think I could get serious about a guy, now did you?"

Mike blushed to the roots of his dark hair and stuck his thumbs in his belt loops. "I always figured you could get serious. But with Norris Hymes? Give me a break! I thought you had more sense than that. He's not much of a catch, Dee."

She put her hands on her hips. "Norris is sweet…and he treats me good, which is more than I can say for 99 percent of the guys I've dated and 100 percent of the jerks I married. And besides, he's young. He just needs a little grooming—"

Mike snickered. "You can say that again."

She ignored his comment. "All he needs is guidance. I can teach him a lot, and maybe, with a little luck, he'll turn out to be exactly the kind of man I need."

He guffawed, holding his stomach. "You'll need more than a little luck with that one. How about starting with a bar of soap and a hair cut?"

At this, she shrugged. "Think what you like, but love can work miracles. Just you wait and see."

Still chuckling, he pointed toward the dining area. "How about you wait on table four?" After she walked away from the kitchen, he shook his head as he added oil to the fryer. "Miracles, my ass."

Eddie Speers sat on the examination table in Doc's parlor, dangling his feet so the rubber heels of his Nike high-tops tapped rhythmically against the metal drawers under the table.

He glanced over at the pictures on the walls—framed paintings of trees and one of acorns, stacked like a pyramid. He'd seen these all his life and they hadn't changed over the years, nor did Doc replace them with different scenes.

A sprig of mistletoe hung over the door. Doc always cajoled his mother for a peck on the cheek whenever she brought Eddie in for a checkup, even though it was hardly ever at Yuletide.

Doc's weird, he decided, even though Doc's hands delivered him into this world and even though he'd come to check on him in the middle of a blinding snowstorm when Eddie had a fever.

This didn't mean he disliked Doc Putnam. Doc treated him kindly and never forgot his birthday. When he'd turned eight, he bought him a shiny red bicycle with license plates that had his name on them. Because of Doc's kindness, Eddie had decided long ago that someday he'd like to become a doctor himself.

But I won't be weird—and I'll have cooler pictures on my office walls, he thought to himself. *And no mistletoe hanging over the door, either.*

Doc entered the room and sat on his stool, the short one with wheels, and he rolled up beside Eddie with a boyish grin.

"Hey, Ed. Your mom tells me you've been having those episodes again. And that you don't much care for taking my syrup."

He put his hands on his knees, not wanting to upset Doc but he had to be truthful. "Well, yeah. It sucks."

Doc laughed. "Well, that's one of the kindest descriptions I've ever heard. Maybe it would interest you to know that it now comes in capsule form. Would that be better?"

"You bet it would." Eddie returned Doc's smile. "Say, what's going on? I saw the Constable's cruiser when we drove in. And Mr. Kelwick's truck. And there's a Volvo out there, too. Who's it belong to?"

A cloud passed over Doc's eyes and he turned away. "Nothing to worry about, son. Just a search. Someone's lost in the woods again, but I'm sure they'll find him soon enough."

Eddie frowned. "You sure? They never found the others."

Doc faced him, his expression cautious. "What others?"

"You know. Those guys who got lost in the woods a few years ago. The hunters—they still talk about them. And that couple who went camping in there a long time ago."

Doc gave him a serious look as he lowered his voice. "Some people don't *want* to be found, Ed. Do you know what I mean?"

"Uh uh." Eddie couldn't imagine why anyone would want to disappear.

Doc rubbed his chin in thought. "Okay, imagine you were married to a controlling woman. A real shrew, if you get my drift. Maybe the only way to get away from her and still provide for your kids would be to get lost. Disappear forever. Or maybe you owe someone a lot of money and there's no way to pay them back when they demand repayment? Who knows? If you vanish, it might be reported as an accidental death and your family would receive the insurance money. Then you've got yourself a free ticket, a clean slate so to speak, to start a new life somewhere else. See?"

Eddie shrugged. "I guess so. But there are stories about those woods."

Doc nodded gravely. "I know. But they're just stories. Not truths but well-constructed lies. Don't you believe them, Ed."

He looked up, feigning shock. "So what's the truth, then?"

The doctor raised an eyebrow. "If I tell you, you must keep it to yourself. Understand?"

Eddie nodded. He was good at keeping secrets.

Doc Putnam stood up and told Eddie to open his mouth. He talked as he checked his tonsils and ears. "Among the first settlers at Gotham Creek were the Speers, your father's ancestors, and the Putnams, who were mine. They came here with the Kingsleys, the Elwins, the Hymes and the Browns. All were from southern Britain, and these families swore a sacred oath to keep their old religion alive."

"Religion?" Eddie wondered aloud. His parents only went to church on Christmas and Easter. Church was held in the back room of the town office, the same place where votes were cast on Election Day and where the adults gathered for town meetings.

"Druidism," Doc whispered. "They worshipped the old gods and they guarded the sacred oak. They planted our forest with special acorns from their homeland."

"Sounds almost as hard to believe as the tales about those woods being haunted and the old Indian story about the man-eating trees," Eddie remarked.

Doc shook his grizzled head. "Now listen carefully and it will make *perfect* sense. Their faith started this town and the faith of their descendants continues it. Those stories were made up to keep other people, outsiders, out of our forest. Like it or not, Ed, those trees are sacred. Special. As are you."

"Huh?"

"Someday, when you're a little older, you'll understand. The woods aren't haunted, my boy. Didn't your mom ever tell you that you were born at the foot of the great bull oak? If she didn't say anything about it, she should have. I was there. I delivered you."

Eddie shot Doc a startled glance. "I was born in the Old Woods?"

Doc nodded. "Yes, as were most of us in Gotham Creek." He pushed a plastic bottle into Eddie's hand. "This is your headache medicine. I want you to take one capsule a day. Swallow it in the morning along with your orange juice. I can't promise you won't ever have another headache, but when you hear that humming noise, I want you to stop what you're doing and *listen*."

"Listen?"

The doctor turned away and opened a small cupboard. "Yes, listen to what the trees are saying to you."

"The trees?"

Doc reached up and squeezed Eddie's shoulder. "Yes. The sacred oaks. When you start hearing words, come see me. But tell no one else, not even your parents, what you hear. They'll find out when the time is right. Okay?"

Eddie gave him a doubtful glance. "Uh, I guess so."

"The future of Gotham Creek depends on you."

Eddie slid down off the table and pushed the bottle of pills into the pocket of his jacket. "Thanks for not giving me the syrup," he said as he left.

"Well, he's just not here," Pat Nevels declared, looking around. "I don't know why he'd leave his toolbox behind. Maybe something scared him?" He eyed Hap with a hint of accusation. "And if Doc had come along we might have had better luck finding him. No one knows these woods better than Doc."

Hap crossed his arms, trying not to let Pat's anger get the best of him. "Hey now, don't go blaming Doc. He said he had an appointment."

Bruce Kelwick held up the talisman worn about his neck. "I just don't understand why he insisted we wear these things. Suppose old Doc's losing his marbles?"

Hap shrugged. "He's just a bit eccentric. Look, guys, it's going to get dark soon. Evidently, Sheridan Phillips was here and wherever he went, he was in a hurry to get there."

"I bet he fell down a mineshaft," Pat suggested. "These woods are thick with them, they say."

Hap shrugged. "Maybe. But it might be, too, that Sheridan Phillips *wanted* to disappear. Could be he pissed off the wrong group of people. He's fairly outspoken, you know."

Bruce nodded in agreement as he and Pat followed Hap out of the woods. "This place is down right creepy," he mumbled so low that only Pat could hear. "Ever get the feeling like you're being watched? It's like we're intruding or something…it's almost like being in the wrong place at the wrong time. Freaks me out, you know?"

Pat shot him an uneasy glance. "You may be right; this is the wrong time to be here, no doubt about it. I think the sooner we leave, the better."

Hap pretended not to overhear, but their words struck him deep. There was something menacing about these woods and it made him wonder all the more about what happened to his father.

As they passed by the last giant oak, Hap gave an involuntary shiver.

If he'd turned and seen the face locked in the bark on the other side of its trunk, he would have run from the forest screaming.

druid \drü-id\ *n. oft. cap* [Latin: *druides*, Gaulish *druides*, from Old Irish *drui* and Old English *treow* (tree)] (circa 1500s): A wizard of ancient Celtic priesthood. A member of the tree worship cult that may have erected the megaliths of Stonehenge. See druidic, druidical, or druidism.

Eddie looked up the three latter words in his dictionary but he learned little more than he already knew. He closed the book, tossed it back on his desk and looked over at Jess.

"This is pointless. How much do *you* know about the Druids?"

Jess shrugged. "Not much. You doing a school report or something?"

"Or something."

"Why don't you try the Internet? I bet you could find a lot more about Druids online."

Eddie's eyes lit up. "Hey, great idea." He reached over and turned the computer on. Jess pulled up a chair beside him and watched as Eddie opened up Internet Explorer 3.0. He clicked on the Search button and typed 'druid' on the search bar of the MSN web page.

"Whoa, check this out. There's a lot more here than I expected." He scrolled down through the list of sites involving Druidism. There were even newsgroups for people who continued Druidic rituals and worship practices.

He clicked the link to a site that looked fairly interesting. Here he found the information he needed and Jess leaned close to him so he, too, could read the screen.

Jess gasped. "Look at that! *We* have a maypole by the convenience store. I didn't know maypoles had anything to do with Druids."

Eddie shot him a knowing glance. "Maybe more than we realize. Haven't you thought it strange that our dads put out the fires in the fireplaces every Halloween, then go out with the other men to light torches?"

"Doesn't everyone do that?"

Eddie tapped the screen with his finger. "I don't know, but look here. That's what the Druids did. They put out the fires in their hearths, then built a bonfire in the forest and performed some sacrifices. Crops, animals, maybe even people. The Romans who conquered Britain at that time claimed the Druids practiced human sacrifice. But that may have been bad press from the side of the conquerors. Whatever they sacrificed, though, they lit their torches from the fire and brought it home to light their own hearths." Eddie paused, his voice lowered. "Jess, *our* dads do this. Every Samhain festival, they bring home a torch and light a fire in the fireplace with it. Don't you realize what it means?"

Jess slowly shook his head. "Our dads are Druids?"

"Not just our dads. The whole town. Gotham Creek is a town of Druids."

"Do you think maybe they sacrifice people?"

Eddie frowned. "Ever notice anyone missing?"

Jess tapped his finger to his forehead, thinking. He was about to say 'no' when he remembered. "Yeah. Oh, yeah. Those people who got lost in the woods. They're *still* missing, aren't they?"

Eddie cocked an eyebrow. "Exactly."

Jess looked genuinely scared. "What'll we do?"

Eddie rubbed his hands together nervously. "I think we have to run away before the Festival of Samhain. That's on Halloween. That's when they'll perform a sacrifice."

"Where will we go?"

Eddie shrugged. "Cousin Mark's in Gouldsboro. That's not so far away."

"Won't he call your parents?"

"He's twenty-three—and he's real cool—and he won't say a word if we ask him not to. I bet he won't mind if we stay a couple weeks with him."

"When should we leave?"

"Tonight. We have to leave tonight." Eddie reached over and shut off his computer.

"Have you seen Eddie? He's not in his room." Ned Speer's brown eyes bore down upon his daughter, revealing an emotion caught somewhere between anger and fear.

Kate reached over and grabbed her purse off the back of a chair. "I haven't seen him since lunchtime, but I don't mind going out to look." She glanced over at her mother, obviously distraught, pacing in the living room. Outside the window, sallow light from the streetlamp fell upon a cold moonless night. Maisie looked on, shivering, tugging her bathrobe closer around her.

Kate whispered, "Stay here with Mom. Please, Dad. I'll find him, I promise."

Ned nodded, the lines on his face deepening. "Jess is gone, too. Hettie just called to let us know. We think the boys are together."

"Aren't they always?" She gave her father a peck on the cheek, then looked over at her mother. "Don't worry, I'll find them both. Maybe you'd better make Mom a cup of Doc's tea—it'll soothe her nerves."

Ned rubbed his forehead as if his temples were beginning to throb. "Yeah," was all he said before she was out the door and hurrying to her Honda hatchback that waited in the driveway.

"Okay, where'd you go, Egghead?" she asked out loud as she put the car in reverse and backed out into the dark street.

She drove slowly through all of Gotham Creek before it occurred to her that there was only one other place Eddie might have gone. Cousin Mark's home in Gouldsboro, some forty miles away. Mark was older than she and while they'd never been particularly close, he and Eddie struck a chord of friendship from the moment they'd met—when Eddie was just a toddler and Mark was a preteen.

He must be really upset with me for making him tell Mom and Dad about his ears, she reasoned as she turned onto Route 1 and headed west. *I only hope I can make it up to him.*

Jess Brown shone his flashlight in Eddie's face. "You don't look so hot," he said. "You sure you're feeling all right?"

He shielded his eyes from the blinding glare. "I'll be okay as long as we make it to Mark's house soon." Reaching into his pocket, he withdrew his pills—the ones Doc Putnam had given him earlier that afternoon. He struggled to twist off the cap.

"What's that stuff?" Jess shone the light on Eddie's hands.

"My headache medicine. I feel a bad one coming on." Jess watched as Eddie dry-swallowed a capsule.

"I've got root beer in my backpack," Jess offered, but Eddie waved him away.

"No. I'll be fine. Thanks."

He pointed a beam of light at the back of the road sign ahead. "Well, we've made it to the county line. If it hadn't been for that trucker giving us a ride, we'd still be back in Harrington."

Eddie managed a smile, which Jess didn't see because he was still looking up at the 'Sunrise County' sign. "We should be at Mark's house in an hour or so, I think." At that moment, the pain came, flooding his skull, causing him to fall to his knees and clutch his ears in agony.

Jess heard him groan and hurried to his side. "Didn't you just take the headache medicine? Why ain't it working? Maybe it's too soon, huh? Ed—are you going to be okay?"

He closed his eyes, rocking to the throbbing pain. "Listen! Can't you hear them screaming? Tell them to stop, Jess. I can't stand it!"

Jess frowned and draped his arm over his friend's back. "Make *who* stop screaming? I don't hear anything."

Eddie forced his eyes open. "You can't hear that?"

"What?"

"I don't know," he whined, his fists at his head. "Voices, lots of voices."

"What are they saying?"

He groaned again, and repeated the sounds he heard. "Héinne! Héinne! Héinne! An féidir le héinne cuidiú liom?"

Jess grimaced. "I don't hear a thing. Nothing like that, anyway. I don't even know what language that is." He felt helpless as he knelt beside Eddie in the gravel of the highway's shoulder. "Eddie, can you get up? You have to. We have to keep moving." He glanced up at the twin beam of headlights coming down the hill behind them. "Oh, shit. Here comes someone and they're slowing down. Looks like your sister's car."

The car pulled up beside them and the driver rolled down the passenger-side window. "Thank goodness I found you, two" Kate said. "Egghead—are you all right?" She glanced over at Jess. "What's going on? Is Eddie okay?"

Jess shook his head as he got up. "I think he's having another attack."

"Shit." She parked the car on the shoulder of the road and quickly got out. Together she and Jess helped Eddie into the backseat. "Mom's half out of her wits with worry," she said, then turned to Jess. "So is your mother. You boys have a lot of explaining to do."

Jess climbed in the backseat beside Eddie. "Explaining might not be such a good idea," he told her.

She shut her driver's side door and peered at Jess in the rearview mirror. "What do you mean by that? You guys know better than to just take off without a word to anyone."

Eddie looked up, his face stricken. "We had a good reason for leaving."

She started the engine and turned the car around. "Well, do you mind running it by me? I'm more than a little curious why you'd take off like that. Is it because I made you tell Mom and Dad about your ears? Or because Dad put a curfew on your video games?"

Jess gave Eddie a miserable glance then hung his head as Eddie replied. "No. It's because of Gotham Creek. It's a Druid town."

Kate raised her eyebrows. "Yeah, so?"

"You mean you *know*?"

She chuckled as she reached over and rolled up the passenger-side window. "Of course, I know. Everyone knows the history. I thought you knew it, too."

"Well, I didn't. And neither did Jess. Don't you think it's weird?"

She shrugged. "It's weird that no one ever told you two."

Jess lifted his head. "Are you a Druid, Kate?"

She knit her eyebrows. "I guess so. I mean we're all born into it, all of us at Gotham Creek." She paused, then added, "Well, most of us, anyway, with the exception of a few outsiders."

"How can you be so calm about all of this?" Eddie demanded, the throbbing in his head lessening.

She glanced up again at the rearview mirror. "It's just the way things are. Our beliefs, our rituals, our worship practices keep Gotham Creek alive. Look at the other towns in the county. We have a higher tax value than any of them—even double of those with water frontage. No one in Gotham Creek is unemployed. No one there is poor or needy. There's more than enough money to go around. We prosper *because* of our faith. And it's high time you began believing it, too."

Eddie shook his head. "What if I don't want to?"

She gave him a hard look in the mirror. "You don't have a choice. Your blood runs thick with it and so does yours, Jess. None of us have a choice, but all of us have an obligation."

"Obligation to what?"

"To protect the sacred forest and our religion." She tucked a long strand of dark hair behind an ear and asked. "So where were you boys headed, anyway?"

"Cousin Mark's."

At this, she laughed. "Mark would have sent you right back home. It's too near the Festival of Samhain."

Eddie gave Jess a fearful look. "Is Mark a Druid, too?"

"Uh huh. Non-practicing, mind you, but he was born to it like the rest of us. He knows what it means to Mom and Dad. He never would have let you stay with him during the festival." Her eyes softened as she glanced up in the mirror again. "Neither of you have a thing to fear. Gotham Creek looks out for its own. It always has and always will."

Jess reached for Eddie's hand in the backseat and Eddie felt him tremble. He was glad no one could see them holding hands—

others might think them queer for doing so; but holding Jess's hand had nothing to do with physical attraction. Jess was as scared as he...and it made him wonder how many other kids in Gotham Creek didn't know the truth about their town and their parents.

5

Promptly, on the stroke of 9 a.m., the next day, most of Gotham Creek's adults filed one by one into the back room of the town hall. No one said a word but for a few apprehensive greetings. Trouble had come to them. It hadn't been invited and yet it arrived...in the form of an outspoken environmentalist and his disappearance in the woods.

Not just any woods but Old Woods, the *sacred* forest, where no man or woman dare enter without proper preparation and instruction. Old Woods guarded the town, protecting it from plague, poverty and misfortune. And they, in turn, guarded the forest.

Jim Digby took the platform and leaned on the podium to tap the microphone. "Morning, folks. I've called an emergency meeting because, well, quite frankly, we have a problem...and we have to decide what measures to take, if any. For those of you who don't know what's happened, I'll ask Constable Kingsley to come forward and explain the situation."

Hap stood up, rubbing his hands together. He looked around at his friends and neighbors before walking up the short steps to the platform. *I don't know why I'm doing this. Everyone knows what's going on*, he thought to himself. *Word around here travels like wild fire.*

Tall and lanky, he towered over the podium. He had to raise the microphone stand twice, but still had to lean over to speak into it. Clearing his throat, he raised his voice...his *authoritative* voice, the one he'd been trained to use in the Police Academy in Augusta:

"Hello, folks. Two days ago, Sheridan Phillips came to Gotham Creek. For anyone who doesn't know, Phillips is quite a well-known environmental activist. Now at least two of you saw him: Jim, here, and Doc Putnam. Allegedly, Phillips went into Old Woods and he didn't come back out. We conducted a search but his toolbox was all we found.

"Now why he'd come here, posing as an agent for the National Forest Service is anyone's guess. But there's a good chance that if Sheridan Phillips knew about our woods, we have to assume the Feds do, too. If they come, they're bound to disturb the forest. I bring this dilemma before you now: if we allow them in, our secret *may* get out. If we *don't* allow them in, we could all be in a lot of trouble with the F.B.I." Hap held out his hands. "I don't like our choices, either way. So I could really use some input here."

As he stepped down from the platform, Jim came over and lowered the mike. "Thank you, Hap. You're absolutely right; we need to make a decision because either way, what we decide affects us all. Does anyone have any suggestions?"

Bruce Kelwick stood and hitched up his work pants. "Well, I participated yesterday, on that search and I'm telling you—there ain't no sign of Phillips in those woods. The only evidence is the toolbox and his car, which is still parked out by Doc Putnam's. So say we hide the car? We could push it into the deep end of the creek and claim Phillips drove off in it this morning. That should get everyone off our backs." He sat back down with a satisfied grunt. A few people in his row nodded with approval.

Hap stood up in the audience and shoved his hands in his back pockets. "We'll do no such a thing, Bruce. It's against the law, for one. Tampering with evidence and lying ain't looked kindly upon—especially by the Feds. No, I think we've got to come up with something better than that."

Ned Speers stood up before Hap could sit back down. "This may be off the subject, but I think it ties in. Last night, my son, Eddie ran off with Dave's boy, Jess. They were leaving home, I guess. Kate found them and brought them back—but what concerns me is the reason they left in the first place." Ned turned to glance at Doc Putnam, seated across the aisle before continuing.

"Now we were told not to teach Druidism to our children until we were given the go-ahead. Dave and I waited for permission, but we never received it. Not for Eddie and Jess, anyway. Somehow the boys found out and naturally, they're upset. Now I'm done skirting the subject with Eddie…and I don't give a rat's ass if you think I should wait a while longer or not. I can't have him running off in the middle of the night, scared out of his wits because of stories and half-truths about our religion."

Jim nodded slowly as Ned sat down. "Ned, you're absolutely right. Don't you agree, Doc?"

Doc nodded, stroking his long beard. He didn't stand up but called out, "The boys and their fathers should meet with me this afternoon at my house. Come as soon as school gets out. And that goes for any others who haven't told their children—providing, of course, that their children are of age. I'd say around twelve or thirteen. We have to stand together on this, as a community, if we are to stand at all."

Pat Nevels stood up after a pause. "I think we have to get back to the problem at hand—and that's what to do about Phillip's disappearance. I agree with Hap, we can't hide evidence, nor can we lie. Let the Feds come if they want to. Let them open up an X-File or whatever. We all know they won't find any foul play…at least on our part. But I have to ask: since Sheridan Phillip's disappearance is so close to festival time, why can't we consider *him* our ten-year sacrifice?" Pat offered a smile. "It's kind of a poetic justice, I think. After all, Phillips *was* a tree-hugger."

Now Doc Putnam rose, waving his arm. "No, no. We can't do it that way, Pat. The ten-year sacrifice must be a virgin. Substitutes are not acceptable, especially if they're outsiders. The sacrifice *has* to be one of us. There are seven eligible people in town, I believe. But as for the selection, that will be decided later as you well know."

At this point, Maisie Speers put a protective hand on Kate's knee. She saw the question, the apprehension burning in her daughter's eyes, but dared not say a word—not during town meeting, where women weren't permitted to speak. It had only been in the last twenty years that they'd been allowed to sit in on meetings and she didn't want to risk spoiling the privilege.

Jim nodded gravely. "So, shall we put it to a vote? What to do about Phillips's disappearance? All who think we should allow an investigation, if need be, say aye."

Every one but Bruce Kelwick voiced approval.

"The ayes have it," Jim declared. "Hap, do you have any closing words?"

Hap Kingsley stood up, facing his neighbors. "I wish I had an easy solution. All I can tell you is this: if you're asked any questions from outsiders, don't say anymore than you have to. And for crying out loud, don't act like you're hiding something."

Jim nodded. "That sounds like reasonable advice. Will anyone call this meeting adjourned?"

"I call," Ned said, raising his hand.

"I second," said Doc Putnam.

As everyone left the building, Edith Hymes approached Hap Kingsley, her face a mask of angst. "Have you talked to Norris yet?" she asked, her skin as pale as her hair.

Hap shook his head, ashamed that he'd forgotten. "No, Edith. Is he here? I can afford him a minute or two."

Edith's eyes narrowed. "No, he's not here. And neither is that slut he's shacked up with. I've a mind you'll find both of them in *her* trailer, fornicating."

He struggled to keep a straight face. "Well, I'll be sure and knock real loud so they hear me." As she stared after him, he glanced back over his shoulder. "Yes, I'm headed over there right now. But I won't make you any promises that he'll come home."

She frowned and crossed her arms, watching him go. She'd learned a long time ago not to trust the promises of men.

Hap did exactly what he told Edith Hymes he'd do. He drove straight to the trailer park on Old Woods Road and parked his cruiser beside Norris's tractor in Deidre Garnet's driveway. Leaving the engine running, he stepped out of the car and walked up to the door. He knocked hard enough to make it shake. *Wouldn't take much to kick it in if I had to,* he thought. He could hear a stereo playing inside. Music, country music. Patsy Cline, maybe. He knocked even harder and called out, "Police, open up."

Just then the door opened and Deidre Garnet stood before him, loosely wrapped in a red thread-worn bathrobe that threatened to fall open above the knot in her belt. Her hair was mussed, recklessly tangled, and a cigarette dangled between her lips. There were dark circles under her eyes.

Her voice dripped with sarcasm. "To what do I owe this pleasure, Constable?"

Hap cleared his throat and tried look around her without looking *at* her. "Is Norris Hymes here? I need to speak to him."

She plucked the cigarette from her mouth and smiled wickedly. "Oh, he's here all right." She looked back over her shoulder and Hap was instantly sickened at the sight of the round purple splotches on her neck. "Norris, darling. Someone's here to see ya." She turned back to Hap. "Want to come inside, Constable? Norris is probably trying to find his skivvies."

Hap blushed as Deidre stepped aside and one creamy breast poked free from the robe. She quickly pulled it shut, then turned off the stereo, bending low as if to make certain that Hap noticed the firmness of her bare behind. Maybe she wanted him to regret turning her down, but he stared out the window, his face the same shade as her brightly lacquered nails.

Undaunted, she padded barefoot down the dark, cluttered hall leaving a trail of smoke in her wake.

"Norris, didn't you hear me? There's someone here to see you."

Hap heard the bedroom door click open, then shut. He could hear whispers, but couldn't make out the words. Then the bedroom door opened and a moment later both Norris and Deidre came out of the hall, Norris in lead.

"I ain't done nothing wrong," he said as soon as he saw Hap.

"I didn't say you did. Your mother asked me to come over and talk to you."

Norris crossed his arms, as if he didn't quite believe him. "Ma said you were going to arrest me."

Hap smiled, shaking his head. "I can't do that—and I won't—unless you give me a good reason to take you into custody. I only want to talk to you, that's all. Why don't you come out to my car? What I have to say won't take long."

Norris put an arm around Deidre and tilted his chin in defiance. "Whatever you got to say, you can say it in front of my woman. Ain't that right, baby?" He kissed her ear as she nodded with a grin and Hap saw the ash fall from her cigarette to the worn shag carpet between her bare feet. He noticed her toenails were painted the same color as her fingernails.

In all the years that he'd known her, Felicity had never painted her toenails.

Hap swallowed. "Well, your mother's worried about you. She feels you're making a mistake. I guess that's all I have to say."

"Screw her," Norris said and Deidre giggled, puffing smoke. "I got me a woman and I ain't leaving her. Can you blame me?"

Hap shrugged. "It's not up to me to blame anyone. I just told your mother I'd speak to you—and so I have. You both have a nice day."

He was about to turn to go out the door when Deidre untied the knot on her belt. His eyes widened as the bathrobe tumbled to the floor, piling around her ankles. Hap blinked, realizing that she wasn't a true blonde, but he was more amazed that she waxed her bush to a near nothing, just a little dark line of hair. He looked away, quickly, his cheeks afire.

"Just wanted ya to see what you missed out on, Constable," she declared, hands on her hips, her breasts pert at that saucy angle. Norris just stood there beside her, grinning like a fool.

Hap inhaled. He could smell the scent of her now, musky and sexual, and forced his eyes to her face. "Deidre, you have Norris now. Can't you behave yourself?" He turned and reached the door in three steps and slammed it shut behind him.

"Well, I guess a threesome's out of the question," she said, turning to Norris. "Why are you looking at me that way? I just thought it would be wild to flash a cop. Did you see the look on his face? Wild, huh?"

He reached down, grabbed her thighs and heaved her up over his shoulder, caveman style. "I'll give you something *wild*," he said, lugging her back to the bedroom.

Maisie sat beside Kate on the bed in her room, and gazed quietly at walls that bore all the markings of a young college student: the triangular university pendant, the movie poster of Brad Pitt, red and green pompoms from her high school cheering days. It was still a teenager's bedroom, smelling of scented candles and bubblegum, and there were some clothes peeking out of nearly shut dresser drawers. The closet door was open, revealing more clothes hung haphazardly on hangers, a volleyball and a set of tennis racquets.

At least there was some order to the way Kate kept her room—a far cry from the utter chaos of Eddie's bedchamber but it still wasn't as neat as Maisie would have liked.

She did her best to be tolerant, though. Kate was nearly a grown up, spending less and less time at home. There was college now and Maisie hoped, eventually, a husband. She knew it would take someone very special to sweep Kate off her feet. Oh, there were dates, certainly, and there was Bobby Crane; her daughter was too pretty to be overlooked. But she was quiet and studious, meticulately so.

Photos pasted to the mirror over the vanity table bore witness of happy times—of Kate with her friends, of Kate posing proudly beside her new Honda hatchback which she paid for with her own money.

"Honey, I just don't know what to say," Maisie said, putting an arm around her daughter's shoulders. "I don't think they'll pick you. You're in college. Too many people would ask questions. And then there's Bobby."

Kate raised her eyes to her mother's face. "Bobby and I broke up a year ago. What's he got to do with anything?"

Maisie bit her lip while she paused. "Well, I assumed, when I found the birth control pills in the bathroom, that you were...well, that you were having sex with him."

"We thought about it." She fell silent and leaned into her mother's side. "But we didn't. We came close, but I was too afraid of getting you and Dad into trouble with the Elders."

A tear slid down Maisie's face. "Well, the Elders would have been upset, but it would be nothing we couldn't deal with—and not half as hard as losing you. Isn't there a boy you know—a nice boy? Someone in college maybe?"

Kate sniffled. "What are you saying, Mom? That I should go out and lose my virginity?"

Her eyes widened. "Yes, I guess I am. But with a *nice* boy. And soon. Before the festival."

"There are a lot of nice boys at college, but none I'd screw just for the sake of losing my virginity. Isn't there another way? I mean, can't Dad talk to the Elders? He could tell them I'm not a virgin."

At this, Maisie shook her head. "If you're chosen, you'll go through an examination. Doc would know immediately that your virginity is intact."

"I don't *need* a boy," Kate whispered. "I can do it myself. I'll use something. But are you sure you and Dad won't get into big trouble? I've heard of families being outcast from the community for things like this."

Maisie hugged her daughter. "It doesn't matter as long as we still have you with us. And someday, when you're married, you can tell your husband you had some sort of accident. But for now, it might save your life." She kissed Kate's forehead and stood up. "I'll leave you alone, honey. You know what you have to do."

Kate nodded, blinking back tears. "I know. I just didn't think it would ever come to this." She watched her mother leave the room, gently closing the door behind her.

With a resolved sigh, she got up and went over to her vanity table stacked with paperback novels, mostly thrillers and college texts. The mirror over the table was decorated with photos of her friends. Their young shining faces all seemed to say: *Do it, Kate. Save yourself. It'll only hurt for a minute. No big deal. Do it, just do it.*

She tore her eyes away from the pictures and stared at her reflection in the mirror. *Is this what Mom had to do?* she wondered. *Is that why grandma and grandpa had to leave Gotham Creek?*

Slowly, she reached down and grasped a spiral-tapered candle, one that she'd bought on a whim at the college bookstore because it caught her eye. She gazed at it in her hand for a long time, wondering with trepidation, if she really dared to do it.

"I have to be the *only* woman in your life," Deidre said, licking at the beads of sweat on Norris's upper lip.

He was too hot and tired to hold her. "You are, Dee, you are."

She raised herself on her hands, breasts hanging, hovering over him, her breath hot in his face. "No, I'm not! You're still devoted to *Mommy*." The way she said 'Mommy' chilled him to the bone.

His eyes narrowed to slits. "How can you say that? I'm *with* you, ain't I?"

"Mommy's boy, Mommy's boy," she teased with more than a hint of spite.

"Stop that!" He reached up and pushed her off him and she landed on the floor beside the bed. Her shoulders began to shake with sobs, so he reached over and patted her hair. "Hey, sorry. Didn't mean for you to fall so hard. You okay, Dee?"

She lifted her head, glaring at him. Her tears, quick to fall, smeared her mascara, making her look like a black-eyed prizefighter and there was still a lot of fight left in her eyes.

"You don't love me enough," she said, trembling. "No one *ever* loves me enough."

Norris couldn't stand to hear her cry. He rolled over, nearer to her and tried to lift her into his arms. "Of course, I love you enough. I left home to be with you. Soon I'll be handing you my paychecks. I want to marry you, Dee."

She shook her head. "That ain't enough. I want a *nice* house. A *nice* car. I want respect and I blow it every time. It doesn't help that everybody in this hick town hates me, except you. I have to know I'm the *only* woman in your life, Norris…then maybe I can get that nice house and car. And a little respect."

He cast her a look of concern. "You're making no sense, Dee. I can't give you all those things. Not yet, anyway."

She stared back at him, her eyes fiercely bright. "Oh, yes, you can. You could *kill* your mother. Make it look like a suicide. We could have her house and her car—and she wouldn't be spreading any more lies about me."

"Lies? What lies?"

Deidre sighed. "You know, slut this and slut that. She has me doing every man in town and you know that's a lie. Yesterday, she confronted me at the store. Called me a streetwalker in front of everyone. I was so embarrassed. I hate having to hide from her, always going out of my way to avoid running into her in public. That's not so easy in this godforsaken town."

He frowned, giving up on pulling her back onto the bed. Still, he stroked her hair, thinking about how close his mother had come to killing him the day he left. *Ma's crazier than Dee.*

Or so he thought.

6

While the parents and young adults held their emergency meeting at the town hall, Gotham Creek's youth were having a secret meeting of their own. Lacking the formality of platform and podium, they huddled in a tight circle behind the playground swings, twenty anxious and well-scrubbed faces, ranging in age from eight to fourteen. Eddie Speers, Jess Brown and Megan Kingsley were the oldest in the group, and it was Eddie who spoke first.

"Something really weird's going on here and I think we're the only ones who can stop it," he told his peers. "Our parents—every grownup in town—are Druids. And if we don't do something soon, they'll make us into Druids, too."

Amy Sands piped up, twisting her pigtails around her hand. "What's a Druid?"

Jess answered her. "Ever heard of Stonehenge? It's thought to be built by the Druids. They were an ancient Celtic priesthood. Worshipped trees, oaks in particular."

Amy stiffened. "You mean our parents worship trees?"

Jess nodded, his face grim.

"Well, my parents aren't Druids!"

Eddie gave her a sad smile. "Maybe not, Amy, but we can't take any chances. I think the focus of their religion is the Old Woods. Those big oaks. Ever wonder why we aren't allowed to go there?"

Megan knitted her blonde brow. "I was always told it was dangerous—that there were mineshafts all through the ground—and if anyone fell through one, it would be next to impossible to find them. Alive, anyway."

At this, Amy began to cry and Jess put his arm around her. "Hey, we don't mean to scare you," he said, "but we need to come up with a plan. Something to protect us—and ultimately, our families. Our town."

Eddie nodded. "I think Doc Putnam's the Druid leader. Some sort of priest. Yesterday, he gave me this." He pulled a bottle of pills from his pocket. "Doc said to take this for my headaches, but last night, Jess and I tried to run away—and I got another headache. I took one of these pills and I heard voices. Strange voices that were crying. No, screaming. I think they were coming from, well, from the trees."

Barbie Kelwick's blue eyes widened. "Doc has pictures of trees in his office. And he asks me to kiss him under the mistletoe he hangs over his door. Mommy said it's okay—that Doc means no harm by it. But I hate that syrup he gives me."

Eddie stared at her. "He used to give me syrup, too, but now he's changed it to pills."

Megan Kingsley looked up in alarm. "My mom drinks his tea everyday. She acts really weird afterwards, too—like she's in a trance or something. I try not to talk to her when she's out of it like that."

"Let's make a pact, right here, right now," Eddie suggested, shaking the pill bottle in his hand. "I don't know what Doc puts in these medications, but I don't think it's good. I think I know now why he doesn't send us to a pharmacy for our prescriptions. He's probably poisoning us."

Jess nodded. "Or poisoning our minds."

Eddie's eyes gleamed. "Yes. That's it. Mind control."

Megan shook her fist in the air. "So what you're saying is it's all about those woods. I wish they'd just burn down. I want our town and our parents to be normal."

"We can't burn down the forest," Eddie told her. "It's way too dangerous. We could lose our homes...they're too close to the woods."

"If only someone would *cut* them down," Jess said.

Eddie's thought, eyes narrowed. "Well, maybe someone could."

"Yeah, who?"

"A paper company, that's who." Eddie straightened his shoulders. "One of us could make an anonymous call to Piston Paper, down in Portland. Invite them to come up and have a look around. Maybe if they offer Doc enough money, he'll sell out. The woods would be cut and harvested…and the Druidism would stop, once and for all."

"I'll make the call." Megan Kingsley offered after a long pause. "Everyone tells me I sound just like my mom on the phone."

Eddie looked around at his group of school chums, from face to face. He saw fear, apprehension and anger. "We all have to agree to keep this secret between us, just like we have to agree not to take anymore of the medicine Doc gives us. If anyone should tell, our plan will be ruined—and we'd all be in a heap of trouble." He drew a circle in the sand with his finger and tossed in a pebble. "I'll not breathe a word of this to anyone. That's my oath."

Jess tossed in a pebble of his own and repeated the promise. So did Megan, Amy and all the others. When they were finished, twenty small stones were heaped in the circle.

The pact was sealed.

Some distance away, music teacher Rachel Sargent poured herself another cup of Doc's tea from a Thermos. She glanced over at the children, dispersing from their tight circle in the corner of the playground. *Now isn't Gotham Creek a nice little town. See how all our children get along so well. Despite the differences in their ages, they play together with nary a problem,* she thought as she glanced at her watch. *Good, just enough time to finish my tea, if I hurry.*

7

David Hardecastle glared at his secretary and picked up the phone, putting it to his ear. "This had better be damned important," he shouted into the receiver. "I'm busy and I don't have time for bullshit."

"Is—is this Mr. Hardecastle?" A woman's voice asked. She sounded young; there was a sweet naiveté to her voice that caused him to relax a little. For a brief moment, he wondered if the caller might be his estranged daughter, Carla. But why would she call him at work? It had been three years since they last spoke...

David cleared his throat. "Speaking."

"Mr. Hardecastle, the main office told me to call you. I'm from Gotham Creek and see, there's a forest here, teeming with oak. Really big, old trees. They need to be cut. Could you send someone up here to take a look? It'd be worth your while. Cutting them down could mean a lot of money for the paper company."

Obviously, the caller wasn't Carla. David knit his brows; in fact, they were most always knit, either in thought or anger. Usually a combination of both. "Who *is* this?"

"I'm, uh, Shirley. Shirley Mills."

"Do you *own* this woodlot? You sound quite young."

"Well, uh, no."

"Then why are you bothering me? I can't just go in and cut without the owner's permission." His tone was slightly quieter but still clearly showed his irritation.

There was a slight pause before she replied. "I'm calling for my uncle, Doc Putnam. He owns those woods and asked me to call your company. It's time those trees were harvested, Mr. Hardecastle."

David almost smiled. "Well, all right, I'll have someone look into it. Mind telling me where the hell Gotham Creek is?"

"Washington County, Route 1 East. Between Columbia Falls and Jonesboro. You can't miss it, really."

This time, he almost laughed. "I'm afraid you misunderstand me, young lady. *I* won't be coming to Gotham Creek. I'm far too busy. But I'll send someone over tomorrow. Now how can we contact your uncle? What was his name? Putnam?"

"Yes," she told him. "Doc Putnam. His house is the last one on Old Woods Road, at the north of town. He's got a shingle outside with his name on it. But, uh, his phone isn't working right now, so don't bother trying to call."

"Yeah, yeah. Thanks for the information, Miss Mills." He hung up the phone before she could reply, and stood up to press the intercom button. "Bert Colby, come to my office, post haste." He rubbed his dry palms together. Flakes of skin snowed down upon his desk and he tapped his left wing-tipped shoe impatiently, thinking that sending Bert to Washington County was poetic justice. Bert had been taking too much time off, lately. His wife had just given birth and as far as he was concerned, paternity leave was more ridiculous than maternity leave. He planned to tell Bert to take a good look around at one of Maine's poorest counties because if he took anymore time off, that would be the only place he'd be able to afford to live.

No man hated his job more than Bert Colby. Twelve long grueling years stuck in the same position with only marginal and sequential raises in pay to keep pace with inflation. Never a pat on the back or a smile from his boss. He knew Hardecastle would have preferred to shit steel-wool bunnies than to grant him a paternity leave of two weeks without pay.

He'd been given the title of Field Administrator, but that was just an elaborate way of saying that he was Hardecastle's gopher. Not right-hand man, not assistant. Gopher. If Hardecastle said "jump", he'd be expected to do back flips with triple-toe loops and be grateful that the mean old goat had acknowledged his existence.

Bert held his breath, as he always did when entering Hardecastle's office, never knowing what to expect and always dreading the worst. Sometimes he developed hives when he heard Hardecastle call him on the intercom. He didn't have hives now, but a tic in his right cheek was doing a double-time spasm and he hoped it wouldn't be obvious.

He closed the door behind him, eyes lowered but wary, expecting anything from a paperweight to fly past his head—or to be blamed for whatever trivial annoyance that his boss relished to take out on him. It seemed he was safe this time. Hardecastle was standing with his back to him, apparently gazing out the window at the odiferous stack pipe beyond and the greyish haze hanging in the air. Millie always complained of the smell—although they lived across town, where the stink of the paper mill couldn't be detected except on a strong west wind—she swore he brought the stench home on his clothes. He'd noticed that she washed his duds separately from hers, which didn't bother him for he suspected that the *source* of the bad smell wasn't so much from paper chemicals as it was from his boss.

For a long moment, the silence in the office hung as heavily as the haze outside the window. Bert cast a nervous glance upward to see Hardecastle's hands locked behind his back. He was twisting his fraternity ring again...a very bad sign. Hardecastle only twisted his ring—that heavy gold ornament—when he was thinking nasty.

"I received a call today, Colby," he said without turning. "A call from Gotham Creek. Do you know where that is?"

Bert swallowed the sponge of phlegm in his throat. "I'm afraid I don't, sir." From where he stood, he could see the cords in Hardecastle's neck thicken, so he quickly added, "but I can find out for you, if you'd like."

Hardecastle whirled around, teeth bared. "I *know* where Gotham Creek is, you fool. For your information, it's in Washington County. And I expect you to be there tomorrow." He glared at Bert Colby with a gaze as comforting as dry ice packed into an open wound.

"Why? Why are you sending me there?"

Hardecastle sneered. "I want you to find Dr. Putnam of Gotham Creek. Supposedly, he has some acreage he wants cut. Remind him that he receives ten percent of whatever net income his wood is sold for. That's ten percent of the *net*, not the gross. Don't fuck it up like you did last time or I'll dock the difference from your pay."

"Can I be reimbursed for my gas?"

Hardecastle rolled his eyes. "You fucking people want everything, don't you? Look, I'm *not* your parent. I'm *not* your friend. Hell, I'm not even a nice guy." He approached Bert with clenched fists and stopped just inches away from his face. Bert could smell his breath and it indeed smelled worse than what came out of the stack pipe. He wondered if Hardecastle had eaten garlic and raw onions for breakfast.

"Company policy dictates that field workers are reimbursed for their gas—and their mileage, as well. You know that, Colby, but I rather think you like rubbing my face in it."

"So you want me to talk to Dr. Putnam?"

"Yes, but only after you check out that damned woodlot of his. Very likely there isn't anything worth cutting there—but you never know until you look."

"Very well, sir. Is there anything else?"

Hardecastle lifted his head and sniffed. "What have you been rolling in, Colby?"

"P—pardon?"

"Are you wearing perfume or what?"

Bert Colby felt warmth rise from the pit of his stomach to his cheeks. "No, sir. It's aftershave. My wife likes it."

"Well, I don't. Wear it again in here and I'll have you down in the plant bleaching pulp without gloves." He stepped back and looked at Bert as if examining something he'd stepped in. Then he shook his head and dismissed him with an abrupt flick of his hand. "Go on, get out of here. You really stink, Colby."

Bert backed out of the office and closed his boss's door softly. "What goes around comes around," he muttered as he walked back to his cubical the size of a small closet. He shimmied behind his desk and wiped the sheen of nervous sweat from his brow as Fiona Hardison hurried by with a stack of files. "Back from the lion's den, Bert?" she asked with a strong hint of sympathy.

"More like an outpost of hell."

Fiona chuckled but Bert just felt sick. *Well, at least I won't have to be here tomorrow,* he reminded himself.

Doc Putnam gave each child a friendly smile and a pat on the head as he invited them into his living room. He shook their fathers' hands and engaged in small talk, keeping everything light and pleasant. After everyone arrived, he indicated that they all be seated.

"I want to talk to you today about our town," he began. "Gotham Creek is a very special place with very special people.

You all know the rules about the forest. Now I'm going to tell you why we have them."

He smiled and stroked his long, grey beard. "You're all old enough to handle the truth about our religion and our town, so I'll be forthright. The grownups here are Druids. That word means 'draw nigh' and our religion is as ancient as that of the Hebrew, the Greeks and the Romans. This is why we celebrate the Embolic on February 2nd, the winter Solstice during Yule, Ostara on the last Sunday of March, and Samhain during Halloween. As you grow older, you'll understand more about our ceremonies and you'll be encouraged to participate to a greater degree.

"It's up to us to keep our religion alive just as it is our sacred duty to protect our forest."

He reached up and took down the sprig of mistletoe, which hung in the doorway of his office. "This is a truly special plant to us. Mistletoe. It represents life eternal." He held it up so all could see. "Look at the berries. Mistletoe only bears fruit in the winter when everything else is dead. When you are kissed under the mistletoe, you are being blessed with wishes for eternal life in the Summer Land, Tir-Nan-Og." He turned and winked at Barbie Kelwick. "That's the reason why I kiss you, not just because you're cute." When he turned back to the group, his face was somber.

"Although it takes many years of study and practice to become a Druid, you will each be invited to join the grove at an apprenticeship level. You'll learn about Llew, the sun god and the celebration of Beltaine, and Samhain, the summer's end, when the veil between the present and the future wears thin.

"Some of you will learn the ancient songs of our ancestors. Others will study the laws of nature, science, medicine, physics and astronomy. This is the wisdom we are sworn to uphold and pass onto the next generation."

As he rehung the mistletoe, he continued, "But there are many outside of Gotham Creek who would mistrust our knowledge and our ways. Therefore, we keep our practices hidden. Secret. Known only to those in the grove. Does anyone have any questions?"

Eddie and Jess exchanged glances but Eddie was first to raise his hand. "What about the sacrifice during Samhain? Is it ever a *human* sacrifice?"

Doc paused for a moment, reflecting on the answer. "Well, yes and no. Usually the sacrifice consists of fruit and vegetables, the very best from our gardens. Now before I tell you about the other part, I want you to understand that our town is remarkably fortunate. We live rich lives here. There is no poverty, no want. Everyone is happy and lacks for nothing. Therefore, every tenth year, something more is warranted in terms of sacrifice. Something very dear and hard to part with."

He closed his eyes for a moment before continuing. "Once every ten years, we must offer up one of our own. It is no easy thing, nor is it ever taken lightly—"

"Who decides who gets sacrificed?" Jess Brown asked, his eyes full of alarm.

"The forest decides through the Elders and myself."

"How? Do you draw names or what?" Eddie blurted out.

Doc nodded. "Yes, we draw names. It's the only fair way."

"But what if that person doesn't want to be sacrificed?" Eddie maintained.

At this, Doc spread his arms wide. "You have all enjoyed living here. You have been raised in a community of love, of sharing. Is there anyone who would be so selfish as to shirk the most sacred of all duties?"

No one dared answer. Eddie couldn't look at Jess or anyone else. He lowered his gaze, believing himself to be a coward. *They better not pick me*, he thought miserably. *They better not pick me because I don't think I could do it.*

But Doc clasped his hands together and smiled. "Now I don't want any of you to worry. You are all too young to be considered eligible for that sacred duty. And rest assured, if any of you are ever chosen, you will undergo a great preparation. You won't be afraid because you'll be accepting a high place in Tir-Nan-Og. In the meanwhile, live and be happy. Protect the forest and all will be well for generations to come."

He held up a finger and the smile dropped from his face. "There is one thing I must warn you all about. The outside world doesn't understand or respect our ways. If word gets out, they'll send in people who will come in the middle of the night. They'll take you away from your families and your town. They'll arrest your parents, locking them up in jail for a long time. That's why our religion must be kept secret. I trust all of you not to breathe a word about it outside of Gotham Creek. Does everyone understand how serious this is?"

Every child nodded. Some felt fearful; others felt privilidged to be let in on such clandestine knowledge. Eddie glanced quickly at Jess, knowing he was feeling the same depths of apprehension.

Doc called the meeting to a close with a special blessing upon the head of each child. He surmised Eddie and Jess, the oldest of the children, bowed their heads out of respect and humble gratitude.

He couldn't have been further from the truth.

Edith Hymes didn't care for *The Tonight Show*, but it was the *only* program worth watching this time of night. She didn't like the new guy with the big chin because she missed Johnny Carson—it just wasn't the same without him—and often the show failed to hold her interest. She hadn't been sleeping well since Norris left home, but tonight Doc's soothing tea seemed to be doing the trick.

Fifteen minutes into *The Tonight Show*, she felt her eyelids grow as heavy as sandbags and this came as such a comfort that she didn't even bother to clap twice for her clapper to turn off the TV set. Bathed in the bluish light of the screen, she welcomed the arms of Morpheus like a lover.

She never heard the turning of the key in the lock at her back door.

Within moments of closing her eyes, Edith was snoring, her snorts and starts nearly keeping a tempo with Leno's musical guests, Hootie and the Blowfish. Not that she would have listened, anyway. For her, if it wasn't Sinatra, it wasn't music.

She never heard the creaking of the stairs or the soft footfalls approaching her bed. The next morning, Doc would pronounce her dead and as he filled out the certificate, he'd state her cause of death as "natural".

But only her murderer knew how very truly "natural" it was.

The night his mother was killed, Norris Hymes was roaring drunk and Deidre was in a pissy mood, pouting in front of the TV, trying to ignore her inebriated boyfriend and thinking she'd made another big mistake.

Doc Putnam was at the edge of the woods, practicing his nightly ritual of prayer.

Megan Kingsley tossed about in her bed, in the midst of a nightmare in which her parents had chased her into the forbidden woods, intent on killing her for her act of betrayal.

In the master bedroom down the hall, her mother, Felicity, slept, oblivious to the fact that Hap was wide awake, sitting on the side of the bed, staring out their bedroom window at the night, worrying about the National Forest Service representatives that were due in town tomorrow. State Troopers from Machias had already impounded Sheridan Phillip's Volvo. He knew they'd go over it with a fine-tooth comb but they'd never find a scrap of evidence that would lead them to Phillips.

Across town, Eddie Speers woke up, his ears humming like a tent full of bumble bees, only this time, there was no headache, no blood. Just a steady humming. *It's the trees,* he thought. *I think they're contented, at least for tonight. It doesn't hurt so much. Not yet, anyway.*

Over the hum, he heard another noise: the padding of footsteps going down the hall, then down the stairs. He knew by their rhythm it was Kate. *Probably going to the kitchen to raid the fridge,* he thought. He listened to the front door open, then shut.

Letting the cat in, he thought and snuggled down into his bed to fall asleep, lulled by the hum of trees that only he could hear.

Bert Colby arrived in Gotham Creek late Thursday morning, October 3rd. As he left Route 1 and turned onto Main Street, he could see the forest looming like a giant guardian at the north end of town. *It must be a hill,* he convinced himself. *One hell of a hill.*

Trees in this part of the country just don't grow that way.

Normally, trees are affected by climate: short summers and long, cold winters tend to put a damper on growth. A deciduous forest, one made up of mostly hardwoods—the leaf trees—oaks, maples, birch, poplar, walnut and aspen—is considered *old*. It could take hundreds of years, sometimes thousands, for evergreens to reach their prime, die and decay, to make room for the harder deciduous trees. Bert knew this from his years of working at Piston Paper. He also knew that the only thing David Hardecastle loved as much as money were old forests, prime for cutting. They made the best paper, but most of the company's profit would come from reselling the wood to a lumberyard; what was left would go into pulpwood to be made into paper and that would be cream off the top.

He steered his Chevy Cavalier to the curb and stopped to step out, scratching his head and studying his Maine Atlas. Where the forest was positioned on the map, it clearly showed a valley, not a hill. He looked back up at the trees and sighed, thinking it possible that the map was wrong.

But could it be wrong enough to show an indentation in the earth that large? That round? Bert surmised a hole that size and shape could have been made by only one thing: a meteor. A large meteor. Maybe not the size of the asteroid that caused the Barringer Meteor Crater in Arizona, but a good-sized space rock, nonetheless.

Evidently, if it had indeed been a meteor, it might have been the source for the mining endeavor, marked on the map as a small circled 'm' with a line through it. *A dead mine,* he thought as he tossed the atlas on the passenger seat and got back into the car.

He drove slowly up Main Street, past the restaurant and store, past rows of pastel-colored capes and ranches. The order and neatness of the town surprised him, pleasantly. Every lawn was mowed. There were no rusting jalopies decorating yards or trash littering the ground. All the homes looked nice. Old, yes, but well kept. *What a perfect little town!* he thought and glanced again toward the forest. *These people have it made. Made in the shade, quite literally.*

He turned right, onto Old Woods Road. A half a mile later, he noticed a trailer park on the left. Not one of those rancid little parks jam-packed with dented, rusting trailers, but a spacious and well-maintained park boasting newly-manufactured mobile homes. He smiled at a longhaired young man driving a tractor mower along the shoulder of the road and the boy offered him a wave. A one-fingered lift, really. But at least it was the *right* finger. Bert slowed the car and rolled down his window.

"Hey, there. I'm looking for Doc Putnam. Could you tell me if I'm headed the right way?"

The boy cut his engine and gave him a nod, but his eyes narrowed as he noticed the sign on the car door, just below the window. "Sure enough. Last house on the right. Say, you from Piston Paper?"

Bert swelled with pride. "Why, yes. I take it you've heard of us?"

Tractor boy scowled and Bert realized he was a bit older than he'd first thought. One pale and hairy knee poked through the rip in his faded jeans and he couldn't help but stare at it as the young man replied, "Who hasn't heard of Piston Paper? What you here for, anyway?"

Bert never let his smile falter. He had years of practice grinning and bearing it on the job. "Business," he told the kid as he rolled up his window. In his rearview mirror, he could see tractor boy turning in his seat to watch him continue up the road.

He pulled into the gravel drive beside the last house on the right, a spacious, yellow-painted farmhouse with several ells running hap shod from the main part. From where he sat, Bert could see its paint had peeled like a bad sunburn. Some of the decorative gingerbread under the eaves had crumbled and he could see heavy spider webbing around them, no doubt holding the rest together. *So different from the other houses in town,* he thought sadly. *The doctor must be old or sick. Or both.*

He rolled his window down and listened to the rusty grind of the doctor's shingle swinging on its post in the breeze. He got out of the car and stepped out to walk up the spongy moss-covered footpath to the front porch to knock on the door.

It didn't take him long to decide that the good doctor wasn't home. Perhaps he had an office in town? Bert pulled out his wallet and removed a business card from its inner pocket. He folded his wallet and put it back, safe and snug, then took the pen from his shirt pocket and wrote on the back of the card:

Dr. Putnam, we need to talk. I'll be in town all day today. If I miss you, please call me at the number on the front of this card. Ask for Bert Colby. Thanks.

He left the business card wedged in the door jam and stepped off the porch to gaze at the woods, looming up from a distance. He didn't see a PRIVATE PROPERTY or NO TRESPASSING sign and shrugged to himself.

Instead of returning to his car, Bert began walking into the forest.

"Oh my God!" Hap Kingsley exclaimed as soon as Doc Putnam pulled back Edith's bed sheet. "Who'd do such a thing? And why?"

Doc rubbed at his nose, feeling an intense itch. "That's *your* job to find out, Hap, not mine. You know as well as I do who could have done this, but you'll never prove it. You and I both know that. Edith always kept this place locked tighter than a drum, especially at night. You won't find any signs of forced entry. But you already know that, don't you? Just look at what's been done to her."

Hap stared down at the corpse, the acorns packed into Edith's skull through her eyes and mouth. "I can't believe it," he murmured, shaking his head as his stomach did a double flip.

"And that's not all," Doc added, as if reading his thoughts. "There's more acorns jammed into her rectum and vagina. She must have done something wrong, but what, I don't know…"

"Why don't you know? You're our priest, for crying out loud! You're supposed to know these things."

Doc hung his head. "The gods haven't spoken to me lately. They may be talking, but not to me." He gave a nod at the corpse on the bed. "I've listed her death as Natural Causes. That should keep the State out of it."

"Natural Causes?" Hap swallowed nervously. "There's nothing natural about the way she died."

"Would you rather have outsiders involved?"

"No." Hap backed away from the bed, feeling the sting of bile rising in his throat. "Just get her cleaned up and we'll give her a proper burial. Has anyone notified Norris?"

Doc shrugged. "Not to my knowledge."

"Then I'll go talk to him."

Doc looked up. "Give me half an hour, huh?"

"Sure thing." Hap hurried from the bedroom, his stomach a twist of knots.

"So sorry it had to go down like this, Edith," Doc whispered as he opened his medical bag, preparing to extract the rather large acorns from her corpse.

8

Bert Colby looked up at the sunlight filtering down through the leaves towering over him. *They're changing color,* he thought. *In a couple of weeks, the autumn foliage ought to be spectacular. Especially on these trees.*

He looked down at his feet and picked up an oak leaf that had recently fallen. He carefully laid it over his hand, amazed at its size. It more than covered his palm—it was large enough to cover *both* hands. *Almost the size of a turkey platter,* he mused. He flipped the leaf over.

A thick vein ran up the middle of the leaf and smaller veins shot off from it at 45-degree angles, each running to a point on the side of the leaf. Strangely, this was a perfect specimen—with no signs of tree cancer, fungi or holes from hungry insects. *I should take it back to Piston Paper,* he decided. *Let Hardecastle shit himself when he sees the size of this thing.*

Holding the leaf, Bert drew deeper into the grove of giant oaks, taking care not to slip on the acorns scattered about the forest floor. Acorns, the size of golf balls. He'd already pocketed a few, thinking he'd take a couple of them home to surprise Millie, and maybe keep a few for paperweights on his desk.

Overhead, he heard a sudden snap, a dry wooden sound. He looked upward just in time to hear a crow scream and the rustle of branches and leaves. What he witnessed next caused him to drop the leaf in alarm.

The screaming crow was caught in the branches of a tree and fought to free itself, squawking with fright. Bert saw the branches move the way branches were never meant to move, passing the bird down the tree trunk like hands. The movement ceased for a moment, pausing with the bird, near the middle of the trunk. From where he stood, Bert could see the bird's oily eyes, wide and wild, as the bird continued to struggle. Then he saw the tree branches choke the life from it. A few shiny black feathers fluttered down to the forest floor.

He stepped back, rubbing his eyes in disbelief. As he did, something *opened up* in the trunk of the tree. A hole, opening like an eyelid. No, more like a mouth. A gruesome mouth, full of sharp splintery teeth lining its entire perimeter. He saw the branches move again, bringing the dead bird into that awful orifice, which closed around it with a horrible dry crunch.

Then Bert realized he'd wet himself, the hot sting of urine burning his thighs and scrotum. His eyes widened as a number of branches began to slither down in his direction, moving slowly like cautious snakes as if they could detect the odor of his urine, mingled with the sour smell of terror leaking from his pores.

He broke into a run, not knowing or caring where he was going—as long as he could get away from those terrible branches. In his haste, he stumbled over a large root and fell headlong into a thick bed of rotten leaves. He scrambled to get up, hearing the branches snapping behind him, closing in fast and lashing at the air.

He made it to his feet and broke into a sprint. Suddenly, there was no ground beneath him. In that single fleeting moment, he thought, *I'm caught! I'm caught!* but he couldn't feel anything holding him. Daylight disappeared as he fell, plunging downward.

He screamed in agony as he landed with a crash—he heard and felt the muffled snap of his left ankle, the first part of his body to touch down. Rocking in pain, he tasted the coppery tang of blood in his mouth. It wasn't from internal injuries, as he'd first thought, but from biting his tongue.

He looked up at the hole thirty feet above his head, letting in only a marginal beam of light, not nearly enough to allow him to see his surroundings. He groped around with his hands. At least he was on a flat surface. Not rock ledge, but gravel. His ankle throbbed with every beat of his heart, the painful swelling inching slowly up his calf.

"Help! Someone, anyone. Can you hear me?" he shouted, hoping his voice was loud enough to travel through the hole above. "Please help me. I think I've broken my ankle. I'm down here. Please, please help me."

A shadow fell across the beam of light and Bert breathed with hope. Someone *had* heard him! They were up there, moving about. "I'm down here," he called out. "Send down a rope. And a flashlight. It's dark. So dark. Please, hurry."

He watched a rope being lowered down through the hole and he crawled toward it, reaching out, grateful that help had come so quickly.

When it moved, Bert realized it *wasn't* a rope at all.

He screamed, trying to ignore the agony in his ankle as he scrambled away from the long thin branch. He pulled himself along the ground with his hands and good leg, feeling gravel dig into his palms. Then he could move no more. He'd come up against a wall, hard and unyielding. It was darker here, almost pitch black, and while he could see the branch several feet below the hole, where it was headed was anyone's guess.

Bert drew still, trying to breathe through his nose so as not to make a sound. The dry rustle of leaves drew closer now. He forced himself not to shudder, to remain perfectly still, as he felt the tip of the branch with its scratchy twigs pass over his knees. The rustling sound moved on, then grew quieter. He watched the branch ascend slowly back up through the hole.

What the hell was that thing? he wondered. *I'll go nuts if I don't get out of here!*

He felt with cautious fingers along the rock wall, rough and cool, almost cold to the touch. "I'll be okay," he assured himself aloud in a whisper. "This passage is man-made, therefore, it has to lead somewhere." He stopped, pressing his hand against the wall. "Wait. Oh, my God. I *know* where I am. The mine. That old mine on the map. This is part of it, I'm sure. Now keep your head, Bert, old boy. There's a way out. If I just follow this wall…God, I wish I had a flashlight."

He moved slowly, not knowing which direction he was headed. The mine floor was solid, the passage wide. He pulled his broken ankle behind him, the pain dancing from his foot to his calf like live wires.

His fingers bumped into something that he assumed must be a rock. As he lifted it out of the way, he thought it much too light to be stone. A chunk of wood, perhaps? He turned it over in his hands, feeling three holes, not unlike a bowling ball. But below the three holes, he felt a larger hole…one with loose jagged edges. Teeth.

With a yelp of disgust, he dropped the skull and it rolled away from him in the darkness. Pushing on ahead with added urgency, his palms came down upon something that felt like sticks. Rows of them. "Ribcage," he whispered. "Just some poor guy's ribcage." It broke apart as he tried to move it out of the way, and he ended up having to crawl over most of it.

He turned a corner, following the wall, and now could see a wide shaft of light illuminating the floor in front of him. Again, he dared not to call out as he crawled to the lit spot on the floor. *What if that branch—thing is still up there, waiting for me?* He stopped and looked upward.

This hole was larger than the one he'd fallen down through. Although it was wider and emitted more light, enough so that he could see his surroundings without too much difficulty, it was still a good thirty feet or so over his head. He knew there was no way he could reach it without a rope or a ladder.

I'll just rest a moment, right here, he decided. *Pain has a way of washing the strength right out of a man. I need to rest. Not for long. Just enough to find my guts again.*

Two strangers approached Hap Kingsley's desk. Hap hadn't had a very good day—seeing Edith Hymes's mutilated corpse and then having to tell Norris about his mother's death—didn't make for a very pleasant morning and it wasn't even noontime yet. Weary, he looked up at the pair who'd just entered his office and gave them each a brief nod.

"Hello," the tall, thin man said. "I'm Dick Oliver and this is my assistant, Susan Mills. We're representatives from the National Forest Service, in case you hadn't already guessed."

Hap stood up and extended his hand in greeting. "I thought as much," he said, managing a tentative smile.

"We've come about Sheridan Phillips. He hasn't turned up yet, has he?" Dick asked.

Hap shook his head, his faint smile falling. "No. I conducted a search, but it's as if he just vanished into thin air."

Susan spoke up. "I beg your pardon, Constable, but no one just vanishes into thin air. He's caused us a lot of problems in the past and we mean to find him."

Hap cleared his throat. "His car's over in Machias at the State Police Headquarters."

Dick Oliver smiled thinly. "We know. We've just come from there."

Hap held out his hands. "Well, I don't know how else to help you. He's not here, I can assure you of that."

Susan cocked a perfectly plucked brow. "I beg to differ with you, Constable. No one in the surrounding towns has seen him, either. Don't you think someone would notice a man traveling on foot? Especially someone as well known as Sheridan Phillips?"

Hap swallowed, nodding. "Yes, I suspect so. But that's only if he *wanted* to be found. Have you checked him out? Perhaps he owed somebody money? Perhaps he had it out with his girlfriend? A person might have a thousand reasons to disappear."

"Phillips was rich. And gay, although unattached for the last several years, as far as we know." Dick said.

"We'd like to take a look around town if you don't mind," Susan added.

Hap held out his palms. "Hey, it's a free country. Help yourselves. But I'm telling you, he's not here."

Susan smiled. "We'd like to decide that for ourselves, thank you. We've notified the F.B.I. and they're sending two of their agents here today as well. Just thought we'd warn you." She struck Hap as a no-nonsense type of woman. Strictly business and probably sporting a master's degree in physics or engineering. Her dark hair was pulled back in a harsh bun, and her glasses were plain, framed in black plastic.

There isn't anything pretty about her, Hap reasoned, but he kind of liked the way she smiled. He felt she hadn't come to destroy Gotham Creek; she just wanted to catch Sheridan Phillips.

Dick Oliver, though, was another story. There was something crafty about him that Hap didn't trust. Could it be his lack of eye-to-eye contact? The man seemed too smooth, too greasy and false. Hap shook his hand again when he bade them both goodbye and good luck—and when they turned away, he rubbed his palm on his pant's leg.

He watched them leave his office, then he sat back down in his chair to rub at his forehead. For a long time, he just stared down at his paperwork, barely able to think.

The Feds were coming. Dear God, what next?

Once in their car, Susan Mills glanced over at Dick Oliver. "The Constable's hiding something. He's nervous. I sensed that much about him. Didn't you?"

Dick shrugged. "Maybe. But why? I can't really imagine anyone holding Sheridan Phillips hostage. But you're right; we can't count anything out."

"Phillips was last seen going into the forest," Susan said. "I think we have to start there first."

"Yeah, I agree." Dick turned the key in the ignition and put the car into gear. As they drove through town, northward toward the woods, she peered out the passenger side window.

"Nice, little town, huh?" he commented.

She turned and gave him a skeptical look. "Nice or not, I bet we'll find Phillips here. Or at least discover what happened to him."

Bert heard human voices, male and female, wafting down from the hole above. He couldn't make out their words, but he could hear people talking. He gazed up at the light, filtering down from the hole and called out:

"Help! Please help! I'm down here—and I'm hurt. Can you hear me?"

The voices stopped, so he shouted even louder. "Please, don't go! I know you're up there. Can you hear me? I need help. I've fallen. I've busted my ankle and I can't get out. Please, talk to me. Please."

The voices began again, this time closer.

"I think it's coming from over here," said the female.

"Careful now, watch your step," said the male.

"Please help me," Bert yelled. "I can hear you up there."

"We hear you just fine," the man called down. "Phillips, are you all right?"

"I'm not Phillips. My name's Bert Colby and I'm from Piston Paper. I need your help."

"Piston Paper? Did he say Piston Paper?" the woman asked. "That means he's one of David Hardecastle's men. Perhaps we should let him stew down there a while longer?"

"Don't be so heartless, Susan. He's hurt and he needs our help."

"Who are you people?" Bert called out.

"National Forest Service," the man answered.

Bert groaned. "Just figures. You *will* help me, won't you?"

"Of course. Say, Sheridan Phillips isn't down there with you, is he?"

"Phillips? The tree-hugger?"

"Yes, that's the one."

"Heck, no. What would he be doing down here?"

"Just asking." There was a pause and the woman called down, "We're going to have to go back to the car for a rope. Can you hang on a bit longer?"

"I'm not going anywhere." An alarming thought sent shivers through his mind. "Hey, you two better watch out—there's something up there. It was chasing me. I saw it kill a bird. Just stay away from the trees, okay?"

"What the devil?" the man asked and in a lower voice added, "I think the paper company guy landed on his head."

"Probably nuts from the pain. He did say his ankle was broken," the woman said. She started to say something else when her words were cut off by a shrill and sudden scream.

Bert looked up at the hole and scooted away from the light. Now the man was screaming, too. Over their shrieks of terror, he could hear the sounds of rustling leaves. He lowered his face to his hands and wept.

"What the hell is this?" With growing agitation, Doc examined the business card that had been stuck in his door. "Piston Paper! What do they want with me?"

He took the card inside and immediately dialed the company number, eventually winding up with David Hardecastle on the other line.

"I gave *no one* permission to come to my woodlot to take a look," Doc said. "What makes you think I want my trees cut down?"

"Your niece called us yesterday. Shirley Mills. Does that ring a bell?"

Doc shook his fist at the phone. "I don't have a niece and I never heard of Shirley Mills! Now your man's car is parked right here in my driveway, and when he comes out of the woods, I plan on slapping him with a lawsuit. Trespassing is still illegal in this state."

Hardecastle paused. "If your land's posted, I'm certain Bert Colby wouldn't have gone there."

Doc gnashed his teeth. *I should have listened to Hap. Why, oh, why didn't I post that land?* But he asked out loud, "How many men did you send here?"

"Just Colby. No one else."

"Damned funny thing—there's *two* cars out here."

"Colby drives a Cavalier."

Doc peered out his kitchen window. "Yep, there's a blue Cavalier out here. There's also a black Oldsmobile."

"Well, I can't help you there. Look, have Bert Colby give me a call before he leaves town. I'd like to get this mess straightened out. Meanwhile, I'm going to have this prank call checked into. At least we might be able to tell where it came from. It costs the company a great deal of money to send out men on fool's errands—and whoever that caller is, she'll pay. I'll see to that."

"I'd appreciate it." Doc hung up the phone, stroking the edge of the business card with his finger. "Do we have a traitor in our midst?" he murmured. "Who *are* you, Shirley Mills?"

9

Norris remained solemn during his mother's funeral. The whitewashed walls of the town hall seemed to echo and magnify his melancholy. The framed photographs of Gotham Creek's stern forefathers glared over her casket and he wanted to stand up and scream at them to stop staring. They would not have approved of the things he'd done that upset her, despite how crazy she'd acted. It gave him little comfort that she'd died in her sleep; somehow it just didn't sit right. She'd always been healthy, didn't smoke or drink. She exercised regularly with her Richard Simmons tapes. She was 42 years old and not yet menopausal, thanks to Doc's good care.

And yet here she was, cold and unmoving, beneath the cover of her coffin. Norris had insisted on a closed casket; Edith never liked being gawked at, and cremation was out of the question; only *special* people were cremated in Gotham Creek. He was thankful his mother hadn't been deemed *that* special.

He glanced over at Dee, perched on the bench beside him, dressed in a black lacy gown and ruining her makeup with crocodile tears. Dee hadn't like Ma one bit. She now had what she wanted—to be the *only* woman in his life. As he looked at her, it occurred to him that he wanted to slap her as much as he wanted to tear those portraits down off the walls. *Why do you have to be so melodramatic?* he wanted to scream. *You never liked Ma. And she hated you, too. Who do you think you're fooling, sitting there bawling like an orphaned calf?*

He remembered that from the moment she'd learned about Ma's death, Dee had insisted on moving from her trailer into the house. "There'd be so much more room for my things," she'd told him. "And besides, you'd be more comfortable there; after all, it's where you grew up." She'd given him a sly sexy smile and added, "We can christen every room if you'd like, the way we christened every room in my trailer."

Not once did she ask how he felt about his mother's death. She offered no words of comfort or compassion. *I've lost my only parent,* he thought, *and all she cares about is what she can get her hands on. And sex. What have I gotten myself into? Ma was right about her all along; I should have listened.*

Deidre caught him staring at her and she looked up, dabbing at her eyes with a tissue. With a sorrowful sigh, she leaned against him, resting her blonde head on his shoulder. Norris frowned and put his arm around her, feeling her shoulders heave with each sob.

"I didn't think you liked Ma that much," he finally whispered in her ear.

She looked up, blinking. "I didn't."

"So why are you crying? You're making a spectacle out of yourself."

She gave him a slow smile, looking like a wet raccoon. "I'm crying because you won't. You haven't shed a tear since she died. I'm crying for you—not for *her.*"

He scowled and shook his head, looking past her to the pine casket mounded with flowers. *You needn't waste your tears,* he felt like saying. Dying was Ma's way of punishing him—castigating him for moving in with Dee—and guilt was her tool of correction, proving far more effective than the leather strap that hung behind the stove.

I broke her heart and she died in her sleep, he added, miserably. He looked back at Dee. *All because of you.*

A hand on his other shoulder caused him to turn abruptly. "We're very sorry about your loss," Ned Speers told him. "If there's anything we can do, you'll let us know, won't you?"

He nodded with a sigh and shook Ned's hand, then Maisie's, who followed close behind her husband. He then looked up into Kate Speer's eyes and found them damp.

"Hey, Norris, I'm real sorry," she whispered, taking his hand in both of hers. Her touch was soft and warm.

"Katie," he murmured, feeling for the first time tears blurring his vision, then she was gone, following her parents back to their bench.

Dee stiffened beside him. "What's with *her?*"

He shrugged. "What are you talking about?"

"You *love* her, don't you? I can see it in your face." Her tears stopped as quickly as if someone had twisted a knob on the kitchen faucet.

"I've always liked Katie—I mean, Kate," he whispered. "We went to school together."

Dee huffed and sat back. "I saw the way you looked at her. You want *her*, not me."

"Now that's not true."

She frowned and nodded. "Look, Norris, I've been around the block a time or two. I know what I see when it comes to men. And I know *that* look. My god, you're head-over-heels in love with her, aren't you?"

"I ain't either. You're the one moving in with me, in Ma's house," he said loudly. "Now you can sit here and behave yourself or go back to your stinking little trailer. Alone."

She bit her lip and bowed her head. Beneath her veil, he couldn't see the hatred burning in her eyes.

Later that afternoon, while Deidre Garnet was moving the rest of her things into Edith Hymes's house, she was shocked to find the closets filled. Not with shoes, coats, sweaters or the ordinary barrage of clutter. No, every closet except the one in Norris's old bedroom was filled with acorns. Boxes of them, garbage bags stuffed with them. Hundreds were loose, tumbling out as soon as she opened the doors. They rolled across the floor like wooden marbles.

She shook her fists at Norris, who sat in the living room nursing a beer and looking particularly sullen. He'd offered no help whatsoever moving her stuff in.

"Your mother was a crazy old coot!" she screamed, throwing the acorns she held from both fists, sending them pinging against the walls, the lamp, the television and his chair.

His eyes remained expressionless as he plucked an acorn from his lap. "No crazier than you," he muttered.

While Deidre threw acorns and screamed at Norris, a black Ford sedan pulled into the parking lot of the town hall. Not the hearse— no, that was a powder blue Chevy and it had long since carted off Gotham Creek's latest deceased. Two men in matching black suits stepped out of the sedan and entered the town hall, single-file. Their dark glasses gave no indication of the color or shape of their eyes. Both had pocked morticians' complexions and closely cropped dark hair. But for the difference in their heights, they could have been twins.

The first flashed his badge at a very surprised Jim Digby. "F.B.I., Special Investigations Unit. Where's your sheriff?"

Jim's jaw dropped nearly a foot. "Uh, we don't have a sheriff. Constable's around the back."

Neither man thanked him, but the one who spoke gave him a curt nod. Jim shook his head as he watched them walk to Hap's office door. A question entered his mind at that moment, and the answer came screaming at him with all the subtlety of a derailed train. *Oh God, oh God, oh God—we're in a heap of calamity now!* Jim jumped at the sound of Hap's door closing behind them and was glad, for the moment, that he wasn't a sitting duck on their hot seat. But his turn was coming, of that, he was sure.

Hap looked up from his desk as the two men entered his office. His eyes widened, but he managed to conceal his surprise that they'd arrived so soon. He tried to relax and forced a small-town, friendly smile. "Hello, gentlemen. How can I help you?"

"F.B.I." Their badges were opened, flashed, then shut in a matter of seconds. The taller man spoke first. "I'm Agent Bullock and this is Agent Kent. We're conducting an investigation on the disappearances of two people: Sheridan Phillips and Bert Colby. Seems Gotham Creek was the last place they were seen...alive."

Hap nodded. "Well, you're not alone. The National Forest Service has already sent two of their representatives here to investigate as well. They'd said they'd like to nail Phillips on a string of charges."

Agent Kent spoke up. "We know. They're working with us on this case. Now we're not insinuating that something *happened* to Phillips or Colby. We're just here to determine the facts. I think you'll agree, it's a strange coincidence that *both* men apparently vanished in Gotham Creek within the past few days. So you won't mind if we take a look around town? Ask a few questions?"

Hap shook his head, holding his palms up. "No, of course not. Go right ahead."

Agent Bullock approached Hap's desk and sat down in the chair across from him. "We'd like to begin with you. For security reasons, we're taping this conversation, so you might want to start off on the right foot and tell us everything you know. We'd hate to have to come back and arrest a fellow lawman."

Hap no longer felt very relaxed at all. "Start your tape, gentlemen," he told them.

F.B.I. File 103669
Tape #1, Gotham Creek, Maine
Constable Hugo "Hap" Kingsley
10-10-96, 3:17 p.m.

"Do you know Sheridan Phillips?"

"Personally, no. I know who he is—hell, everybody knows Phillips, the tree-hugger. I've seen him on TV but I never read his books. He's a bit too radical for me, I guess. Jim Digby, that's our town manager, said Phillips came here October 2, wanting to look at some maps and asking questions. You'd have to talk to him about exactly what was said, word for word, but on a hunch I guess Jim sent him up to talk to Doc Putnam. I saw Doc that morning and asked him whose car was parked in his yard. That's when he told me it belonged to Sheridan Phillips. But no, I didn't speak to Phillips personally, nor did I see him here."

"It sounds to us that you suspect something might have happened to Phillips."

Long pause. "I don't know what you're talking about."

"We think perhaps you do. This isn't the first time someone disappeared in the woods at the north of town, is it?"

"No."

"We've opened a file for an in-depth investigation on Gotham Creek's history. Your own father disappeared in those woods, didn't he, Constable?"

Another pause. "Yes."

"We've come up with a total of twelve missing since 1935. That's a lot of people for one small town, wouldn't you say?"

"I guess so." Another pause. "But you've got to understand—they were *lost* in the woods. That forest isn't like any other—it's so dense you could hardly drive a rabbit through it. And then there's the old mine."

"Yes, we know. Putnam's Silver Pit. Don't look so surprised, Constable. We've checked into that as well. Excavated in 1931, after Malcomb Putnam, Sr. discovered a vein of silver while digging a well. He saw the mine as an answer to the Depression so he hired men to work it for fifty cents a day. But silver wasn't the only thing they hauled out of that mine, was it?"

"I wouldn't know. I wasn't around then."

"Allow us to clue you in: it didn't take long for the silver to peter out, ten years at best. The vein was thin and the silver wasn't exactly the best quality. The miners then happened upon a substance glowing inside some rocks. They touched it with their gloves and their gloves began to glow. Not white, but greenish-yellow. They called the substance 'Lumin'", but scientists would later determine it to be 'Radia-anthracite'. Worked better for illuminating clock hands than Radium because Radia-anthracite didn't require exposure to light to work. It glowed all by itself. I'm surprised you didn't know this."

"That was a long time before I was born."

"Were you also unaware that all the men who mined this material were dead by 1945?"

"Huh?"

"Severe radiation poisoning. Of course, they didn't call it that back then. But I suspect that even today, if you held a Geiger counter over their gravesites, it would tip off the scale. You see, Radia-anthracite has never been found in any other place on the planet, except in Gotham Creek, Maine. It was a rare and deadly find but it made Malcomb Putnam rich, and he poured that money back into the town. Then by 1950, he closed the mine permanently."

"The mine ran out of Radia-anthracite?"

"No. People were getting sick. Miners, as well as their families, started coming down with strange cancers. Some of them took the stuff home for their children to play with. The workers at the clock factories began falling ill as well and by the time Malcomb Putnam realized the Radia-anthracite was dangerous, even deadly, it was too late to save anyone. He saved many more lives by shutting down that mine forever."

"I didn't know that."

Pause. "No, we don't expect you did. It's not something Putnam wanted up for discussion. In fact, he did his best to hide it. Paid in full, out of his own pocket, for healthcare and funeral costs. Dealt out stipends to widows. Even went so far as to take orphans to a home in Augusta. No, it's very unlikely you'd have heard about it."

"Well, I know the mineshafts are still there in the forest. Maybe you'll find bodies down there somewhere."

"I suspect you may be right, Constable. We're going to leave no rock unturned until we find Phillips and Colby. We'd like to start by taking a ride out to the cemetery. And we want you to come with us."

"Why the cemetery?"

"Just a theory, a hunch, Constable. If it checks out, it'll save us some time."

<End of Tape #1>

Doc peered at the faces of the men in his cellar—his friends, his neighbors—and felt distraught that Hap couldn't attend this important meeting. *What if something goes wrong and someone loses their temper?* he wondered grimly. *It's happened before and I don't want to see it happen again. I'd just feel better if Hap were here to keep the peace.* He took a deep breath.

"Before we draw the name of the Chosen, I'd best warn all of you," he said. "There's a traitor in our midst. Someone, posing as my niece, called Piston Paper and told them I wanted my woodlot cut. I don't know why anyone would do such a thing, but I have the feeling she lives right here in town. She might well be one of the girls whose name is in that box. We've had them panic before, but nothing like this."

He looked up, rubbing his hands. The light from tallowy candles cast wavering shadows across the stone cellar walls. "And on top of that," he added, "there's another man out in the woods today, I'm fairly certain of it. He left his car in my yard and a note in my door. He's from the paper company and I have a bad grue about this one. By ill fortune Sheridan Phillips disappeared in our forest. Now he's got company." Doc rubbed his fingers together then wiped at the sheen of sweat on his forehead. "Well, we'd best get on with this and have done with it. The sooner, the better."

Silently, each man passed the black box along the circle, giving it a firm shake so the slips of paper inside could be heard rattling about. Hand-to-hand it made its rounds with a series of Gaelic blessings until it finally came to rest in Doc's grasp. He stared down at it, his knobby fingers trembling. He never enjoyed this part of the priesthood. Reading the name of the Chosen was a harsh task because it was always someone he knew and cared about, a girl he'd helped bring into this world by assisting in her delivery. Every sacrifice stole another piece of his soul, and in the twilight of his life, he felt in his heart this would be his last drawing.

"Now's the moment of truth," he said at last, lifting the heavy metal cover. He reached in and withdrew a slip of paper, unfolding it in his trembling fingers. His eyes narrowed as he read the name, then he looked up with a somber expression, carefully guarded lest he break down and sob.

"Kate Speers is to be the Chosen."

Ned groaned and fell into the arms of his neighbors.

10

It didn't take Hap Kingsley long to realize that things were about to go from bad to worse. He didn't like either of the Federal agents; being around them made him feel as comfortable as sleeping naked in a tent full of chiggers—only these bloodsuckers were capable of tearing apart an entire town. His town.

Agent Bullock was the taller of the two and maybe a half a degree warmer than his partner; but Hap found both to be humorless, devoid of personality. Since neither removed their dark glasses, he slipped on his own mirrored aviators as soon as he got into his car. He followed them out to the cemetery, and couldn't help but wonder if they might be the infamous 'men-in-black' who were sent by God-knows-who—the government maybe?—to scare silence into U.F.O. witnesses. He'd had heard such stories but never put any stock in them. Until now.

They turned right, onto Celt Street, a narrow lane with pavement as dark and crinkled as the surface of a chocolate cookie. Thick lilac bushes lined both sides of the road, their brown leaves scattered upon the tar like confetti. Up ahead, the bushes gave way to a shaded lawn and a stately house, one of the oldest in town, a three-story structure with a mansard roof. A sprawl of ivy, now brown, had crawled up its south side and clung to the blue clapboard siding. The mailbox beside the road hung from a metal post bent like an upside-down J. The name on the box read: Edith & Norris Hymes.

As Hap passed by the house, he noticed Deidre's red Mustang parked in the drive and stacks of cardboard boxes by the front door. *Deidre's moving in. Edith must be rolling over in her grave,* he thought. That notion was followed by an eye-opening realization: *Oh God, Edith's grave. It's fresh and damned if the G-men aren't going to start asking questions. How can I keep them away from that mound of dirt? Surely, they're bound to notice it. How could they help it, what with all those flowers? If they ask, I'll just have to tell them that poor Edith died of a broken heart over her son's affair with the town slut. That should satisfy their curiosity.*

Ahead, the black sedan pulled to a stop at the gate, a tall grill of rusting iron with the words: ETERNAL REST CEMETERY spanning over its middle in crumbling letters.

Wonder who shut the gates? he asked as he pulled in behind the sedan, stopped and got out. "I'll open them," he shouted to the sedan's driver's side window that had rolled down only a crack. He pushed at the gate, swinging its screeching doors open wide, then stood aside, watching the sedan slide past him, then he went back to his cruiser.

They parked at the foot of the hill and both front doors of the sedan opened simultaneously. The agents stepped out at the same time, looking around.

"This cemetery is somewhat larger than we expected," Bullock called out as soon as Hap turned off his engine.

His eyes narrowed behind his sunglasses. "Well, it's old, so of course it's big."

Bullock slipped his hands into his pockets and turned away as Hap got out. Kent was already poking his way between headstones. Hap pointed his finger, catching up with Bullock. "That's the oldest section over there. The newer section is further on."

Bullock stiffened. "Agent Kent's quite capable of reading dates, I assure you, Constable."

Hap bit his tongue and followed Bullock to where Kent knelt before an old whitened stone, leaning precariously to one side.

Agent Kent looked up, his fingers still on the stone. "October 31 appears to be a concurrent date for your townspeople's deaths. Females in particular. Can you explain this phenomenon, Constable?"

Hap leaned down and read the timeworn information engraved on the stone: Bethany Brown, born June 2nd, 1928. Died October 31st, 1946. He straightened up. "Sorry, I don't know about her. That was a bit before my time."

Kent pointed to the grave next to hers. "Melody Kelwick died ten years later on the same day. Strange coincidence, don't you think? And there's Betsy Brown, born in 1939, died on Halloween, 1956. Jane Turner, born 1951, also died on Halloween, 1966. Serena Haskell, age 17, died on Halloween, 1976 and the latest, Arienna Nevels, who died on the same date in 1986. I'd like to know what's going on here. Why Halloween? Why every ten years?

And why the mounds are so small? And why are they all buried in the same row instead of with their families?"

Hap felt a lump rising in his throat and struggled to clear it by coughing into his fist. "I suspect they were cremated. It's a local custom. As for dying on the same day of the year—Halloween's always been a dangerous holiday. Kids die, sometimes, when pranks go awry. They overdose at parties or get run over while trick-or-treating. Accidents happen. What more can I say?"

Kent stood up. "I'm very good at math, Constable. And statistics. The years of these deaths are staggered by ten and they were all young women. Would you mind telling me what the hell's going on here?"

Hap shrugged with a sigh. "Nothing that I'm aware of."

"Why don't you go back to your car and wait for us?" Bullock asked. "We won't be much longer." As soon as Hap was out of earshot, Bullock whispered to Kent. "He knows more than he's admitting. What do you think is going on here?"

Agent Kent shook his head with a sigh. "It's anyone's guess. An occult practice of some sort, maybe. But even if it turns out to be something like that, it doesn't explain what happened to Phillips or Colby." He frowned and tapped his finger to his lips, thinking. "Suppose there is a secret in this town? Let's say black magic, for example. Suppose those men discovered what's going on here. They'd have to be silenced, wouldn't they?"

"Perhaps. But I wouldn't think so in this day and age."

Agent Kent shot his partner a grim look. "Don't forget where we are." He added a bit of nasal twang to his voice and inserted, "These are country folk, simple and unsophisticated, prone to superstition and backward ways. Maybe they're practicing a little voodoo on the side? Maybe they kill outsiders who come snooping too closely around these parts?"

Agent Bullock shook his head. "But the bodies would have to be hidden."

Kent nodded. "So where would be the most feasible location?"

Bullock shrugged. "I don't know. The woods, maybe? With the old mine there, it would make no sense to dig graves for the bodies."

Kent frowned and pushed his sunglasses further up the bridge of his nose. "So you're saying you think the bodies may have been dumped in the old mine?"

"If Phillips and Colby were murdered, yes. It would be the most likely place."

"That mine has to be riddled with radiation."

"Perhaps. But we'd have to be careful. Exit at the first sign of Radia-anthracite. We've got bulletproof vests in the trunk. The lead in them should afford us adequate protection, at least for a little while."

Bullock scratched his head, unsure. "If you say so."

"I say so."

He glanced at his watch. "Let's go there tomorrow. It's almost five now and it'll be dark soon."

"Fair enough. There's a restaurant next to Route 1 and I'm getting hungry."

"I could use something to eat myself. So we're done here?"

Agent Kent gave a lift of his head. "Not quite. There's a fresh grave over there on the hill. I'd like to take a quick look at it before we go."

Bullock sighed, shaking his head. "You've always been drawn to morbidity, Kent. Why is that?"

"The dead never lie," he replied.

Cuffy's restaurant hadn't changed much in the last 35 years. The green-leather cushioned booths and chrome-trimmed tables, the black and white checkered floor and red melamine-covered walls indicated that it had been built back when big-finned Chevys lined up in the parking lot and Elvis Presley's "Jailhouse Rock" was number one on the Hit Parade. Back in the days of poodle skirts and bobbie socks and the war in Korea.

Mike Elwin looked out the window and noticed a black sedan pull into the lot. He watched two men in black suits get out and approach the front door and he shouted, "Hey, Dee, there's some big spenders coming in. Put them at table four and we'll split the tips."

She shot her boss a look of disgust. "Like hell we will."

Mike chuckled and turned back to his fryer, watching out of the corner of his eye as she led them to a table. He couldn't help but notice the sway of her hips exaggerate just a bit more than usual. He saw the shorter one smile at her and say something which she jotted down on her pad. Then she hurried back to the kitchen.

"Two sirloins, medium rare. Baked potatoes, slaw."

"Gotcha," Mike said. "And what are they drinking?"

"Martinis, shaken not stirred." She gave him a wave. "Don't worry, I'll fix the drinks. You'd water them down too much, anyway." She went to the bar and grabbed bottles of vermouth and vodka. "Hey, where are the olives?"

"We ran out a month ago. Nobody around here likes olives, anyway."

"Great." Deidre made the martinis, hoping that her handsomely suited customers wouldn't miss the olives too much. *With any luck*, she thought, *I can take their minds off what's not floating in their drinks*. She hurried back to their table, expertly balancing their cocktails on a tray.

"Here you go, gentlemen," she said with a smile that could melt a glacier. "Could I get you some hor d'oeuvres?"

"What are you offering, sweet thang?" the shorter man asked.

Deidre's smile broadened as she felt his hand slide up her thigh and come to rest on the right cheek of her ass. She could feel one of his fingers slip under the elastic band of her underwear and move back and forth sensuously. "What's your pleasure?" she asked in a husky tone, turning slightly so no one could see that his hand was up under her skirt.

The shorter man glanced at his partner and lowered his voice. "We'll order dessert later. Privately." He gazed back up at her. "When do you get off, missie?"

Deidre grinned. "Every chance I get."

The taller one toasted her. "I'll drink to that." He didn't smile and she couldn't see his eyes behind his dark glasses, so she leaned over and whispered in his ear. "I'll fake cramps and get off work right now, if you boys want to party."

The shorter man lifted his glass to clink with that of his friend. "A lady after my own heart."

"You don't have a heart, Bullock," the other said with a snicker.

After a lingering gaze at her tits, Bullock looked up at her face, his fingers steadily kneading her ass. "We've got a room at the Swan Motel. Number 14. Meet us there at seven. And wear that cute apron."

Deidre nodded. "That can be arranged. Now let me see about getting you fellars fed." She started to walk away and as she did, she felt the waistband of her panties snap against the small of her back. She flashed him a flirty smile on her way to the kitchen.

The Swan Motel was a line of neat white rectangles just inside the Jonesboro town line. It catered to tourists during the summer months and was about to enter its off season; therefore, the parking lot was empty but for a few cars. Sports and luxury vehicles, mostly. The travelers with children in minivans and station wagons had left state a month ago, at the onset of the school year.

Deidre parked her red Mustang beside the black sedan in front of door #14. She checked her watch. 6:58 p.m. Then she examined her makeup in the mirror and everything was perfect.

With any luck, she surmised, *I'll be able to leave this god-forsaken place and go somewhere warm, where it never snows. Someplace tropical. If I can just get one of these guys interested in me I'll have them eating from the palm of my hand. Then I can leave Norris Hymes with his sloppy kisses and that smelly old house of his behind. Damn, I was born for luxury! And if I have to use my ass to get it, so be it.*

She got out of the car and quickly scanned the lot. Sure that no one was watching, she hurried up to the #14 door and rapped lightly. The lights were on in the room, she could tell from the crack in the curtain of the window. Her heart felt as if about to explode out of her chest; it was beating so hard. Then the door opened and she was pulled inside.

Bullock laughed and welcomed her with a hard kiss. She felt his hands cup her ass and squeeze it firmly. "Glad you could make it," he told her. He glanced over at the other agent, seated in a chair at a small round table in front of two beds. "Ain't she something, Kent?"

"You boys ain't seen nothing yet." She quickly undid the buttons on her jacket. She was wearing nothing underneath except her apron, that short ruffled thing.

Bullock pulled her jacket free and tossed it on the bed. "We want to see it all," he said, putting his arms around her. "Show us everything you got."

After a hasty session of stripping foreplay (there wasn't much left to take off), Deidre was on her hands and knees on the bed, taking the tall man's cock down her throat as Bullock knelt behind her, pumping and sweating. She gave them her all—in as many ways as a woman can take two men.

And when it was over, she had five crisp new $100 bills in her pocket. Not nearly enough to get her out of Maine, but it was a good start. Bullock, the shorter man, liked her a lot; he'd want more, she could tell.

She trusted she could abide their eccentricities long enough to raise the $1500 she needed to escape Gotham Creek forever.

Agents Bullock and Kent had no reason to tell the blonde party girl that they'd ordered Edith Hymes's body exhumed. Nor did they tell her that they suspected murder. They had no need to try to wrest information about Gotham Creek out of her.

That would come later and by then, she'd give it all away for free.

The man and the woman from the National Forest Service were dead and Bert reckoned it was now waiting for him. *But what exactly was it? Some sort of tree monster?*

I've seen hundreds of thousands of trees in my life, he reasoned, *and I know trees don't move that way. They don't just grab people up and eat them. But I also know what my eyes have seen. That branch moved like a snake. The oak ate that bird. Plucked it right down from the sky. And here I sit, in the dark with a busted ankle—even if I could climb out of this place, I'm not so sure I would dare to. It's out there, I know it's out there and I think it knows that I know. It's just biding its time.*

God, I'm so hungry. I'm so scared, I shouldn't be hungry. And yet, I am. All I can think about is food: steak and home fries and flapjacks as big as dinner plates smothered with real maple syrup. No, scratch that. I don't think I could eat maple syrup. Not now.

Millie always made the best pies. Chocolate cream, mincemeat, apple. No, don't think about apple pie. Ah, I can't help it. I remember back when I was a boy in Bridgeport, Connecticut…we had this apple tree in our backyard, a rough-barked, twisted monstrosity. Dad always threw a net over the entire tree every spring just before the blossoms came out and those apples never had worms.

But they were the strangest apples, weren't they? Pink and grainy inside with a blood-red clot at the core. And we ate them—how we ate them! Mom baked pies and cobblers with them. Oh God, I wish to hell I never heard of an apple. Or maple syrup, for that matter.

I suppose the trees have every right to be mad at us, he thought soberly. *We drink their blood, eat their babies, build our homes with their flesh, burn them in our fires. Why shouldn't they wage war on humans? Especially on people like me. How many of them have I sentenced to death at the paper mill?*

Too many to count.

A tear rolled down Bert's cheek and he caught it with his tongue. *I'm so thirsty. I think I must be losing my mind. Maybe I'm dead and this is hell? But hell's hot, so I can't be there because I feel cold. Not shivering. Not yet. Just cold.*

Except for my ankle. Feels like my foot's stuck in an oven. He reached down and gingerly touched his lower leg. *Yep, swollen to twice its size, too. I'm in a world of hurt and the only people who knew exactly where I am are gone. Eaten alive, probably, just like that bird. No one's ever gonna find me. Please, God, don't let me die like this! I've got to get back home to Millie and Jason; they're counting on me. I'll make you a deal, God. If You can get me out of here, I'll think kind thoughts about David Hardcastle. I'll even kiss his feet, if You want. Just please help me...*

Bert Colby buried his head in his arms and wept as the last bit of daylight flickered over the mineshaft, then total darkness settled in.

Ned pulled Maisie into his arms and stroked her hair, trying to calm her down. She hadn't taken the news well. There'd been no easy way to tell her that the elders had selected Kate as the Chosen.

"Our poor baby," she sobbed into his chest. "Why'd they have to pick her? Why?"

"The decision was as fair as always," Ned said. "I was there and I tried to convince them to change their minds but it was impossible. The Chosen is chosen and that's that." He kissed her hair and added, "But I want you to know, I tried."

She pulled away from him, a glimmer of desperate hope gleaming in her wet eyes. "We have to leave. Pack up what we need, take Kate and Eddie and get out of town. Tonight."

Ned reached down and grabbed her by the hand to lead her to the living room window. He pulled aside the curtain. "Look, Maisie. They're not going to let us leave."

She saw four men standing under the streetlamp. They wore white robes and their faces were painted blue. She gasped and covered her mouth with her free hand, remembering what she'd heard about a family that tried to escape twenty years ago, when their daughter had been selected as the Chosen. Vincent and Maria Haskell had been shot to death along with their nine-year-old son, Marcus, by men with blue faces. Serena Haskell was the sole survivor.

But not for long.

"This is wrong, Ned! So very wrong. My parents were right all along—it's a wonder they ever got out alive. Oh god, why'd I ever come back to this godforsaken town?"

Ned let the curtain fall back into place and put an arm around his sobbing wife. "You came back because you wanted to. Because I was here, waiting for you."

She shook her head as she wiped her face with her hands. "I was so stupid, so naive! I really thought everyone got thousands of dollars on the fireplace mantle every Yule. But it's not that way on the outside, Ned. No Yule money ever comes." She sniffled and added, "You're right. I came back to be with you but I also came back for the money. Now my greed is going to cost our daughter's life."

Ned started to disagree, but she stopped him. "I told Kate to lose her virginity. I told her to go have sex with someone or do the job herself."

His eyes narrowed. "You did *what*? Maisie, how could you? You have no idea what they'll do to us, do you?"

She stepped back, instantly defiant. "I was thinking of the safety of our child! That's more than you did for her!"

Ned shot her an ugly sneer. "You're dead wrong. If they find out Kate's *not* a virgin they'll run us out of town. We'll lose everything—the house, our businesses, our land, the cars, even the bank account. We have no IDs, no birth certificates or social security numbers, either. Nothing. It will be as if we never existed. Do you want that? Where could we go with just the shirts on our backs? How could we start over with nothing and no one to help us? Where will we live with winter setting in?"

Maisie sank to her knees in despair. She knew what it had been like for her parents when they fled Gotham Creek. They lived for two months in their car while her father tried to find a job. At last he landed one, at a sardine factory as a general laborer, a far cry from owning the convenience store at Gotham Creek.

From their car, they moved into an old, abandoned school bus that they managed to convert into a makeshift home. There was no running water but at least they had an outhouse.

Maisie enrolled at Naraguagus High School but her two years there were miserable. She wore clothes donated by the Salvation Army and old hand-me-downs her mother bought for nickles and dimes at yardsales.

And of course her classmates took careful note of where she lived and what she wore. Those who didn't tease her shunned her. There was only one boy; one out of the hundreds enrolled there, who was kind to her. He took the time to talk to her and always had a smile. His name was Henry and he dreamed of becoming an airplane pilot someday.

But she refused to go out with him. All during those two long years, her heart longed for Ned Speers, the boy she'd left behind at Gotham Creek. She secretly kept in touch with him by letter and as soon as he got his driver's license, she started dating him on the sly.

On her eighteenth birthday, she left home and returned to Gotham Creek on Ned's arm, as his wife. Now the Elders couldn't touch her and she was safe from being selected as the Chosen. The only person to kick up a stink about her return was Felicity Kingsley. Maisie didn't know why Felicity was treating her that way; she'd gotten what she wanted: Hap.

The year Kate was born, there had been a fire in the old schoolbus and Maisie's parents died without ever setting eyes on their granddaughter.

Ned's right, she thought miserably. *I came back because of the money. I love the finer things in life and I loved being a part of this town. I was so wrong to ever return.*

Ned dropped to his knees on the carpet and pulled her into his arms. "Try not to worry," he vowed. "I'll come up with a plan to save Kate. Trust me."

Hap Kingsley hadn't relished the thought of exhuming Edith Hymes's body, but he had no choice in the matter. If he'd put up a fuss, the two agents would think he had something to do with her death. He didn't—but that wouldn't stop them from pointing fingers, now would it?

To cooperate, he called Underbrother's Construction to send someone over to operate the backhoe. It didn't seem right asking Norris to dig up his own mother's grave. It was hard enough having to tell him what the F.B.I. had ordered.

Norris had been upset, expectedly so. "But Doc said Ma died in her sleep. Why do they have to look at her?"

Hap rested a hand on his shoulder. "I know it's hard, but it'll be just a routine autopsy. She'll be back where she belongs in no time."

He shot him a look of disbelief. "I just don't get it. Do they think someone killed her?"

Hap shrugged. "I don't know, Norris. I just don't know."

This was the kindest lie he could think of.

Voices. I hear voices. Oh, no. Not from above. Please, not from above. Don't let it get them, too. I think I'll go stark raving mad if it happens again. Bert giggled and the sound was eerie, teetering on the edge of insanity. *I'm really losing it. I can feel reality slipping away from me with every breath, with every throb of my ankle, with every rumble of my empty stomach. Are the voices real—or are they coming from inside my own head? I wish I dared to yell for help.*

He began to shake uncontrollably; fear, pain, hunger and thirst were taking a toll on him. Some say the insane never question their sanity, but this is not so. Whether or not they admit it, it's the *first* question they think of.

Bert tried to crawl in the direction of the voices, but they seemed to be coming from all sides. He managed to swallow; the dry click in his throat sounded loud. He opened his mouth wide, turning his head to make sure he was far enough away from the hole in the ceiling and the beam of bluish early morning light that filtered down through it to the mine floor.

"Whaa," he managed to say, no louder than a hoarse whisper. "Whaa."

The voices became louder, almost ringing in his ears. He dragged himself closer to the sound. Closer still. *Whaach. Whaach oww.*

He could see them now. Two beams of light floating through the darkness ahead like uneven eyes, bouncing off the walls, off the floor. Closer now.

And he held out his hand to them, wishing his voice was stronger so he could tell them to watch out, but he could only manage to say, "Whaa. Whaach oww." Finally, one beam strayed across his arm; his hand and the voices became louder still. Then all went hazy. Bert felt himself being picked up, caught by the arms by the thing with the glowing eyes. One of the eyes shone into his face, blinding him with its light. He heard the voices again, but was unable to understand what they were saying.

"Whaach oww," he whispered, more to himself than to the four-armed creature holding him upright as he screamed inside his head: *Watch out! Watch out!*

As he collapsed in a dead-weight faint, Agents Bullock and Kent struggled to keep from dropping him.

"Well, looks like we found Colby," Bullock said, shining his light on the prone body. "Geez, what do you suppose happened to him? His skin. Looks like a bad case of road rash. And that ankle."

"Let's get him out of here." Kent nodded. "And take care with his foot. It's either sprained or broken."

Slowly, they half-dragged, half-carried Bert Colby through the mine's winding labyrinth and out into the light of day.

"What's wrong with him?" Bullock asked, his eyes fearful. The man looked even worse in the daylight.

"Radiation sickness, dehydration," Kent replied, then added. "I think."

"Were we exposed?"

"I don't know. One thing for certain, this man needs more medical assistance than we can provide. I suggest we take him to the nearest hospital."

"He was trying to tell us something back there. What do you suppose it was?" Agent Bullock asked.

Agent Kent shrugged. "I don't know. He was incoherent. Here, open up the back door of the car and let's get him in."

"I don't like touching him. His skin looks like, feels like...well, melted cheese."

Agent Kent grimaced. "Just check the map and see where the nearest hospital is."

Bullock flipped open the glove compartment and pulled out a Maine road atlas. After studying it for a moment, he looked up. "Machias. Route 1 East."

11

A week passed until the autopsy report on Edith's death came to rest in the hands of the F.B.I. The report stated that she'd had been strangled to death with a blunt object. The manner in which her windpipe and larynx were crushed and the outer bruising round that area indicated the use of a weapon, a club or stick. Or more likely, the branch of a tree, an Oak to be exact, given the tiny splinters and microscopic shreds of bark left embedded in the skin around her throat.

The report also showed that her body had been grossly mutilated after death. There was no pooling of blood around her lungs and heart, as there would be, had she been tortured before she died. Numerous acorns were found as deep as her broken windpipe and as far up inside as her large intestine. One was discovered resting firmly against her cervix.

The woman's eyes had been crushed by the insertion of acorns, evident by the shards of shells imbedded in the orbital area. These acorns had been removed before burial, as had several others, it was suspected.

Now the F.B.I. had a focal point for their investigation: the doctor who falsely filled out the death certificate.

But by then it was evident Doc Putnam had also vanished, along with Sheridan Phillips, Dick Oliver and Susan Mills and if anyone knew where any of them had gone, no one was talking.

Bert Colby would be a long time recovering from his ordeal. His speech was incoherent, a disjointed series of the words "tree", "eat" and "watch out" were most prevalent. The F.B.I. notified his family and Piston Paper of his condition; in the terms used by the staff of doctors: Bert was suffering from exposure, dehydration, radiation sickness and Post Traumatic Shock Disorder.

The time needed for his recovery period was anyone's guess: days, weeks, months or years.

"Or he may never recover at all," the Chief of Staff was heard to say.

Bert's wife, Millie, arrived the next day and while she was going through his personal belongings, she found two acorns in the pockets of the pants he'd been wearing when he was found. They were the largest acorns she'd ever seen in her life and she made a vow to plant them on her lawn come spring. For it wasn't likely Bert would ever return home.

She'd plant them for him.

Deidre Garnet showed up at room #14, Swan Hotel, at seven sharp, just as she had every night of the week. The door opened at her knock and this time, the Federal boys weren't waiting for her in their Fruit of the Loom's, ready to party.

Instead, they were waiting for her with a tape recorder and microphone and because she could be trusted to keep a secret or two, as a special treat they allowed her to read Edith Hymes's Autopsy Report before turning on the mike.

F.B.I. File 103670
Tape #2
Deidre Garnet
10-17-96, 7:20 p.m.

"How well did you know the deceased, Edith Hymes?"

"Oh, better than I would've liked, really. See, I live with her son and she didn't like that. Not one bit. I guess she thought I was corrupting her darling little boy."

"What is his name, age, and occupation?"

"Norris. Norris Randolph Hymes. I think he's around twenty or twenty-one. He takes care of the cemetery. Does odds and ends around town."

"What's his address?"

"5 Celt Street. You know, the big house just before the cemetery. We both live there."

Pause. "So you and the deceased didn't get along?"

Laughter. "Now that's the understatement of the year. She hated my guts."

"So you were enemies?"

Pause. "Good gosh, no. I didn't have a beef with her. I just tried to stay out of her way."

"Do you know anybody who wanted to cause her harm?"

Another pause. "No. No one really liked her, but I don't think anyone wanted to kill her."

"Someone did. Where's Norris's father?"

"Who?"

"We'd like the name of Norris Hymes's father."

"I honestly don't know. I always assumed Edith was a widow."

"You say you live with Norris in his mother's house. Were you living there before she died?"

"You're kidding, right." Giggle. "Of course, not. Norris insisted I move in the day she was buried."

"Where was Norris on the night of October 3?"

"We were in my trailer out on Old Woods Road."

"Was he with you all night long?"

"Hmm. Yeah, I guess so."

"You don't sound so sure."

"Well, quite honestly, I'm not. I can hardly remember one day to the next. We get drunk sometimes, you know, but Norris is usually home at night."

"That will be all. You may be questioned later. Thank you for your time, Miss Garnet."

<End Tape #2>

Deidre looked up at the agents and pushed her hair back with a flip of her hand. "Well, how'd I do?"

"Splendid as always," Agent Bullock answered.

"Are we gonna party?"

Agent Kent shook his head. "Not tonight, dear. We have paperwork to do."

"Will I be paid for this?"

Agent Bullock reached over and patted her ass. "Consider this a freebie, sweet thang. Just doing your duty as an American citizen."

12

With his lantern in hand, Doc Putnam ventured deeper into the forest. It was a bone-chilling evening and he pulled his cloak tighter around him for warmth and comfort.

He wished it wasn't dark. He'd spent more than a week in the forest, preparing for the Samhain Festival and trying to make certain everything was perfect. But he knew it wasn't wise to be here at night, alone, and especially at a time when his visit might not be welcomed.

Outsiders had been here, desecrating the sacred woods with their presence. Carefully hidden, he'd watched when the Feds carried a man out of the mine. That man had been extremely sick, and Doc felt tempted to try to help.

But he couldn't. The woods demanded his attention.

That, and he was terribly afraid, as badly as he hated to admit it.

The ghost of his father's voice kept echoing through his mind: "You didn't touch him, did you? Forget you ever saw him, Doc. Just forget about all of this. It was just a bad dream…"

Only it wasn't a dream and he knew it.

He'd seen only one other person stricken with what appeared to be the same sort of sickness. He was five years old in 1943 and his real name was Dickie but his father had dubbed him 'Doc' and for some reason, the nickname stuck.

He was playing outside in the yard when the truck drove up to the house. It was a Saturday and his father had bought him a baseball the day before. He was practicing tossing it into the air and catching it but stopped to look when the truck arrived. It was one of the mineworkers' trucks, with a rusting hood and a homemade wooden body. There was a lot of moaning coming from the back, so while the driver headed for the house, Doc dropped his ball and climbed up on the rusty bumper to take a look at what was inside. A man lie there, groaning and writhing in obvious agony.

Only it didn't look like a man anymore.

He'd been a large black fellow; Doc remembered his name was Big Joe for he was the first Negro he'd ever seen.

Poor Big Joe looked like a melted tire. His skin was a terrible sight—plastered with giant blisters and some had split to reveal the wet pink flesh underneath. What wasn't blistered was speckled with some sort of greenish stuff that looked like powder. Or mold spoors, like the kind that grew on stale bread.

The man opened his eyes, staring directly up at Doc's face, and when Doc saw those eyes he screamed. He jumped down of the truck to bolt toward the house as fast as he could.

Those eyes, Big Joe's awful eyes, were blood red with pupils that glowed green. Light green like the color of a new leaf and glowing like those of a cat in the dark. No human should ever have eyes like that.

He screamed for his father, who came rushing out of the house, tugging at his suspenders as he hurried toward the truck. Doc stayed up on the porch; his father was angry about something, shouting at the driver. Maybe he was mad about the man in the truck but Doc wasn't sure.

As they drove away, he could hear the man in the back crying.

"What's wrong with Big Joe, Daddy?"

His father's jaw tightened as he approached and he got down on one knee to look eye to eye with Doc. "You didn't touch him, did you? Please tell me you didn't touch him."

Doc shook his head. "I didn't."

"Good." His father ruffled his hair but he didn't smile.

"I saw Big Joe. He looked just awful."

His father shot him a stern look. "Forget you ever saw him, Doc. Just forget about all of this. It's just a bad dream, son. Never happened. Okay?"

Doc nodded but he never forgot. Oh, there had been plenty of things he'd forget about but never this.

His father had lied to him. It *had* happened and it was worse than a nightmare.

Something's gone wrong, same as before, Doc thought to himself as he walked along the overgrown wood road. He could feel the *wrongness* in the air all around him. Was it because outsiders had intruded the forest? Or was he just worried about how the Speers were taking the news about their daughter, Kate? Or maybe ghosts were haunting him? Not literally but figuratively. Doc reasoned the other lost people must almost certainly be dead by now.

He stuck to the old road. He knew it well; there were no mineshafts here. Gradually it became a footpath, almost impossible to spot if you didn't know exactly where it was and difficult to follow even if you did. It led, twisting and turning, through the forest glade and straight to the foot of the great bull oak.

Here Doc knelt, humbled, bent in supplication.

This was one of the most sacred spots on earth, as holy than the megaliths of Stonehenge. Doc had been born here, as had his father and many generations of Putnams before that. It was here that he'd helped bring forth life, and every baby born beneath the oak was consecrated in the Druid tradition, blessed with dew from the leaves above. This was also the spot where the Chosen were sacrificed; the iron shackles and chains still hung from the tree, ready and waiting.

Everyone in Gotham Creek had been born at the foot of this tree with exception of the outsiders. Doc didn't care much for those who moved in from the outside; it meant all of them had to take more care in concealing their beliefs and protecting the forest. They were a necessary evil; new blood was needed, as bad as he hated to admit it.

And of course there was always the danger of outsiders seducing Gotham Creek's young, enticing them to move away to find better jobs. Doc had every confidence that he and the council of Elders could prevent such things from happening; it mattered little that they sometimes had to threaten people into obedience and that occasionally they had to do things to scare them.

It was only for the good of the town.

Breaking up teenage relationships between belivers and outsiders was often necessary, but no big deal when it came down to the bottom line. There was always the delicate matter of religious differences and in Gotham Creek's history, there'd only been a handful of true conversions.

He had just begun to pray, this time in the ancient Celtic tongue, when he heard the wind pick up, rustling through the trees. Then a twig snapped behind him. He stopped praying and lifted his head, half-expecting it to be a deer but knowing that was next to impossible. Nothing lived in these woods. Not for long, anyway.

He pulled down the hood of his cloak and slowly turned, still on his knees.

What he saw towering over him caused his heart to quake. He'd only seen it once every ten years but then from a distance. *Always* from a distance. Now Doc Putnam knew something of the terror the Chosen experienced.

His jaw dropped; his eyes bulged with fright and yet he could not pull his gaze away.

This was not the arrival of his gentle natured god but of something infinitely cruel, full of malice and consumed with lustful hatred.

And it glowed, bright green and blindingly so, staring down at Doc with menacing eyes, as the wind blew leaves in a spiral around its massive form.

"F-father forgive us!" he managed to whisper.

The forest god pointed a glowing, stick-like finger at him. "How dare you call me 'father'! You have done this to me, you and your kind. Have I not been good to you, protecting you always from the outside world? Why have you hurt me? Why?"

Doc faltered as he sought his voice. "What did we do? Where have we gone wrong? All my life I've observed the sacred rites. Why are you so angry?"

The glow grew even brighter, like a green fire. "You've let outsiders desecrate this holy ground! Because of them my brothers have tasted blood and they want more. They have become insatiable. Perhaps I should feed you to them so you, too, can experience their agony?"

Doc held up his hands to protect his eyes. "No, please. What can I do to appease you? To make things right? Just say the word and I'll do it!"

The being opened its arms wide. "There is only one way. Become one with me."

Doc shuddered. He'd witnessed the mating of the forest god with the Chosen. It always consumed the young women, setting their flesh to melt away from their bones. Their screams echoed in his darkest nightmares but afterwards, the forest god would become sated and he'd return to his benevolent form: a kindly being of generous nature, adorned with mistletoe, acorns and leaves.

Although fear seized Doc, he managed to stand up and face the glowing monstrosity. "What will happen to me?" he asked. "Will I burn up like the Chosen?"

The forest god roared. It was a horrible anguished sound that echoed through the trees. "I consumate and consume—then I give again. That is my nature. You understand, for it's your nature, too. But I tell you this: the Chosen will be a corrupt woman, unfit and unworthy. Do you not think my trees have ears? They hear and know everything! This is the only way now. Come to me. Let us become one and set the wrong to right."

Doc shook his head. "But I'll die if you touch me."

"You don't believe you deserve death," the being bellowed, "but I say you do! I know what you did twenty years ago. You stole the Chosen from me. Have you forgotten? I never forget. Never. But she was mine in the end."

Doc hung his head. "We were in love and planned to get married. It wasn't fair—"

"I decide what's fair! You are barely fit for priesthood. Choose your fate, little man. My brothers can smell you and they are ravenous."

Doc heard the rustling of leaves and looked upward just in time to see branches hurtling down at him. He couldn't move quickly enough and four of them grasped him, wrapping around him with the strength of boa constrictors.

Screaming, he was lifted into the air, brought face to face with his terrible god.

"Make your choice, human. Will it be my brother or me? Live or die, it makes little difference. Others are doomed to die. Many others. Which do you choose?"

Doc felt the circulation pinching off in his arms and legs. Something was opening up in the bark of the tree that was holding him: a terrible hole widening, lined with sharp wooden teeth. He could hear them grinding together, and a long string of sap ran like drool down the back of his cloak, wetting his neck.

It's going to eat me, he thought frantically as he struggled in vain. Finally the pain and the fear were too much to bear. He shouted at the forest god, "You! I choose you!"

The branches let go instantly and he felt himself fall, but only for a half second.

The forest god caught him in an embrace and as the green fire danced around them, Doc felt his fear turn into something else.

Something darker that burned much more brightly.

In the backseat of the Mustang, Norris sat up, watching Deidre go into the motel. Sure, he'd done a sneaky thing, hiding in her car—but he'd suspected for some time that she'd been messing around behind his back. Now he had proof.

It hurt him more than he thought it would. Hadn't he been good to her? Treating her nice even when she was in a foul mood? He had to admit sometimes he felt more like a jockey than a boyfriend, but the sex was great and frequent—so who was he to complain?

But it went deeper than that. He loved her. Or at least he'd thought so until now.

Ma was right, he decided, gritting his teeth as he pulled a Lucky from the pack in his shirt pocket. *Dee's nothing but trash. Who does she think she is, making a fool out of me?* He lit the cigarette and inhaled deeply.

This must be where she's been going all those nights she told me she was working. I know Mike Elwin hates me but he wasn't lying when I called asking for Dee. Of course when Mike said Deidre didn't work nights—and hadn't worked nights in a long time—Norris felt like a complete buffoon.

I trusted her, dammit! He punched the back of the front seat, wondering if he was man enough to walk up to door #14 and confront the weasel she was screwing around with.

But what if he's bigger than me? Is she worth losing a few teeth over? And what point would it prove, anyway? He flicked the ash from his cigarette onto the leather of the front seat. *Take that, bitch.*

With his free hand, he reached down into his coat pocket and felt for the bottle of chloroform and the rag he'd tucked there. Oh, he'd make her pay. By the time he finished with her, Deidre Garnet would never so much as look at another man. Norris concluded his plan by grinding his cigarette out on the top of the dashboard right where she'd be sure to see it. Then he sat back and waited.

It took her a little over an hour to come back out of the motel and as she trotted toward the car, keys in hand, Norris ducked behind the seat. He heard the door unlatch and felt the seat shift as she got in. Then she shut the door, turned the key in the ignition and gasped as she spotted the cigarette butt on the dashboard.

"What the fuck?"

That's when Norris sprang up from the back and grabbed her by the hair. "Yeah, Dee—that's *my* question, too. What the fuck? You not getting enough at home any more? Is that it?"

She froze in pain and fear. "Norris? It isn't what you think. Please stop pulling my hair—it hurts!"

He gave a cruel laugh. "That ain't nothing, Dee. I'm not letting go, either. Now you're going to drive back to Gotham Creek and then we're going to settle this once and for all. I'm not going to stand for any woman stepping out on me. Nobody makes a fool of Norris Hymes. Nobody. So drive if you want any of that bleached-out hay you call hair left on your scalp." He gave her another short tug just to let her know he meant business. "And don't think about pulling any tricks, either. I have a gun, all loaded and ready."

Deidre gulped and put the car into reverse. She backed out using the rearview mirror because Norris wouldn't let her turn her head.

"It really isn't what you think," she told him in a squeaky voice.

He chuckled again. "I suppose you were seeing a sick friend. You've been seeing that friend a lot lately, huh?"

"No!" She shifted into drive and stepped on the gas pedal.

"Take it slow, girl. No peeling rubber and calling attention to yourself." With his free hand, he reached over and pushed down the lock on her door just in case she tried to jump out.

Once they were on Route 1, she blurted, "It was the F.B.I. agents, ok? I'm working with them. You can go back there and ask them for yourself if you don't believe me."

The F.B.I.? Norris remembered seeing them snooping around town in their suits and sunglasses and that big black car. "Well, you're a regular Miss Bond, aren't you? What do you possibly know that can help them? All you know about is spreading your legs." He reached around the seat with his free hand and slipped it inside her jacket.

The car swerved a bit and he tightened his grip on her hair. "Keep it on the road, Dee. You don't want your pretty red car all dented up, do you?" He felt her waitressing apron and slid his hand underneath it.

She had nothing on, save the apron, her jacket and shoes. "Some sick friend," he growled, giving her left tit a hard twist.

Yelping, knowing she was caught in a lie, she began to cry. He let go of her flesh and seriously considered shooting her right then and there. But that wouldn't be wise; it would likely get him killed in the process—and shooting her would be the kindest fastest way out for her.

She deserved a far crueler fate.

As if reading his thoughts, she asked, sobbing, "W-what are you going to do?"

"Does it matter?"

"Yeah—ouch! Of course it matters. Just say the word and I'll leave. Pack up my shit and hit the road. I think I can still get my trailer back." She swallowed forcefully and added, "I'm really sorry. I don't know what else to tell you."

He shook his head in disgust. The only thing she was sorry about was getting caught. "You could start by telling me the truth. The 'real' truth, not the Deidre Garnet version." He saw her teary eyes glance at him in the mirror.

"You want the truth? Okay, I was seeing them. The F.B.I. agents."

His own eyes widened. "Both of them?"

"Yep, at the same time. Are you satisfied now, Norris? Huh?"

Despite his anger, he felt himself getting hard at the thought of her with two men. "Not quite satisfied yet, but I will be soon enough."

She began crying again. "What more do you want from me?"

"I'll decide later."

"You're scaring me. Please, just let go of my hair and my boob. We can talk this out and get it settled—I just know we can."

"Just shut up and drive." Her blubbering was interferring with the twisted scene playing in his mind: of his woman serving two men at once. Strangely, it turned him on and angered him all at the same time.

At least she wasn't talking now and that was a help. Every few seconds, she'd let out a frightened sob but for Norris, it just added to the fantasy.

When the car reached Gotham Creek, he suggested that she drive out to Old Woods Road. She asked he wanted to see if someone had moved into her old trailer. But he didn't answer; he had something else in mind. Something darker.

She slowed down as they neared the trailer park but he indicated that she keep on going.

"Why? There's nothing out here but the woods..."

"Exactly," he told her.

"Oh, no, Norris, please. You know I've never liked that forest! It's creepy, especially at night!"

His fist tightened again in her hair. "That's our *sacred* forest, Dee. You'd best show some respect for it."

Sacred forest? What the hell was he talking about?

He told her to park the car in Doc Putnam's driveway.

A glimmer of hope sparked in her heart but was soon extinguished when Deidre saw no lights on in Doc's house. She parked the car, not daring to disobey.

"Shut if off and kill the lights," Norris said.

Breathlessly, she did so, her muscles coiled for the first chance to escape. He finally released her breast and she sighed with relief.

"Now just breathe," he whispered, pulling her head back against the top of the seat. "I'm going to let go of you now and you're not going to move. Wanna know why?"

"No." Her voice sounded like a mere mew.

"Because I've got a gun and my finger's on the trigger. Taking a bullet in the liver is a hard way to die, Dee. A *real* hard way to die. Very slow and painful. One move and you'll know just how it feels."

"Please, Norris…" She began crying again.

Trusting that she was plenty scared, Norris let go of her hair and reached into his pocket for the chloroform, which he poured onto the rag.

"That's it, just breathe," he whispered, pushing the soggy rag over her face.

"What is that? What are you doing? What—"

Her body sagged back against the seat, and he lifted the rag, satisfied that she was out like a light. He moved her head to the side, then her upper body and unlocked the door. It wasn't easy crawling over the seat without squishing her but he managed. Then he opened the car door and stepped out.

He stretched, gazing up at the starry heavens. *The night has a thousand eyes,* he thought grimly, *but I doubt they'll want to watch this.*

He reached down and pulled Deidre from the front seat of the car. Her body was limp, a dead weight, seeming heavier now than when she was awake. He heaved her upward and slung her over his shoulder, then nudged the door shut with his boot.

Carrying her in the direction of the forest, the grass felt crunchy, stiff with frost under his feet.

She doesn't like the woods, he thought. *She'll like them even less after tonight.*

He knew the forest well; perhaps the only person who knew it better was Doc—but Doc was nowhere to be found. He'd virtually vanished after the selection of the Chosen. Maybe this was what he always did—Norris wasn't sure. It had been his first time on the selection committee and he'd only served as one of the Elders for less than a year.

He remembered Ned Speer's shock when Doc announced Kate was the Chosen. Norris had also been stunned. He'd always liked Kate, even though she was often rude to him. She wasn't half as rude as Deidre, though. Lugging her into the woods was no easy task. She felt as heavy as a sack of rocks and twice, so far, he'd nearly lost his footing.

He didn't need a flashlight. There was enough moonlight to see by and his night vision was quite sharp, almost cat-like. Deidre moaned once when he started to slip the second time, causing him to stop and reshift her weight across his shoulder.

Many leaves had fallen during last night's wind, and his sneakers made a shuffling sound as he plodded over them. Most people would have been frightened to death to venture here alone at night, but Norris wasn't the least bit scared. The woods knew him as they had since he was a ten-year-old child, hiding in the shadows, watching the Chosen being mated to the forest god.

He wasn't supposed to see the ritual; it had come about quite by accident. He'd run into the woods to get away from his mother for a while. This was his secret haven, a place to sort out his thoughts, an area of solitude and comfort. Norris had fallen asleep, burrowed in leaves, and when he awoke, he heard voices. He crept up behind a tree to see what was going on.

Even though their faces were painted blue and despite their long white robes, he recognized all of them as the men of Gotham Creek. His baby sitter, Serena Haskell, had been chained to a tree, scantily clad and weeping. Her death had been a terrible and yet fascinating thing to watch, even though part of Norris wanted to rescue her.

The shackles were still there, attached to the great bull oak with heavy chains, and he could think of no better punishment for Deidre. Why not scare her half to death? He lowered her to an upright position, pinning her against the tree with his body as he reached upward for one of the shackles. The sound of the chains made metallic clanks that echoed through the dark woods.

The shackles were held shut by metal pins and it didn't take him long to bind Dee, her wrists and ankles stretched, her body forming a human X.

She woke up when he pulled off her apron.

"Where am I?" she asked in a groggy voice. "Norris?"

He reached up and took her face in his hands none too gently. "Are you scared yet, Dee? I bet you'll never mess around on me again, huh?"

She quickly realized she was bound to the tree and began to struggle. "Norris, what have you done? Why? I'm cold and scared—please let me go..."

He shook his head as he zipped up her jacket. "There, you're warm enough now."

She began to cry. "I'm sorry I cheated on you. I really am. Can't you forgive me? I love you, Norris, I really do."

He stepped back. "You never loved anyone but yourself. So I'm just going to leave you here to think about it."

She looked up at him, tears washing down her cheeks. "Please don't go! I've learned my lesson. We can go home and talk. We can get past this—I have faith in us. Don't you?"

"I used to." Norris started to back away when he saw something flash in her eyes. Sheer terror spread across her face in an instant.

"What the hell is that?" she screamed.

He whipped around and saw what she was screaming about. The forest god was coming, making its way through the woods, glowing green and terrible. The ground shook with its footsteps. Norris glanced back at Deidre, knowing there was no time to change his mind and save her. Her fate was sealed.

"Help me, please!" she shouted at him. "Get me out of here! Don't leave me alone with that thing!"

But he ran, sprinting through the woods without daring to look back. He could hear her bloodcurdling screams and it chilled him to the bone. He was nearly breathless by the time he made it back to her car. Hurrying, he got in and turned the key in the ignition and sped away.

Within moments, he was back on Main Street. He wanted to get back home so he could have a few drinks and settle down. His heart was beating so hard he could feel it pounding way up in his throat, and his skin was slick with sweat.

Up ahead, bathed in the Mustang's headlights, he saw someone walking along the sidewalk. Not wanting to call attention to himself, Norris eased up on the gas and slowed the car down.

Kate saw the lights of the approaching car. It seemed to be moving quite fast, then it slowed down. The speed limit was 25 m.p.h. in Gotham Creek and the penalty for getting caught for speeding was a hefty fine. The car was barely creeping now, and the passenger's side window rolled down as it pulled up beside her.

She recognized the red Mustang as the one belonging to Deidre Garnet. *Wonder what she wants?* Kate wondered, after all, they barely knew each other.

"Hey, Katie, can you help me?" The voice was that of Norris Hymes and she stopped walking.

"I'm busy, Norris. What do you want?"

"It's Dee. She's hurt and I really need some help."

She could hear the urgency in his voice, the angst of desperation. She turned and bent down by the car window. "What happened?" No sooner than she'd asked the question, Norris grabbed her head and pressed a rag over her nose and mouth.

Then all went darker than the surrounding night.

Kate woke up in a dimly lit room with rock walls and a dirt floor. Even though her head throbbed with pain, she knew almost instantly she was in the cellar of a house. The last thing she remembered was talking to Norris and he'd put a damp rag over her mouth.

She tried to reach up to touch her head but found her wrists were bound by rope behind her back. She glanced down. Her ankles had been tied as well, to what appeared to be the legs of a cot.

Her mind raced as best it could despite her headache. *Norris, you sick fuck! Why have you done this?* She began to scream for help and as she gulped for breath, she heard a series of heavy footsteps and looked across the room at the stairs.

Dirty work boots were descending the steps, attached to the ripped legs of faded Levis, and she knew it was Norris long before she saw his face.

He grinned as he reached the foot of the stairs. "You're awake," was all he said.

She had no patience for his dull-minded observations. "Why am I here, Norris—and why did you tie me up?"

"I've saved you," he said, approaching the rusty cot she was tied to.

She knit her brows in frustration. "Saved me from what? Any why did you see fit to drug me and tie me up? Why, Norris?"

He knelt down near her face. "You really don't know, do you? You're the Chosen, Kate. I was there at the meeting. They chose you…"

Her eyes filled up with tears. That might be the reason her parents had been acting so strangely these past few days, hardly speaking to one another. Her mother had been jumpy; her face filled with anxiety—and she'd assumed it was because of Eddie's ongoing problem with his ears. Her father, however, could hardly bear to look at her and she hadn't understood why. Until now.

"You're going to be in trouble with the Elders," she told him. "They'll punish you for this just like they punish anyone who gets in their way."

He shook his head. "Aw, no, they won't. Not after tonight."

"What are you saying?"

He sighed and brushed a long strand of hair away from her face. "The sacrifice has already been made. Tonight. I didn't mean to do it, but it happened anyway."

She stared at him in alarm. "What? Who?"

Norris smiled. "Never mind. It's over and done with."

"Do the Elders know?"

"Nope, not yet."

Kate shook her head, confused. "So they're still going to try to kill me. Maybe even you, too."

"I doubt it."

"Can you untie me? Please? My wrists hurt."

At this, he frowned. "You'll be safer if you stay here for the time being. I don't know if I can trust you not to leave."

She shook her head, pleading. "I won't go, I promise."

"It's too risky. Too dangerous. We'd best wait until after the Festival."

"But that's three days away."

He stood up, wiping his hands on his jeans. "Are you hungry, Katie? I can make you a peanut butter and jelly sandwich…"

"No. I don't want food; I just want to go back home. Please, Norris. I'll be safe, especially now that you *fixed* things."

He shook his head. "Well, I can't be sure you'll ever be safe here in Gotham Creek, especially since they think you're the Chosen. Maybe I'll pack things up and head west. Maybe I'll take you with me."

She began to struggle, trying to loosen the bonds that restrained her. "I don't want to go anywhere with you! Let me go, dammit!"

He backed away. "Nope, I can't do that. Not yet, anyway. Go ahead and scream if you want to. There's no one around for miles."

"You fucking bastard!"

At this, he reached up and shut off the overhead light. "Nobody calls me a bastard," he told her. "Now you can just stay down here in the dark and think about what you said. You should be grateful for what I've done to save you. It's more than *your* father ever did for you."

Kate heard his footsteps going up the old wooden stairs and she screamed in frustration. When the cellar door shut, she was submerged in total and complete darkness.

She screamed even louder…

"Have you seen Kate this morning?" Eddie asked his parents as he poured himself a bowl of crisped rice cereal.

Maisie shook her head and shot a glance at Ned. "No, isn't she in her room?"

"Well, I thought so. But her alarm didn't go off, so I went in to wake her up and she's not there. Her bed's still made up, too."

Ned frowned and headed for the stairs, shouting Kate's name.

"Where do you think she went?" Eddie asked his mother as he peered out the window. Kate's car was still parked in the garage.

"I don't know. Wasn't she here last night after your father and I went to bed?"

Eddie nodded. "Yeah. She went out for a walk around nine. I figured she'd be right back and I fell asleep on the couch. When I woke up, I think it was around eleven, and I thought she must have come back and gone to bed."

Maisie cupped her mouth, stifling a sob, and ran from the kitchen. Eddie heard her rush up the stairs, calling for Ned.

It wasn't like Kate to just take off like this, he thought. He could hear his parents arguing about something upstairs. He didn't know what that was all about, either. They hadn't been getting along very well lately.

He ate quickly and tipped the bowl up to finish off the milk. He thought about going to school—but he couldn't. Something bad happened to Kate; he could feel it, and he had to try to find her. Grabbing his coat, he hurried out the door. Across the street, he spotted Jess getting ready to walk to school and he ran over to him.

"You have to help me," he told his best friend. "Kate's gone. And I think something really bad has happened to her."

Jess's eyes widened. "Where do you think she is?"

Eddie shook his head. "I don't know. She went out for a walk last night and never came home. She's somewhere here in town, though; I can feel it."

Jess lowered his eyes and his voice. "I wasn't supposed to tell you this, but…"

Eddie grabbed him. "Tell me what? What is it?"

"I heard our dads talking last night. I think the Elders are planning to sacrifice your sister."

Eddie let go of Jess's coat. "Are you sure?"

He shrugged, feeling helpless. "I only caught part of the conversation, but that's what it sounded like to me."

Turning to glance at the woods, Eddie frowned. "There's only one place she could be then, isn't there?"

Jess nodded solemnly. "I think we'd better go rescue her."

They raced through the neighborhood, trying as best they could not to be seen by their peers who were walking to school. Both were panting, nearly out of breath, by the time they made it to Old Woods Road.

"You know Doc's gone, too," Jess told Eddie as they came to his yard.

Eddie nodded. "Yeah. I bet he's the one who took Kate. He's probably keeping her out there in the woods, too."

"Did you stop taking the medicine he gave you?"

"Yeah."

The boys halted to look at the woods before going in. This place had been off limits to them since they were born, and it was hard to shake free of the fear that surrounded it. Eddie could hear voices clearer now, hundreds of them, calling out to him and this time his ears didn't hurt: *An féidir le héinne cuidiú liom?*

Héinne! Héinne! Héinne!

"Can you hear that?" he asked Jess.

"Hear what?"

"It's the trees," he whispered. "They're saying something but it's not in English."

Jess looked at him, trying to understand. "What are they speaking, then? French? German?"

He shook his head. "No, but it's close, I think. They sound like they're in trouble. Does that make any sense?"

Jess shrugged. "About as much sense as you hearing them, I guess."

"Are you ready to go in?"

Jess nodded. "Yeah."

"Just stick close by me, ok."

"Don't worry, I will."

The forest appeared even more ominous, dark and hungry, as the boys approached. They followed the old road, where it wound past Doc's driveway and became swallowed up in the woods, making it difficult to follow.

Something caught Eddie's eye and he pointed at the ground where the long dying grass had been crushed. "See these?" he asked Jess.

"Yeah, footprints. Someone's been here and recently, too."

"Probably Doc."

Jess shook his head. "Are his feet that big?"

"Well, who do you think it was? Bigfoot?"

At this, Jess paled. "Don't joke around, Eddie. Not now. Okay?"

He sighed and looked up at the trees towering overhead, their nearly bare limbs reaching into the morning sky. He could still hear them calling out to him and they sounded like they were in pain.

Héinne! Héinne! Héinne! An féidir le héinne cuidiú liom?

As the boys plodded onward the trunks of the trees blotted out the sun. It grew increasingly dark and the old road became a narrow footpath, almost impossible to follow. All the while they walked, both boys felt as if they were being watched but neither said a word about this, lest they scare themselves into a blind panic.

The footpath ended at the base of a huge tree. The boys stopped and stared wordlessly. The trunk appeared burned, scorched in the shape of a human.

Then they noticed the iron shackles hanging there.

Eddie's throat squeezed up and his eyes watered. "I think we're too late."

Jess shook his head. "No, Festival is the day after tomorrow. They wouldn't sacrifice her before then. Would they?"

"I doubt it. But someone died here recently. Burnt to death by the looks of it."

Héinne! Héinne! Héinne! An féidir le héinne cuidiú liom?

"I think we'd better get out of here," Jess said, shaking Eddie's arm.

"But what about Kate?"

"She's not here, and I don't know where else to look."

Something moved in the leaves by Jess's foot. A snake, maybe? Eddie reached out to pull Jess away from it but then it sprang up and wound around his ankle.

Jess began yelling. "Hey, get it off me! What is it? Can you tell?"

He bent down and tried prying it off Jess's leg. "It's the root of a tree," he shouted. "You're all tangled up in it. Hold still so I can take it off you."

But Jess couldn't hold still. The root was hurting him, digging into his sock, and it was winding its way higher up his leg.

That's when the branches rushed down.

Eddie could only watch in horror as his best friend was lifted into the air by the boughs of an oak. Jess was screaming, his arms and legs flaying at the air, his body twisting like a worm on a hook.

"Go get help!" he yelped. "You'll need a saw to cut me down."

Eddie ran, wondering all the while if the tree limbs were going to come after him and swoop him up just like they'd done to Jess. But after half an hour, he made it out of the forest unscathed, except for some scrapes and scratches.

He ran down the middle of Main Street and waved down the first car he saw. The tinted window opened just a little and a man with dark glasses asked, "Slow down, son. What's the problem?"

Eddie panted as he pointed at the north end of town. "It's my friend, Jess. The trees got him—we have to get him out of the woods or something worse is going to happen!"

"He's in the woods? What were you boys doing out there?"

Eddie swallowed. "Look, my sister's been kidnapped. Jess and I went to the woods to rescue her and now he's in trouble. He's going to die if someone doesn't help him!"

"Get in the car," the man told him. "We're going to talk to your parents and straighten this out."

Eddie gave them directions to his house as he climbed into the backseat. "Please, we gotta hurry."

Jess struggled for what felt like an eternity, dangling upside down in the air. He felt his limbs growing tired, heavy as lead. After a while, he just hung there, waiting, praying for Eddie to return with some help.

As soon as he heard footsteps, he twisted around in the direction they were coming from and called out, "Hey! I'm over here."

"I see you."

It was Doc Putnam's voice but it didn't look like him at all. His skin was leaf-green and blotchy; leaves and twigs sprouted out of him everywhere.

"Doc? Is that you? Can you help me down?"

Doc shook his head. "Sorry, I can't touch you. If I did, you would die. Now listen carefully, Jess. It's all gone wrong, falling apart. You have to get everyone out of town as soon as you can. Our forest is poisoned."

"Poisoned? How?"

Doc gazed up at him and his face was sad. "The old mine. Radiation, my boy. What happened here was a mistake. We thought it was a sure sign that the gods were smiling down upon us but we were wrong. They weren't smiling at all."

Jess's eyes narrowed. "Where's Kate? We came here looking for her. Figured you had her because you wanted to sacrifice her."

Again Doc shook his green head. "We were wrong. We polluted the old religion and now the forest is dying. It's too late, too late."

"So where's Kate?"

"If I tell you, you'd have to promise not to hurt him."

Jess could feel blood tingling in his cheeks. "Hurt who? What are you talking about?"

"Norris. Norris Hymes has Kate. He's keeping her safe in his cellar."

"Why?"

"So she won't be sacrificed."

"Is she okay?"

"Yes, for the time being. But you have to get out of town. Tell everyone we were wrong, that we've been wrong all along."

"What about you? What happened to you?"

Doc paused, thinking. "Let's just say I'm getting what's been coming to me for a long time." There were voices off in the distance and before Jess could ask another question, Doc reached out and touched the trunk of the tree. "Thank you for sparing this boy," he said.

Then he walked away. Jess watched him disappear into the forest and wondered what he'd meant about polluting the old religion, and what had happened to him to make him look like...well, like a tree.

One thing he knew for sure. Nothing was ever going to be the same again.

13

Ned used his handsaw to cut Jess down out of the tree and for a long moment, the boy couldn't speak. It wasn't just because of hanging upside down—it was seeing Doc all green with things growing out of his skin—and what he'd said.

If I tell them will they believe me? he wondered. Eddie would, of that he was certain. But what about the grownups? There was only one way to convince them.

"I know where Kate is," he said when he finally found his voice. "She's at Norris Hymes's house, in his cellar. Norris is keeping her safe, so please don't hurt him."

Ned's eyes narrowed. "Hurt him? I'll kill the bastard!"

Jess grabbed his sleeve. "No, Mr. Speers, please, just listen to me. Norris wouldn't do anything to hurt Kate. He didn't want to see her sacrificed so he saved her the only way he knew how. Please don't hurt him."

Ned glared down at Jess. "How do you know? If you knew where Kate was, why didn't you tell anyone?"

"What does he mean about Kate being sacrificed?" Agent Bullock asked. "What's going on here?"

Jess held up his hands, fingers splayed. "Listen, please—just hear me out. Doc told me where Kate was. He was here just a few minutes ago."

Ned shook his head. "I don't believe it. Where's Doc now? Why didn't he stick around?"

Agent Kent asked, "Why don't you tell us what's going on?"

Eddie put his arm around Jess like a brother. "Don't any of you *get* it? Huh?" He looked up at his father. "Dad, you had to cut Jess down out of that tree. Have you ever seen branches and roots wrap around anyone like that? If he says Doc was here, then Doc was here." He glanced over at the F.B.I. agents. "And as for what's going on, it's over and done with."

Agent Bullock pointed at the shackles hanging from the bull oak and the charred human-shaped burn on the trunk. "So what's the meaning of this?" He walked over and began examining first the shackles, then the bark of the tree, finally stooping to sift his hand through the pile of light colored ashes at its base.

"It's nothing. Nothing at all," Ned said and turned to the boys. "We're done here. We'd best go rescue Kate."

Agent Kent started off after them but Agent Bullock flagged him over. "Let them go...for now. There's evidence here. Those are human remains, I'm sure of it." He pulled a baggie from his pocket and put some of the ashes into it.

"They've been sacrificing people here, haven't they?"

"We won't know for sure until the Crime Lab examines the evidence. But from the way they were talking, yeah, it does sound like it."

Agent Kent stood up with a sigh, studying the ground where the leaves had been disturbed. The crime scene had been virtually ruined; so many people had been here already, tramping around. Then something caught his eye. The bark of a nearby oak didn't appear quite right. There appeared to be a burl growing on one side of it. He approached the tree to take a look and that's when he noticed the compass lying there in the leaves.

Not an ordinary pocket compass, this one was a prismatic compass with a prism sighting arrangement and a lid with a hairline on top. Expensive, not the sort of tool for a layman. It was quite possible Sheridan Phillips carried such an instrument and probably the National Forest Service representatives did, too.

He knelt and put the compass in another baggie, then looked up at the tree trunk and gasped.

The burl in the bark looked exactly like a human face, not carved but molded out of wood.

"Bullock, come here and look at this." When Agent Bullock approached, Agent Kent reached up and touched the strange growth. "What do you make of this? Weird, huh?"

"Well, it's strange. But it's probably just an anomoly of nature."

"But it looks so...life-like."

Agent Bullock pulled a penknife out of his pocket and used it to pick away at the burl. Flaky pieces of bark fell away and in one brief moment, he realized there was something under there, locked in the fibers of the wood. Something meaty.

That's when the trees sprang to life. Branches rushed down and wrapped around the two men before they could move away. Agent Bullock was first to be devoured; his partner watched, screaming as one of the oaks opened up and swallowed him whole. Then came his turn and when it was over, the forest fell silent once again.

As Ned pulled into the parking lot of the town office, Eddie rubbed at his left ear. There was no pain but when he looked at his hand there was blood on his fingers. He glanced over at his father."I think the F.B.I. agents are dead. The trees got both of them."

His father shot him a bewildered look as he got out of the car and headed into the building to get Hap Kingsley. Jess had urged him not to get the police involved in Kate's rescue but Ned wasn't listening. The town wastrel had his daughter and he meant to get her back.

Norris Hymes was raking leaves in the Eternal Rest Cemetery when the police cruiser pulled up past the gate. As soon as he saw the car, he dropped the rake and broke into a sprint. But Hap was faster. He tackled Norris and they slammed onto the ground together between two headstones. They rolled a couple times over graves and the struggle ended with Hap on top, straddling his back.

"I didn't hurt Kate," he shouted as Hap slapped the cuffs around his wrists.

"You're in a heap of trouble, boy," was all Hap said as he yanked him to his feet.

Ned wasted no time kicking in the Hymes residence's front door. He'd only been in the house a couple times before—when Edith's car had broken down and he'd brought her a replacement to use while he fixed hers. She'd kept her house spotless, immaculately so, and it would have killed her to see what it looked like now.

Beer cans littered the livingroom, scattered across the coffee table, windowsills and carpet. The ashtrays overflowed with cigarette butts. Snack food wrappers and potato chip bags were everywhere, along with acorns. Thousands of them.

Ned waded through the mess and found the cellar door. Seeing the hook and eye lock on the outside made him grind his teeth, evidence that Norris had imprisoned Kate down there. He unlocked the door and swung it open. He switched on the light, calling out:

"Kate? You down there?"

"Daddy? Is it really you?"

"Yeah, honey, it's really me."

He took the steps two at a time and saw her before he got to the bottom of the stairs. She'd been tied to a rusty cot, but when she looked up at him, he knew she was all right. "I knew you'd find me," she said in a hoarse voice.

He hurried over to her, knelt down and cut the ropes with his jackknife. "Did he hurt you?"

She shook her head and sat up, rubbing at her wrists. "No, I'm fine. Norris scared me but he didn't hurt me."

"Scared you?" Ned began rubbing her ankles. The ropes had made such deep indentations in her flesh that he could see them through her socks.

"Yeah, I think he killed somebody. I don't know who. But he was saying some strange things."

"I'll kill him!" Ned growled.

She put a firm hand on his arm. "Daddy, there's no need to do that. You know Norris is simple-minded. He really thought he was saving me." She stopped and looked into his eyes. "You weren't going to let the Elders kill me, either, were you?"

He shook his head with a sigh. "Your mother and I were trying to come up with a plan to stop the sacrifice but Norris beat us to it. You sure he didn't hurt you?"

She nodded. "I'm sure. Let's get out of here. I've seen enough of this cellar to last me a lifetime."

Norris cried as the men dragged him into the woods. They'd tied a rope around his neck and were pulling him by it, forcing him to follow them.

Along the way, he'd heard Pat Nevels express concern that the Federal agents were still in the woods but Mike Elwin snickered. "Let them watch us lynch the son-of-a-bitch! That way, they can get a taste of Gotham Creek justice. We take care of our own, always have, always will."

They yanked Norris to the trunk of the bull oak, where just the night before, he'd shackled Deidre Garnet.

"I didn't mean for her to die," he wailed, looking down in horror at the ashes at his feet. "I just wanted to scare her a little."

Jim Digby glared at him. "Norris Hymes, you are sentenced to hang by the neck until dead for the murders of your mother and girlfriend as well as the kidnapping of Katherine Speers. Do you have any final words?"

Norris dropped his head. It was useless to try to convince them that he hadn't killed his mother and that he hadn't meant to kill Deidre. He'd only kidnapped Kate to save her from what *they* were going to do to her but they weren't at all interested in hearing his side of things. They were out for blood now; the time was right and so was the season.

"All right, string him up," Jim Digby yelled.

14

"The acorn falls not far from the tree," Doc declared, stepping out from behind an oak. The men gasped in shock when they saw what he'd become: some kind of cross between human and tree, a mutated monster.

"Doc?" Hap asked, blinking in disbelief. "What the hell happened? Is it really you?"

He nodded and held up his hand. "Don't come any closer. You don't want to get what I've got."

"My God, what happened to you? Is it some kind of disease?"

"Never mind, it's a long story. What's going on here?"

"You heard the charges, right? Norris Hymes has to pay for what he's done."

Doc pointed a moss-covered finger-twig at Norris. "He's done nothing wrong. Well, nothing that merits being executed for, anyway. You hate him because he's not like you. He's not as bright or as articulate or as clean. But he isn't the one who did wrong here. It was me. It's *always* been me."

"What are you saying?" Hap asked. "We've always trusted your judgment, your wisdom. You've never led us astray; I just don't get it."

Doc shook his head and held up his hand. "No, listen to me. It all began with my father and the old mine. When the silver ran out, he found Lumina. Radia-anthracite. It's a hundred times more radioactive than pure uranium and even after people started getting sick, he refused to shut the mine down. He still had money to make. Bundles of it.

"To keep people working the mine, he created a religion, part Druidism, part Malcomb Putnam-ism. He knew what the Radia-anthracite was doing to the forest and to the people living here, so he decided to make it the center of his new religion. I was even duped into believing it."

"New religion?" Hap shook his head. "I'm not buying it. Druidism is older than Christianity; you've told us so yourself."

Doc frowned and crossed his twig-covered arms. "That's true. But what we've been practicing is a polluted form of it. Let me explain. You're all used to getting Yule money every year on the fireplace mantle. Well, *I'm* the one who's been supplying it. It's what's left of my father's estate, nothing more. So you see, Virginia, there really is no Santa Claus after all."

"And what about the sacrifices of the Chosen?" Hap asked. "We've all seen what happens—we've seen the god himself."

Doc shook his finger at him. "Don't you know that if you believe in something hard enough, you make it real? The sacrifices were all part of the plan to keep everyone under control. The Christian church has its brimstone and hellfire; we have our tenth year sacrifices. Even there, I failed you all."

"Failed us how?" Pat asked, not wanting to believe any of this.

Doc paused. "Twenty years ago, when it came time for *me* to make a sacrifice, I couldn't let her go. None of you knew about the affair that corrupted the celibacy of my priesthood." He pointed his finger at Norris. "That boy is proof of my failure. And now you know. Yes, I'm his father. And I did the worst thing a father can do. Last night, I took his woman."

"But Doc, we *believed*."

"I know you did—and for that I don't expect your forgiveness. All I ask is that you leave this place. The forest is dying and it will take you right along with it if it can. Take your families and go. Let me die in peace here." Slowly, he walked up to Norris and removed the noose from his neck. "Come walk with me?" he asked. Norris nodded, rubbing at his throat.

The mob stepped aside to let them pass through, watching them disappear together into the thick glade.

Hap held up his hands. "Okay, folks, let's all go home and think this whole thing over."

15

"We're dying, ain't we, Doc?"

Doc Putnam looked at his son in the semi-darkness and sighed. "The forest is dying and so am I, but there's something I need you to do."

"What?"

Norris had done so much for him already; he'd helped him down to the creek for water. He'd fashioned a comfortable bed of leaves for him to rest on. It was getting hard to move and harder still to think. He could feel the disease eating up his brain, little by little, and he knew twilight was setting in, yet there was something that needed to be done before he was totally consumed.

"Go to my house," he told Norris. "You'll find a file cabinet in my office. There's a big manila envelope in the top drawer, right in front. Get it and take it to the town office. Leave it on the doorstep where Jim will find it. Don't stop and talk to anyone, and for godsakes, don't touch anyone or let them touch you. You'd do well to not let anybody see you, either. Then come back here, okay?"

Norris stared down at his own hands. They were beginning to show signs of the same green mottling that had taken over Doc's body. "It's contagious, ain't it?"

"I'm afraid so."

"Why do I have to come back here? Why can't you come with me?"

"I'm dying, son. You'll have to return to bury me."

Norris looked up from his hands. "You said back there that the old religion was a lie. That's not really true, is it?"

Doc took a moment to answer. "No. I said that to set the people of Gotham Creek free. Our forest god has become just as sick as I am. Maybe sicker. He's part of me now and he's dying, just like me."

"Is there such a place as Tir-Nan-Og?"

"Yes. Yes, that you must believe."

Norris pushed more leaves under Doc's head. "And Ma is there?"

"I believe so."

"Who killed her?"

"The forest god," he said. "I think she died because of what we did. I wanted to marry her after you were conceived, but she refused, saying it would reveal our sin. I think in her heart, she still loved me, but you can't imagine what the Elders put her through. Must have been something terrible. She was never the same afterwards..."

"How can the forest god be *in* you?"

Doc grimaced as he raised his hand to jab at his chest with his twig of a thumb. "He took me a few nights ago. I think he wanted to be inside me because he's dying. Maybe it was my fault. My father created him and made him an object of worship. I saw him once when I was a boy, after he got the disease. He was in the back of a truck, the worst thing I've ever seen. I can feel his rot spreading through me now."

"The rot," Norris said with a nod, "I've got it, too."

"I'm sorry, son. There was no other way to save you. They would have killed you if I hadn't taken you away from them. Hurry now and get that envelope to the town office. I don't think there's much time left."

As Norris began to stand up, Doc reached for his hand. "I want you to know I'm proud of you."

"I'll be right back. Doc...Dad."

"Be careful."

"I will."

Doc watched him leave, wishing they'd had more time together as father and son.

Doc's envelope was fairly easy to find but on his way out through the kitchen, Norris stopped in front of the refrigerator. Instinctively, he pulled the door open and looked inside.

The nauseating stench of spoiled food hit his nose with all the subtlety of an oncoming train.

Shutting the fridge door, he gagged and ran outside. Night had closed in now, starless darkness without moonlight. His hands were glowing, though, sort of the way a firefly glows; only this was a steady shine.

His vision was sharper, too. He could see each individual tree surrounding the lawn and looking up the road, he saw the trailers in the park, set in rows, with automobiles parked beside them.

Tucking the envelope under his arm, he ran, avoiding the road where he could be seen, taking a route across lawns and driveways. Hettie Brown's Great Dane started to bark at him but as he approached, the animal raised his hackles and the fur stood straight up along his spine. Then it turned with a yelp and ran back inside the doghouse.

Norris kept running. Gotham Creek Convenience was shutting down for the night; the lights over the gas pumps went off as he jogged past the back of Cuffy's Restaurant. Mike Elwin, who'd been having a cigarette by the back door, called out, "Hey, who's there?" But Norris didn't answer or slow down.

He didn't stop until he reached the town office. It was closed but there was a light on in the constable's office. He set the envelope down against the front door and jumped off the steps. As he landed, the side door opened and Hap Kingsley stepped out.

They looked at one another for a brief second. Then he saw Hap reach for his holster. Norris took off, sprinting, and behind him he could hear Hap yell "Freeze!" but that didn't stop him.

Again, he raced across the back lot of Cuffy's and made his way across town toward the woods. Looking over his shoulder, he could see the flashes of blue light coming from the strobe atop the cruiser.

Felicity Kingsley was letting out her cat when he cut through her backyard. He heard her cry out in alarm. When he ran across the Brown's lawn, their dog didn't bother to bark. He made it to Old Woods Road and stopped for breath near the trailer park. There was a stitch in his side, a tight mean cramp, and he lifted his shirt to rub at it.

His stomach was as green and glowing as his hands.

Strangely, though, he no longer felt sick but more alive than he'd ever felt in his entire life.

Hap Kingsley watched Norris dart into the woods—there was something seriously wrong with the man. Back at the town office, he'd come closer to killing Norris than when they were going to lynch him. Deep down, he knew why. It was fear, plain and simple, fear of the unknown, of something he could not understand.

He didn't know what to think anymore and he wasn't sure he could trust his own feelings. Even Felicity was losing patience with him. She'd pitched a fit when he threw away all the tea Doc had given her, screaming that she wanted a divorce.

But she hadn't seen Doc and she didn't know what he'd become.

When Hap tried to tell her, she didn't believe him. *It's a strange irony*, he thought, *how a man created the religion in Gotham Creek and how it was ended by a man, yet women would cling to it and keep it alive. They'll hope against hope that the forest will continue to protect their way of life and they'll be shattered when no Yule money arrives in December.*

With a sigh, he turned the cruiser around and headed back to the office. Norris was probably better off in the forest where everyone—including Hap—would leave him alone.

As he got out of the car, he noticed something on the town office steps. A package or envelope of some sort. He walked over, picked it up and took it inside.

'To the citizens of Gotham Creek' was written across the front of the envelope in bold black marker. He raised his brows and sat down, wondering if it was from Norris Hymes.

He put the envelope down and started to do some paperwork but his eyes were continually drawn back to it. Finally, curiosity got the best of him. He reached over and tore it open.

Doc's last will and testament was tucked inside, written in his scrawling handwriting. "I, Dickie "Doc" Putnam, in sound mind and body, do bequeath my earthly belongings…"

The phone rang, jarring his thoughts away from the document. He set it down and picked up the phone.

"Gotham Creek Constabulatory."

"Hap, you have to come home right now!" The alarm in his wife's voice brought him to his feet in an instant.

"What's going on? Are you all right?"

"I'm a nervous wreck! You'll never believe what I just saw—I think it was an alien. You know, an extra-terrestrial."

"Slow down, Felly. Where'd you see this uh…alien?"

"He ran across our backyard!" Her voice was so loud he had to hold the phone away from his ear. "I was letting out Silver and there he was, running like his shoes were on fire. He was all weird, Hap, glowing just like in the movies!"

"Did he hurt you? Or threaten you? Is he still there?"

There was a pause on the other end. "Well, no."

He sighed. "I don't know what you expect me to do about it then."

"Please come home. I'm too scared to be here all alone...what, with that alien running around the neighborhood."

He sighed and rubbed his temple with his fingers. "Lock the door, hon. I'll be right there."

Eddie Speers pulled the chair from his desk to his windowsill and looked outside. He could see nothing except for a few lights on in the surrounding homes. His bedroom window faced the north, where the forest was.

"I can still hear them," he said out loud to no one but himself. The trees didn't sound as urgent as before, and since he'd stopped taking Doc's medicine, his ears didn't bleed so much anymore. He listened closer and the words were beginning to make sense:

Help! Can someone please help me?

He knit his brows. *Who wants help? The forest? The trees? And why are the words in English instead of the language they'd used before?*

Please help me...

"I don't know what I can do," he said. "Maybe if you'd tell me how I can help, I might be able to do something about it."

Just then there was a knock on his bedroom door. "Eddie?" his mother called out. "Who are you talking to?"

He got up from his chair, went to the door and opened it. "I wasn't talking to no one, Mom."

"Anyone," she corrected. "You weren't talking to *anyone*."

He shrugged in defeat. "Yeah, whatever."

Maisie raised a brow and reached out to touch his forehead. "Are you feeling all right?"

"I guess so," he said. He didn't have the heart to tell her about the deep, inexplicable sadness tearing away at his soul and the premonition that something terrible was about to happen.

Norris shook Doc but he didn't wake up. He put his ear to his chest and listened but he couldn't hear a heartbeat. He'd only known Doc was his father for a few hours and the loss cut him to the bone.

"What was so important about that envelope that you had to send me away while you died?" he asked through blinding tears. "You shouldn't have been alone. I should have been with you."

He gazed up at the starless heavens. "The least I can do for you is give you a decent burial, right here in the woods. I'll get started on it tomorrow. Rest well in Tir-Nan-Og, Father."

He settled down in the leaves beside the corpse but he didn't sleep.

"We've got trouble," Jim Digby told Hap Kingsley. "The National Forest Service called this morning asking about the representatives they sent here. To top it off, the F.B.I. called, too, asking a lot of questions. Evidently, they haven't heard from their agents either."

"Oh, that's just great," he said as he passed a manila envelope to Jim.

"What's this?"

"Doc Putnam's last will and testament. I think you'd better read it."

Jim knit his brows. "All right, I will." He took it to his office and settled down in the chair behind his desk. A few minutes later, he called out to Hap, "From the sound of it, we'd better call another emergency town meeting."

Norris sat up to watch the sunrise through the trees. It started out rosy-pink and slowly turned gold. He looked down at his father and was surprised by the seedlings sprouting out of his body. They'd ripped through his clothing and the largest of them had already grown a foot tall. Doc's face had a mossy-earth look to it and his eyes had sunken in.

"I have to bury him soon," he thought, "before the forest totally claims him."

That's when he noticed his own hands. They'd turned entirely leaf green, not just mottled splotches of skin. He remembered how sick Doc had been—but he didn't feel ill. In fact, physically, he felt better than ever.

How am I going to bury him? he wondered. *I don't even have a shovel.*

"You'd better hurry or you'll be late for school," Maisie warned Eddie as she poured herself a cup of coffee. She turned around and studied him as he sat listlessly at the table, staring down at his bowl of frosted flakes.

"Eddie? Are you feeling okay?"

He shrugged and poked at his cereal with the spoon. "I don't know, Mom. My head feels kind of funny and my stomach does, too. Do I have to go to school today?"

There was something in his voice that told her he wasn't trying to play hooky. He looked terribly pale. She set her coffee down on the table and reached over to feel his forehead.

"My god, you're burning up. Have you taken any ibuprofen?"

Eddie nodded. "Yeah, I took a couple when I got up. My head really hurts. Still does."

Maisie put a hand on her hip. "Let me look at your ears."

He waved her off. "My ears are fine, Mom, really. I just don't feel good."

"Well, you're not going to school today, young man. If you're not going to eat, you'd better go back to bed."

He set his spoon down so the handle rested on the edge of the bowl and he pushed away from the table. Maisie watched him leave the room, dragging his feet.

This wasn't like him at all and it had her worried.

Jim Digby, the fiery-haired town manager, read from the podium, "I, Dickie "Doc" Putnam, in sound mind and body, do bequeath my earthly belongings to the citizens of Gotham Creek to dispose of at their pleasure. This includes my house and its entire contents as well as the land and the adjoining woodlot. I've done enough wrong to this town and its people. I only ask that my last request be granted. I'm appointing Hap Kingsley as the executor of this will. If anyone understands the forest must be destroyed and the woodlot cleared, then barracaded, it is he. The money from the sale of the wood should be divided equally among you. This is my last and only will. ~Doc Putnam, October 24, 1996."

A hush enveloped the room broken only by the sound of the door opening as a stranger walked in and took a seat in the back. Several people turned around to glance at him, their faces pale with shock.

Jim Digby cleared his throat. "Well, I guess that says it all. Doc wanted the woodlot cleared, and although it will be a hassle taking it out of tree growth, I can have it all arranged by tomorrow. Does anyone have anything they'd like to say? Comments of any kind, before we close this meeting?"

Felicity Kingsley stood up, looking at her fellow townsfolk with tears in her eyes. "Listen to what you're saying! We can't let them just come in and rape our forest. It's the heart and lifeblood of our town. And think of what it will do to the ecology of the area. I just think it's plain wrong." She pointed her finger at Jim and added, "I'll do everything I can to stop it, mark my words, Mr. Digby. And besides, how do we know Doc Putnam is dead? Has anyone seen his body?"

As she sat down, Pat Nevels stood up. "I'd like to add to Mrs. Kingsley's comments. Doc wouldn't have sent his will here if he wasn't dying. Now I suppose we could form a search party and go into the woods to find him, but from past experience, I don't think that's such a great idea. There are those of us who remember what he looked like the last time we saw him. He told us then that he was dying and we have to take him at his word. Now about the woods—are we talking about clear-cutting or selective cutting? And what's to be done with the slash left behind? That's a fire hazard, you know."

Jim cleared his throat again. "Doc wanted the lot cleared, so I suppose it will be clear-cut."

Felicity started to stand up again, her eyes blazing, but Hap put his hand on her arm and pulled her back down to her seat. He stood up instead.

"Is there any possibility Doc *wasn't* in sound mind or body when he wrote his will?" he asked. "We all know how much the forest meant to him. Why would he want it destroyed?"

Jim nodded in sympathy. "You remember what he looked like the last time we saw him? Clearly, the man was sick. But his will is dated before that, so we have to assume he knew what he wanted us to do."

A silent moment followed, then Ned Speers looked around and stood up. "I think it's a good thing," he said. "The old religion is dead; Doc killed it when he told us the truth about what was going on. I wouldn't mind seeing that forest go, myself. It's a constant reminder of the old ways and we have to move on now."

Felicity sprang to her feet, her fists clenched. "You're wrong! Our religion will never die—and neither will those woods. You can cut them down, burn them, whatever. But they'll live on. It may take some time, but they'll come back and when they do, our religion will be revived and it will be stronger than ever!"

Hettie Brown stood up and turned to Felicity. "Listen to you, go on and on about the old religion! It was a poison, Felicity—destroying lives—the very lives of women like you and me."

Felicity bared her teeth. "Maybe they were like *you*, Hettie Brown, but they weren't like me at all. I remember how Serena Haskell used to bat her eyes at my Hap. She wanted him all through school." Her sneer turned into a sardonic smile as she added, "But she didn't get him in the end, did she?"

Jim Digby hit the top of the podium with his gavel. "Enough bickering, ladies, please…"

Just then, the stranger in the back stood up. "If I may address this situation," he began. Both women turned around to stare at him. Glaring at one another, they eased back down to their seats.

"I'm David Hardecastle, president of Piston Paper. Your town manager was good enough to call me here to attend this meeting and I'm glad he did. I believe I can put your fears to rest concerning your forest."

Jim motioned for him to come forward and all eyes were upon him as he walked up to the podium. He was a lean angular man, dressed in a black business suit that brought out the color in his cold blue eyes. "The fact is," he said into the microphone, "that woodlot should have been harvested thirty years ago. Much of what is there will have to go into paper; that's all it's good for. Now some of you have concerns about clear-cutting and that's the issue I'd like to address.

"More trees are killed by *not* harvesting than by clear-cutting a forest. When the canopy is thick, like the one in your woods, light can't penetrate to the forest floor in sufficient amounts for healthy new growth. What doesn't die from lack of sun, remains stunted. You know bio-diversity is necessary—and it is—but in a forest as old as yours, bio-diversity comes to a virtual halt. When was the last time any of you went deer hunting there? Or rabbit hunting? When was the last time you saw a moose in those woods? Or, heck, even a squirrel?"

The room fell silent. Although there were hunters here, none of them ever went in the Old Woods to hunt. Maybe because the forest was considered sacred as well as dangerous; but nothing lived there except the old oaks and everyone knew it.

"We've been conditioned by the media to believe forest fires are bad, but in the days before Smokey the Bear, sometimes Native Americans would burn down forests intentionally. Their purpose in doing so was to destroy the old to make way for the new. Deer, moose and other animals depend on young fauna in order to survive. So do many kinds of insects as well as the mammals and reptiles that eat them. Your forest is in the process of dying. You want to talk about a fire hazard? Few things burn faster than dry, dead wood."

Hardecastle scanned the faces of his audience. "You've expressed concerns about slash being left behind after we cut. Don't worry, we'll put all the waste through a chipper and we'll haul the chips away. We want to give your forest a healthy new start. For those of you who are doubtful, take a look at our track record. Piston Paper has received numerous awards for our work from the National Forest Service."

Felicity stood up and cleared her voice. "Excuse me, but I hardly believe the National Forest Service would condone any of the practices of Piston Paper."

David turned to her, humorlessly. "For your information, ma'am, the National Forest Service was organized to protect forests for the purpose of *harvesting*, not for the sake of the forests themselves. They know nature will always find a way, but cutting the old to make room for the new is safer, faster and more economical in the long run."

She huffed and sat back down, turning to Hap with her arms crossed. "Well, aren't you going to say something about this?"

He shook his head. "Nope."

She glared at him as she stood up again. "Well, fine then." She turned toward David Hardecastle. "I've heard quite enough. You might be able to dupe the rest of these people with your fancy words, but you're not fooling me. I'm going to find a way to stop this nonsense; just you wait and see." With that said, she strode out of the room, chin held high.

Hap watched her go, shaking his head, wondering if maybe he shouldn't have thrown away Doc's tea after all.

Maisie Speers met Felicity Kingsley coming out of the town office. "Is Ned still in the meeting?" she asked.

"Yeah, he's in there—with all the rest of the sheep," she said with a frown.

"What do you mean?"

Felicity leaned forward, her face hard, her eyes narrowed. "What I *mean* is my husband and yours—as well as all the others—are going to let the paper company cut down our sacred forest."

Maisie stepped back, knowing how Felicity's temper could get out of hand. She remembered a scene at the convenience store when Felicity had said some very nasty things to Deidre Garnet, reducing the woman to tears in front of everyone. "Well," she said, "I think cutting down the Old Woods might be a good thing."

Felicity shook her fist in the air. "Ah, why do I even bother wasting my breath talking to you? You're just like the rest of them!" She pushed past her. "I'm going to put a stop to it, Maisie Speers, just see if I don't!"

If that wasn't just like Felicity Kingsley, she thought, wryly, *the snootiest, most high-falooting bitch in Washington County, maybe in the entire state.* She remembered her from childhood, how she'd always been that way and wondered what on earth Hap ever saw in her. He would have been much better off—and probably a damn sight happier—had Felicity been sacrificed and Serena Haskell had lived to marry him.

She sighed and went inside. As she did so, the door to the back room opened and she stood aside, searching the faces for Ned. When she found him, she grabbed his arm.

"Something's wrong with Eddie," she told him. "I think we'd better take him to the hospital."

Eddie sat in the backseat of his parents' car, staring out the window, watching the rush of trees and meadows going by. He remembered his father shaking him, asking him what was wrong, but something inside of him wouldn't let him answer.

I'm dying! he wanted to scream. *I can feel my organs shutting down, one by one. I can hardly breathe, barely even think. Please save me, Dad! Get me some help before it's too late!*

"That's it," Ned had said. "You're going to the hospital. Now."

He felt his father lift him in his arms and carry him out to the car. His mother followed, frantic with panic, pitching her proverbial cow, but his dad remained calm.

I hardly ever tell you I love you, he thought, looking at his father's face as he laid him down in the seat. *You've got to know. I've got to pull through this so you'll know.*

It didn't take Norris long to discover that digging a grave in the woods without any tools was an impossible task. Under the mulch layer of leaves and topsoil, the ground was hard-packed gravel. Three of his fingernails had split when he tried to dig with his hands. He'd found a stick nearby and jabbed at the earth with it, but the dirt was unyielding. Finally, he cast the stick aside and sat down beside the hole to suck on his sore fingers.

Just then, he had a thought. *The old silver mine is somewhere here. Maybe I can bury Doc there.* Taking his fingers out of his mouth, he got up and made his way through the trees back to the place where his father had died.

He knelt down and tried to pick him up, but Doc fell apart in his hands. His body had literally turned into moss-covered sod and the seedlings growing out of him had grown even taller.

He cried out in disgust, looking at the clumps of black soil clinging to his hands.

"I don't understand," he said aloud. "Bodies take years to rot like that. I just don't get it…"

A distant rumble of machinery interrupted him and he stood up, wiping his hands on the legs of his jeans. Through the trees, he saw flashes of orange and yellow trucks headed through the Old Woods Road.

Wood harvesters? What are they doing here?

Distraught, he shook his head, knowing that if they found him, they'd kill him just like the townspeople had wanted to do. He reached down and quickly dug one of the seedlings from what was left of Doc's chest.

Taking the small tree with him, he ran away from the sounds of the trucks. He didn't know where he was headed; he just had to go where no one would ever bother him again.

16

Felicity Kingsley took note of the paper company trucks as she sped out of the town office parking lot. *How dare they even think of cutting down one tree here!* she fumed, her knuckles white as she gripped the steering wheel of her Lincoln Town Car. *Why, I'd like to take Hap's gun and shoot them all! Our town and our religion was built around those woods—and I think, no, I believe there's something there...an alien spaceship, maybe. A U.F.O. That would explain the green man I saw last night. In fact, it explains a lot. Maybe old Doc Putnam found the U.F.O. and he wanted to keep it all to himself. What if he's not dead after all—what if he's living aboard the U.F.O. with those aliens?*

"I've got to do something drastic to stop this madness," she said aloud, tapping her nails against the steering wheel. Knowing the harvesters would begin work soon, she turned right, onto Old Woods Road.

The day was as cold and dark as her mood, the sky heavy with continuous clouds, an off-shade of grey with the promise of rain. Leaves blew across the road and a couple of them landed on the windshield of her car, trapped there by the wipers.

She took it as a sign that she was doing the right thing. She parked her car cross-wise in Doc Putnam's driveway and smiled at her ingenuity in the rearview mirror, then reached into her purse for her lipstick. Warpaint to face the adversity. Carefully, she applied it, deep in thought.

Parking the car here probably won't stop them, she surmised. *But at the very least it should slow them down.* With a sigh, she turned the key in the ignition to off and dropped it into her pocketbook. Then she stepped out of the car.

She tried all the doors one last time to make sure they were securely locked. She glanced over at the woods. *I'll protect you,* she promised, *even if it means risking my life.*

Getting into the forest was no small task, for she'd worn nice clothes to the town meeting. It was important for the constable's wife to look her very best; after all, she was an extension of her husband's power. Her high-heeled designer pumps presented problems, though, making it quite difficult to walk gracefully. She cursed when she snagged her nylons on a bush and her silk skirt caught on the branch of a tree, ripping the hem.

She followed the path as best she could. A leaf, brown and dry, fluttered down from a nearby tree and caught on her mohair sweater. *Another sign,* she thought to herself. *Proof that the forest loves me.*

The loggers have already been here, she noted with dismay. They'd marked some of the tree trunks with splotches of paint—white on some, blue on some and orange on others.

Gradually, the path became less clear as it came to a steep decline. Trees, their limbs bare, towered above her. She stopped, standing at the edge of the slope. *What if the U.F.O. is down there?* she wondered. *How on earth could it have landed? These woods are so thick...*

That's when she heard the trucks, the rumble of their engines carried by the wind. There was no time now to search for Doc's U.F.O.

She walked back up the path to the edge of the forest where she could see the road from across the field. Oh yes, they were coming.

And Hap was leading the way in his cruiser.

Her eyes flooded with angry tears. *How can he do this? Perhaps he's just like all the rest of them? No, that's impossible. Hap's a brave and upstanding man. That's why I fell in love with him. He'll do right in the end; I just know he will. Maybe he's come to help me stop them—*

She gasped when he got out of his cruiser and unlocked her car with his set of keys. Then he drove it close to Doc's porch, making plenty of room for the logging trucks to get by.

She clenched her fists in outrage. *How dare he?! What gives him the right?* Her mascara was smearing, running down her cheeks like black tears but she didn't care. All that mattered now was keeping the trees safe from harm.

The loggers drove into the woods like tanks approaching battle. She ran to an oak, which had been marked with white paint, and she grabbed onto its trunk, pressing her body against it. "Don't fear," she whispered with her cheek against the bark. "I'll protect you. I'll defend all of you, even if it costs me my life."

They were closer now, bearing down on the forest.

Suddenly, she had an idea. She let go of the oak and ran toward the oncoming line of trucks, waving her purse. In the process, she broke a heel and stumbled, falling on one knee, but she got back up and faced them.

The first driver to reach her slowed and rolled down his window. "Move out of the way, lady," he yelled.

Felicity shook her head and her purse. "No, I'm not leaving. What you guys are doing is wrong. I'm staying my ground. You'll have to run me over if you think I'm going to stand here and let you cut down so much as one tree."

With that, she sank to her knees on the leaf-covered ground and flung her arms wide open. "Go ahead," she shouted, taunting them. "Run me over."

The truck ground to a stop, causing all the equipment behind it to brake as well. She watched as the driver reached for his CB radio and said something into it that she couldn't hear.

Moments later, Hap arrived on foot, looking quite unhappy. "Felicity, what the hell do you think you're doing? Move out of the way and let these men carry on with their business."

Spittle flew from her mouth as she sneered a reply. "Their *business*? They've come to destroy, to rape and pillage—and out of all people, I would have expected you to be the one to stop them." She stood up before he could reach her. "Don't come near me, you traitor! Don't you dare touch me!"

He spread his palms in an attempt to make an appeal. "Felicity, be reasonable now. You can't stop this and neither can I. Piston Paper has every legal right to cut this forest." He took another step toward her. "Come on, dear; let me take you home so you can get yourself cleaned up. A nice hot bath and some soft music will do you a world of good. You'll feel better, trust me."

"I'll never trust you ever again!" She screamed and bolted for the nearest tree, the one with the white paint on the trunk. She wrapped her arms around it as tightly as she could, not caring that it was ruining her expensive sweater.

Hap sighed and went after her. "You're embarrassing me," he told her. "In front of everyone. They're sitting in their trucks laughing at the pair of us. Now please, let go of that tree and I'll take you home."

She bared her teeth. "Go to hell."

"Fine, you want to play hardball?" He reached down into a pouch on his belt and pulled out a set of handcuffs. "I don't want to have to do this, but I've had enough of your games. Now either you come with me willingly or not. It's your choice."

"Fuck you, Hap. I'm staying right here."

His eyes widened in shock at her words. This was a woman who wouldn't have said scat if she had a mouthful of it. "What's gotten into you?" he asked in a low voice as he readied the cuffs.

"Don't fucking touch me!" she screamed. "I hate you, Hap Kingsley. As soon as I get back home, I'm getting a divorce."

He said nothing as he reached over and grabbed one of her wrists. As he put the cuff around it, she reached up with her free hand and raked his face with her nails, drawing blood. He caught the other wrist before she could do more damage. "Enough of this," he said in a stern tone. "You can have your divorce; I don't care. Now either you're going to walk out of these woods peacefully or I'll drag you along."

Felicity held her head high, her lower lip trembling. "I'll walk," she said.

Doctor Crabtree at Machias Medical Center shook his head as he glanced from Maisie to Ned. "I don't know what to tell you. I wish I had the answers but I don't. For some reason, your son has lapsed into a coma. Now we'll run more tests but you understand, we've got to keep him here."

"A coma?" Maisie could barely say the words as she clung to her husband. "Will he come out of it? Why can't anyone tell us what's wrong with him?" She locked eyes with the doctor. "Eddie will wake up, won't he?"

"I don't know. If he does, it may take a few days or maybe even weeks. We'll do everything we can but our facility is small. If we have to, we'll move him to Eastern Maine Medical Center in Bangor."

"How soon will you know what's going on?" Ned spoke up.

Dr. Crabtree shrugged. "Maybe in a week or so."

"Can we see him?" Maisie asked.

"Yes. Just keep in mind that people in comas can hear what's on around them, so keep the conversation light. Give him plenty of encouragement; talk to him as if he's wide awake."

Ned put his arm around Maisie. "Will it help him wake up sooner?"

"Again, I can't promise anything. Right now, Eddie's in God's hands. Follow me and I'll take you to his room, but remember, keep the conversation light and upbeat."

Maisie swallowed nervously, then caught her breath as soon as she saw her son lying in the hospital bed. He looked so small and frail. There was a row of machines beside him and some of them had plastic tubes running from them into his arms.

Dr. Crabtree gave her a warning glance and she nodded.

"Can we touch him?" Ned asked.

"Of course. Just take care around the I.V.'s."

Ned let go of his wife and approached the bed. He reached down and lightly shook Eddie's foot. "Hey, sport. How're you doing?"

Maisie followed his cue, went to the other side of the bed and stroked his hand. "Hi, honey. We're right here." She forced herself to smile. "I know you didn't feel like going to school today, but aren't you taking this a bit too far?"

Ned chuckled. "That's our boy, Maisie. He never does anything halfway."

Dr. Crabtree motioned to the door. "You folks are doing just fine. If you need me, have me paged at the nurses' station."

"Thank you," Maisie called out.

After chatting back and forth for a little over an hour, Ned told her he had to go back to Gotham Creek. Kate was due home at noontime and he felt it best if one of them was there when she arrived. Maisie nodded, knowing Kate and Eddie had a special bond. Her daughter was apt to take the news of his coma quite badly.

"I'll stay here," she told her husband. "As long as it takes, I'll be right here."

Ned leaned across the bed and kissed her, then he gave Eddie's hand a gentle squeeze. "Take care of yourself, son, and come back to us as soon as you're able."

David Hardecastle was right; the trees in Old Woods were dying. Some of the higher branches were dry and devoid of bark, laid smooth and bare by wind and weather. He'd had his men color-code the trunks: white for paper, orange for lumber-quality and blue for dead, dry trees which would be harvested for cordwood and pellets for stoves.

Most of the trees were oak, great for lumber and primarily unsuitable for paper—but he'd recently discovered a way of making excellent paper from trash oak. *Cream off the top*, he'd called it with a larger profit margin than woodchips or firewood.

In order to access the entire woodlot, roads had to be cut through the forest in the basic shape of a fish's spinebone—one main road leading out with smaller roads side-shooting at 45-degree angles.

This is where the feller bunchers would come in, to seize each tree, saw it off at the trunk and delimb it, then place it in a pile of logs known as a twitch.

The grapple skidders would come in behind them, waiting to drag the twitches to the clearing where a loader would put them onto trailers.

Ralph Kane was driving the first feller buncher; he was a veteren logger, one of Piston Paper's foremen. In his twenty-seven years of working the woods, he'd never seen a forest quite like this. Old growth, primarily oak—remarkable in its height and density. While he'd supervised marking the trees earlier, he couldn't help but feel he was about to demolish a cathedral. Not that he was funky about trees or religion, but there was something surreal about this forest.

He drove his machine to the first tree he'd marked and positioned the hydraulic jaws around the trunk. Then he turned on the saw blade.

And that's when hell broke loose.

The trees in the forest, all of them at once, began twisting and flailing their branches like arms. Several men jumped from their machines to run for their lives and were caught by the boughs. Ralph Kane fought his panic and reached for his radio. The tree he'd just sawed was dead, not moving like the others. "FB1 to all crew," he yelled. "We have to cut the trees down that have our men in them and we have to do it now! It's the only way to kill them."

No sooner than he'd said that, his feller buncher began to rock. Ralph looked down just in time to see several tree roots jut upward from the ground to seize his machine. "What the fuck is going on?" he screamed as one of the roots smashed against the windshield, cracking it into spider web lines.

Black soil dripped in clumps from the roots and as he tried to jump clear, one of them caught him in the face, knocking him back into the cab, blinding him. He reached again for his radio and felt something loose in his mouth, rolling around on his tongue. A tooth. He spit it out and yelled into the receiver: "FB1 to all crew. Get out now. Abandon operations. If possible, save the machines—and if not, well, just save your asses and run like the devil's on your heels because he is!"

Ned Speers had just finished telling Kate about Eddie being hospitalized when their house started to shake.

"What's happening? Is it an earthquake?" she yelled, grabbing onto the living room couch.

"I don't know," he shouted, confused. Yes, Maine experienced earthquakes from time to time, but most were minor, just tremors that barely registered on the Richter Scale. He remembered one in 1973 that was a 4.8 but that had happened over on the other side of the state in Oxford County. People in other areas didn't even know it had occurred until they'd heard about it on the news.

The house was making strange noises now, creaking and grinding. When acoustic tiles began to tumble from the ceiling, Ned grabbed Kate by the arm and as they fled, they could hear dishes rattling in the kitchen cabinets, smashing to the floor. Pictures thumped against walls; books toppled from shelves. They'd almost reached the front door when the living room floor suddenly burst apart. In an instant, something snaked up from the cellar and grabbed Ned by the leg.

He pushed Kate outside to safety but she reached for him, struggling to pull him free. "What is it?" she cried, "What's got your leg?"

"I don't know—*I just don't know!*" He could feel it winding higher, working its way around his thigh. It felt like a snake but it looked like the root of a tree. "You have to go, Kate. Get to safety."

"I'm not leaving you!" she shot back, continuing to tug on him.

"You have to," he said, glancing over his shoulder. "There's more coming; I can't fight this thing much longer. Save yourself, girl, and make your old man proud."

She looked up at him, bewildered, frightened out of her wits. "But I don't want to leave you, Daddy."

Another root-thing wrapped around his torso, and she screamed as her father was ripped from her arms.

Felicity reached for the rose-scented body wash; Hap was right, having a bath did make her feel better. She loved her tub; it was an old-fashioned oval in mint green enamel with a luxury ledge on the side. He'd bought it for her as a wedding present.

She poured some body wash into her palm and lifted her right leg out of the bubbles. She loved her legs, too, and took special care of them by massage, exercise and a myriad of moisturizing creams. Thirty-eight years old and she still had the muscle tone she had when she was twenty.

Every once in a while, though, a truck would roll by, spoiling her bathtime and she'd frown to herself. *They don't understand what they are about to destroy,* she decided. *After all, how could they?*

They hadn't been in love with Hap so hard it hurt, then to have Serena 'slutface' Haskell practically throw herself at him every chance she got, getting him all confused about who he really loved. *They* hadn't been there in the locker room of the school gymnasium when Serena walked up to her and bragged how *she* was planning to steal Hap away.

Felicity smirked, remembering how both of them were eligible for the Chosen, that October in 1976, only Serena's name had been the one they picked. And her family had put up *such* a stink about it that they all wound up getting killed.

She shrugged as she lathered soap onto her leg. It was a shame about Serena's little brother; he was just a kid in the wrong place at the wrong time with no choice whatsoever in the matter.

But Serena, that little bitch, got what she had coming to her.

And Felicity got Hap.

She lowered her leg back down into the steamy water and reached for the body wash again—and as she did, another truck rolled by.

This time it shook the bathroom so hard that the medicine cabinet door opened and all her toiletries began jiggling. She set the bottle of body wash down and watched her perfumes do a cakewalk from the bottom shelf of the cabinet and into the sink.

"Damn those trucks!"

Even the bubbles in the tub were wiggling from their vibrations.

The shaking didn't stop. When the water in the toilet bowl began to slosh and burp and the window by the sink rattled so hard it cracked, she stood up in the tub to reach for her towel.

Something wasn't right.

It sounded like the whole house was ripping apart—and here she was up in the second-story bathroom without a stitch on. As she snatched her towel from the bar, the entire house *shifted*. She fell back into the tub, smacking the back of her head on the porcelain neck-rest.

She was aware of falling—the entire tub was falling with her in it—crashing through the floor, down into the dining room, then through the floor again and into the basement. It happened so fast, she'd barely had time to scream.

But she had plenty of time now, in a basement full of woody snakes.

While Felicity succumbed to the onslaught of roots in her basement, Pat Nevels was driving out of the Gotham Creek Convenience parking lot, his backseat laden with bags of snack food: ice cream, soda and chips. There was a basketball game on Channel Four at eight o'clock he'd planned to watch.

He'd been Gotham Creek's leading center on the high school team back in the mid-eighties, though none of those games were ever televised. The latter part of the eighties was a major bummer, beginning in 1986 when his twin sister, Arienna, was the Chosen. It had all been down hill from there; he lost interest in playing ball and his studies.

They say twins have a special kind of psychic connection, and Pat believed it was true. There were times when he could almost feel his sister's last agonies; he'd get a flash of impending doom and his stomach would fill with knots.

This was one of those times.

He'd just passed the old Maypole when he began to lose control of the car. Something lifted it into the air and it bounced down hard on its shocks, fenders grinding against the tires. "What the hell was that?" he shouted. Then it happened again.

This time, he wasn't so lucky. Coming down, he turned the wheel too hard and the car flipped over onto its roof. Fortunately, he was wearing his seat belt, but now he was hanging upside down and he couldn't get the latch to work.

The window beside him had broken and something that looked like a snake slithered into the car with him. Pat, who loathed snakes, began to shout, trying to slap it away while he fumbled with the seat belt.

Only it wasn't a snake and this realization became his last thought.

Bruce Kelwick, like Felicity Kingsley, was in the bathroom when the shaking started. He'd just settled down on the toilet to read and have what his wife Jasmine referred to as a "B.M." That meant crap to him, but she didn't like him using what she called "foul language".

In his eyes, that made her a real lady. *It's not always easy living with a real lady*, he thought soberly, glancing over at the toilet paper. Yep, she'd done it again, hung it the wrong way so the end of the paper went over the top of the roll. That was one of the little things she did that drove him crazy.

But Bruce was a fixer; he couldn't help himself, it was just the way he was wired. With a resigned sigh, he took the paper roll from the dispenser and put it back the *right* way. Then he opened the newspaper and began to read.

He started with his favorite part, the funnies. Jasmine had beaten him to yesterday's paper and had clipped coupons from various pages, making it almost impossible to read—and the comics' page had been damned near indecipherable because of the money-savers on the back.

He knew his reading in the bathroom drove her nuts, too. Afterwards, she'd handle the paper as if it was smeared with "B.M." and he thought it was funny in a sick sort of way. Of course it didn't have "B.M." on it, but she *thought* it did and that's what made it count.

He looked up from the newspaper when the mirror on the wall began to rattle. It was probably just vibrations from the logging trucks. They'd been driving past the house ever since the town meeting ended.

A cramp in his gut told him it was time to push and he did so with a grunt, hoping that when the "B.M." came out, it wouldn't make the water splash his bottom. That was just plain repulsive; whenever it happened, he'd have to take a shower afterwards.

There was no splash this time. Bruce breathed through his mouth so he wouldn't have to smell "B.M." as he scanned down through the funnies. His guts told him he wasn't finished yet, though, so he was contented just to relax and let nature take its course.

The house shook again and this time the water in the toilet sloshed. He thought about getting up but it was too soon. Another cramp was on its way.

That's when *something* touched him. Something coming up from *inside* the toilet bowl. He screamed in shock, dropped the paper and started to get up.

But he wasn't fast enough.

Something hard and cold nailed him right in the butt; he felt it rip past his ring of sphincter muscles in an instant surge of pain. He tried to move away from it as it wound its way into his rectum and further up into his large intestine. Jasmine began pounding on the door.

"Bruce!" she called out. "Are you okay in there?"

No, he definitely was *not* ok. Whatever was penetrating his body was very long and rough and it hurt, dear God, it hurt. It was in his stomach now; not only could he feel it in there, he could see his abdomen bulge and dip as it moved through him.

He kept screaming and Jasmine kept beating on the door. Why he'd locked it was anyone's guess; she'd always given him plenty of privacy.

He began to choke and vomit blood, splashing the floor and walls as he thrashed about. It was in his esophagus, worming its way up into his pharynx, stretching and tearing. His last scream was cut off as it flew out his mouth and his eyes grew wide with sheer terror at what he saw.

He didn't recognize what it was at first. It was dripping with gore, tinted red with blood. He gripped it with his hands, trying to pull it free from his body, but there was no end to it. *What is this thing?* his mind screamed. *It's killing me and I don't even know what it is!*

That's when he saw the rough scaly bark that came off in his hands.

He writhed on the floor, watching more of it shoot out of his mouth. The tip end slithered toward the door, smearing the tiles with something that looked like red curry. It took a stance like a king cobra, five feet high and ready to strike. Bruce's hands slipped away and he fell forward, dragged by it as it stabbed right through the door.

He heard Jasmine scream again. Then he heard no more.

Hap Kingsley and Jim Digby were talking outside the town office when the ground beneath their feet began to tremble.

"Must be an earthquake," Jim said, slipping his hands into his back pockets as he looked around.

"Could be, I suppose," Hap commented. "It's not like we've never felt them before." He glanced across the road at the diner as frightened people began boiling out through the front door, screaming.

"What's got their knickers in a twist?" Jim asked, turning toward Cuffy's.

"I don't know. Maybe something fell over inside and it scared the daylights out of them?"

Just then, something, no—many somethings—burst from the sides of the diner, crashing through the windows and busting through the walls. To Hap, they looked like snakes—huge snakes—and they were moving, slithering with lightning speed toward the running crowd. Before he could draw his pistol from its holster, the snakes had already grabbed five or six people, lifting them into the air and smashing them down onto the pavement of the parking lot like they were nothing more than rag dolls.

"Holy shit!" Jim said, taking a few steps backward. "Hap, what the hell are those things?"

But Hap was running, trying to get a good aim at the snakes with his gun. "Get in the cruiser," he yelled back to Jim. "Get in there and stay put."

He fired five or six shots at the snakes but the crowd was making it difficult. Hap figured he might have had two sure hits but it didn't stop the snakes or slow them down.

The town office began to shake, then the windows smashed outward all at once. The building groaned as it sagged and over the fracas, Hap could hear Jim screaming in the police car.

There was another scream, this one higher in octave, and closer than the crowd that had come from the diner. It was Missy Sands, running for her life, sprinting across the convenience store parking lot, her long blond hair waving like a banner behind her.

Five or six of the snakes were chasing her and closing in fast.

Hap dashed back to his cruiser and got in. Jim stopped screaming and pointed out the window. "You'd better step on it, Hap," he said in a shaken voice. "Something's coming out of the ground right beside the car."

Hap wasted no time. The tires squealed as he backed up, then squealed again as he turned onto Main Street.

"Whew, that was a close call," Jim said, turning in the seat to watch the snakes slither along behind them.

Hap was rolling down his window as he drove closer to the running girl. "Missy!" he yelled, stepping on the brake pedal. "Get in!"

As she dashed for the safety of his cruiser, the snakes that were chasing her picked up speed. Panting for breath, she managed to open the door and jump into the back seat. One of the snakes had wound its way around her ankle and it broke off when she slammed the door shut.

It fell to the carpet and she reached down to pick it up.

"What the hell is it?" Jim asked her.

Missy passed it to him. "You tell me."

He turned it over in his hands, bewildered. "It's a tree root. Well, a piece of one. That's what it looks like." He glanced over at Hap. "What is going on here?"

"I don't know. I just don't know." Hap didn't pull his eyes from the road; he'd had to speed up again to outrun the tree roots that had been chasing Missy. Up ahead, there had been an accident and he recognized the car almost instantly. It had belonged to Pat Nevels but there was no sign of Pat anywhere.

As Hap sped by, he saw the inside of the car was filled with tangled roots.

Someone in the distance was running toward him, straight down the middle of the street, waving their arms. "It's Kate Speers," Missy cried out. "We've got to save her," she added, reaching across the seat to unlock the opposite door.

Hap gritted his teeth as he stepped on the brake pedal. It was going to be close and he hoped the car wouldn't fishtail when he tried to stop.

As Kate ran up, Missy opened the door for her and she dove inside.

"I can't believe it," she said, hugging herself, her eyes wide with fear. "I thought they were going to get me. They're everywhere!"

Jim turned in the front seat to face her. "How many people do you think are still out there alive?"

Kate shook her head. "Just look at the houses and you tell me."

Jim bit his lower lip. There were no more houses left standing in Gotham Creek. All had been demolished into piles of rubble. It was the stuff of nightmares, a Dante-like scene, with a bit of Dali thrown in for good measure.

Thinking of Felicity, Hap said nothing as he drove toward Route 9.

17

Norris ran until he could run no more. It was nearly dusk and he collapsed to the ground in exhaustion. He didn't know where he was, only that he was safe for now.

Bathed in sweat, he shivered. The temperature was dropping with the approaching night. His stomach rumbled with hunger and as he caught his breath, he could hear footsteps on the forest floor, snapping twigs. Something was moving through the underbrush and it was large, from the sound of it.

He sat up in alarm and tried to remain perfectly still, believing if he did so, whatever it was that was out there couldn't see him.

When it moved into a clearing, he saw it was a large black bear. And despite his stillness, it *did* see him, backing away with a low growl.

Norris watched its eyes as it disappeared into the forest, eyes that were Mt. Dew-green with the reflection of his glowing skin, and he knew right then he'd be safe and would remain so, if he could manage to stay away from people.

When the last remnants of twilight faded into full-fledged nightfall, it began to rain. Water drops fell in a soft patter at first, then the sky broke open with a crash of thunder.

Norris crawled to huddle beneath a thick pine, using its low sweeping branches as protection from the storm.

Mike Elwin lifted his head from where he'd hidden inside the dumpster just outside his ruined diner. All was silent now. There were no more screams, no sounds of the diner being ripped apart, no shaking and rumbling from beneath the ground.

He reached up with shaking hands to grip the greasy edge of the metal box and slowly, he peeked up over it. It was raining now in hard fat droplets, a bone-chilling kind of drizzle. He heard a roll of thunder and a moment later, forked lightning lit up the sky.

That's when a loud crack ripped through the air, sounding like a gunshot, only a hundred times louder. Afraid to move, he stood there, knee deep in garbage, looking around.

The fire at the northern end of town caught his eye. The tallest tree, the one called the Great Bull Oak, was burning, split in half by the lightning's strike. Mike watched the fire rage for a moment, then the flames died down in the rain.

He looked around. As far as he could tell, the snake-things had stopped their destruction. There was nothing slithering across the parking lot, nothing whipping up from the cracks in the pavement. He'd seen what had happened to some of the people, at least to those who'd run around to the back of the diner. They'd reached out and squeezed those people to death, like big Amazon snakes.

But where had the bodies gone? he wondered. *And more importantly, where were the snake-things now?*

Jess Brown lifted the corner of the blackboard and poked his head out to look around. Their classroom was a disaster. Desks and chairs had been toppled, books and papers scattered. But all was quiet now. "I think it's over," he told the girls who'd been hiding with him. Megan Kingsley pulled herself out from beneath the blackboard, then she helped Amy Sands and Barbie Kelwick.

They looked around their classroom in apprehension, each of them knowing they might not have been there if they hadn't stayed after school for band practice. Megan glanced at Jess, then at the huge hole in the floor surrounded by broken tiles.

"Do you think Miss Sargent is down there?"

Jess shrugged, rubbing his chin. "Beats me. I saw those things grab her, and then the blackboard fell down on us." He pointed at the hole. "She might be down there, somewhere. But I'm not going in there to find her. Hard to say how deep it is."

"Well, we have to *do* something!" Megan crept as close as she dared to the hole and called out, "Miss Sargent...are you down there? Can you hear us?"

Her voice echoed through what was left of the school building, then the row of windows facing the playground broke as the roof began to sag.

"We have to get out of here now," Jess said, reaching out to grab her arm.

Megan looked over at the windows. "You're right. Let's get out before the whole building falls down."

They'd just made it outside to safety when their school caved in.

"Wow! We could have died in there!" Amy exclaimed.

Jess nodded. "Yeah, and by the looks of things, we could have died out here, too."

Eddie Speers could hear his mother's gentle voice, the comforting rise and fall of her tones. He could even hear her breathing, but he couldn't understand what she was saying. It was as cryptic as the teacher's voice in the Peanuts cartoons, yet it soothed him and soon he felt himself falling asleep, knowing he was safe because she was near.

He opened his eyes. The sky above was darker than the deepest black and filled with a billion stars. The ground beneath him was hard, solid as rock, and very cold. He sat up slowly, looking around, trying to figure out where he was.

The terrain appeared alien and surreal, with what resembled stalagmites shooting up from its surface. They glittered like ice sprinkled with bits of shiny silver.

He stood up and walked over to one of them. It was very windy here and incredibly cold, looking very much like a scene from one of his video games. *Deathvoid Fighter Pilots* or something like that; he really couldn't remember the title.

I'm a stranger in a strange land, he thought. As he ran his finger along the side of a stalagmite, he heard a whirring noise. He looked around but saw nothing except the weird landscape surrounding him.

The sound grew increasingly louder, then he saw a movement out of the corner of his eye. He looked upward in silent wonder.

It was a rocket of some sort. No, it was more like a spacecraft. As it got closer, he could see it was shaped like a sphere and a row of white lights circled its equator. He quickly knelt behind the stalagmite, his heart racing.

It's a U.F.O.! Oh God, it's landing and something's coming out of it. Some sort of projection, like the legs on a stool. It's touching down. I sure hope they don't see me—I don't want them to find me unless they're the friendly sort and go figure the odds on that.

When the legs of the spacecraft made contact, the ground shook. Eddie watched, transfixed, not daring to blink or look away for an instant. A column of blue light came out of the bottom of the craft. It was like an arc welding light, too bright to look.

Eddie shut his eyes and heard the ground where the blue light shone began to sizzle and pop. He thought it sounded a lot like bacon frying in a pan. *What are they doing?* he wondered. *Why are they here? Heck, why am I here?*

Within moments, the sizzling stopped and he looked up. There was a steaming hole beneath the starcraft and now something was being lowered into it. It was a cylander, glowing neon green. It disappeared into the hole, then something else came out of the craft.

This object was disc shaped and quite heavy, for when it dropped, the ground shook even harder than it had when the spaceship landed.

Evidently, it sealed the hole. Then the whirring started again, and the legs of the craft retracted. It shot upwards into the sky. Eddie watched it disappear as quickly as it had arrived.

In the silence that followed, he crept over to the place where it had landed.

The seal over the hole was hard and smooth, appearing to be made of some kind of metal he couldn't identify. He knelt down and tapped it with his fingers.

That's when something tapped *him* on the shoulder.

Eddie jumped and looked up into his father's face.

"Geez, Dad! What are you doing here?"

Ned smiled. "Well, I was going to ask you the same thing. I've come to take you home."

"Do you know where we are?"

"Yes. We're on the surface of a meteor, somewhere in outer space."

Eddie shook his head, grinning. "Sure, we are. Did you see the U.F.O.? Do you know what's in here?" he asked pointing to the metal seal.

"That's toxic waste, son."

"Alien waste?"

"Yep."

Eddie frowned. "Why'd they put it here? It makes no sense that they'd do that."

"They're desperate, Ed," Ned told him. "They've poisoned their planet, and they're running out of options."

"Sounds like Earth."

"Just because they're more advanced doesn't mean they've got all the answers."

"What will happen if this thing crashes into a planet?" Eddie asked.

"Same thing that happened in Gotham Creek. It's radia-anthracite, a poison that works as a growth stimulant to some forms of life and as a lethal toxin to others."

"Like the trees in Old Woods," Eddie said. "That's what made them grow so big."

"It did other things to them, too. But that's over now." Ned ruffled Eddie's hair with his hand.

"This is just a dream, isn't it?" he asked, looking up at his father.

"Well, yes and no. You're in a coma and you need to wake up. If you listen real hard, you can hear your mother talking to you. I want you to go to the sound of her voice. No matter how scary it seems, you have to reach her. Can you do that?"

Eddie stood up. "Yeah, but what about you? How are you getting back?"

Ned put an arm around him and hugged him close. "Don't worry about me. I know the way home." He kissed Eddie's forehead. "Now go to your mother. She needs you now more than she even knows."

Eddie closed his eyes as his father released him. He strained to hear his mother and a moment passed, then he heard it, sounding like she was quite distant. He smiled back at his dad.

"Hey, I love you."

"I love you, too, son."

Eddie started walking in the direction of his mother's voice. She sounded closer now, but he was reaching the edge of the meteor. Small pieces of it had broken off and were zipping past him. He turned around but his father was gone.

"Mom, I'm here," he shouted. "Can you hear me?"

"I felt you move," she was saying. "Squeeze my hand again if you can hear me. Come back to us, Eddie. Please come back."

"I can't, Mom. I've reached the edge and there's nowhere left to go."

"I know you're in there somewhere. If you can really hear me, I know you'll come back to us." Her voice was beginning to grow distant again.

"Mom!" Eddie reached upward. Gathering up his courage, he jumped from the edge...

...and into her arms.

He could smell her before he opened his eyes. She smelled nice, like soap and citrus. It was the best feeling he'd ever known, being back with her. His eyes fluttered open and the first thing he saw was her face, her sweet face, smiling down at him.

"Welcome back," she said, stroking his cheek.

He looked around the room, a bit surprised to find he was lying in a bed and there were all kinds of machines nearby, some of them whirring, with tubes coming out of them and going into his arms.

"Mom, where are we?"

"In the hospital, in Machias."

"Where's Dad? He was with me on the meteor then he told me to come back and—"

Maisie patted his hand. "I think you must have been dreaming, Eddie. Your dad's gone back to Gotham Creek so he could be there when Kate got home. I think they'll be coming by tonight to check in on you."

Feeling exhausted, Eddie closed his eyes.

18

Jess was right; Gotham Creek looked more like a battlefield than a town. There wasn't one building left standing and the roads had been torn up.

"Do you think our parents are okay?" Barbie Kelwick spoke up, shielding her eyes from the rain. She was the youngest in the group and until now hadn't said a word after the blackboard fell on them.

Jess glanced over at Megan and then at Barbie. "I'm sure they're fine."

"I want to go home," Amy wailed, starting to cry. Megan put an arm around her. It would have been hard to tell where any of their homes had been in the daylight, and it was virtually impossible in the dark.

"Where can we go?" Megan asked. "We can't stand out here in the rain."

"Grab hands," Jess told the girls. "Grab hands just like we did inside. We'll find shelter somewhere but we have to stay together. You know that hole in the classroom floor? Well, I think there are probably a bunch of them, everywhere, anywhere. If we stay together, maybe we won't fall into one."

Megan shot him a look, hoping he was right.

Slowly, taking great care, the children made their way along the refuse that had been Main Street. Jess had thought it best to head toward Route 1. Perhaps along that stretch of highway they could find some help.

They'd just made it past the convenience store when they heard someone call out, "Hey, you kids—stop—wait up!"

It was a grown up's voice, a man, who hurried out of the shadows carrying a flashlight. The children watched the light bob and bounce as he jogged toward them.

"Mr. Elwin? Is that you?" Jess called out. He only knew one man who wore white pants.

"Yeah, it's me."

As he came closer, they could see the mist of his breath blown about by the wind. "Thank goodness you kids are okay," he said. He knew all of them, as well as their parents, many of whom he doubted were still alive after today.

"We're headed for Route 1," Jess said. "It's too dangerous to walk around town in the dark with everything torn up."

"I agree."

"What's that smell?" Amy asked, wrinkling her nose in disgust.

Mike gave her a sad smile. "I'm afraid it's me. I dove into the dumpster when something started busting up the diner."

Jess looked into his eyes. "Do you know what it was? What wrecked our town?"

Mike shook his head. "I haven't a clue. They looked like snakes to me."

"Yeah," said Megan, "big snakes."

"But they're gone now? Right?" Jess asked.

"I think so, sonny. At least I hope to hell they're gone."

"Have you seen anyone else?" he asked, hoping for some good news.

But Mike shook his head. "I saw Hap Kingsley in his cruiser. He picked up Missy Sands and there was someone else in the car, but that's all I know."

Megan and Amy started to hug each other, then stopped, realizing that Jess and Barbie might not have been so lucky.

"Come on, gang," Mike said, trying to sound cheerful. "Let's hike out to Route 1 and see if we can get some help."

Brad Davis was driving home from a trip to Campobello Island when a man and four children flagged him down from the side of the road in the rain. None of them were wearing raingear and he thought it strange, but perhaps their car had broken down?

He pulled over to the shoulder of the highway and rolled down his window as the man trotted over.

"Can you give us a ride?" The man sounded desperate. Maybe it was the look in his eyes or the fact that he was soaked to the skin.

"Where you headed?" Brad asked.

"We need to get to a phone, but I want to get these kids out of the rain first."

Brad nodded, "Sure, hop in." The man motioned to the children and they bundled into the car, the older ones in back. He put the smallest girl in the front seat between them before getting in himself.

"So what were you all doing out there in the rain?" Brad put the car into drive and pulled back out onto the highway.

"I think maybe we should talk to the police first," the man said. Brad glanced over at him and turned off the dome light. The guy was creeping him out a little; the children were a bit too quiet, too.

After a moment passed, he decided he needed to break the ice in order to get them to talk. "Well, my name's Brad Davis and I'm from Milbridge." He turned again to look at the man. "And you folks are?"

"Mike Elwin," the man said. "From Gotham Creek."

"Gotham Creek? Where's that?"

"It *was* back there a ways, between Routes 1 and 9."

There was something about the way he said it that put Brad on edge. "Are these your children?" He really didn't think they were—none of them looked like they belonged to the same family, but with all the marriages and divorces these days one never knew.

Mike shook his head. "They're not mine, no. They're neighbors, friends' kids."

"Did your car break down or something?"

"No."

Brad slowed down, thinking. Something was going on here and it just didn't feel right. He pulled the car over and looked hard at Mike. "I think we'd better get out and talk for a minute." He glanced at the children, then back at Mike and added, "Privately."

Mike sighed and opened his door. "Fine," he said as he climbed out of the car. The kids looked nervous—they'd been frightened enough already, but he'd pretty much gathered that Brad was nosy and had the wrong idea about what was going on. "You guys stay put," he told the kids. "It will be all right."

Brad met him at the front of the car. "So what's really going on here?"

Mike looked up, searching for the right words to say. "There was some kind of...well, accident, I guess you'd call it, back in town. I think a lot of people are dead. I was beginning to believe I might be the only one left there alive then I found these kids. We've got to get help."

"What kind of accident was it?"

Mike shook his head, looking down at his feet. "It was bad. Real bad. Let's just leave it at that."

Brad saw the hopelessness in his face and instantly he felt a bit ashamed of putting the man on the spot the way he had. "I'm sorry," he said, offering his hand. "I just wanted to make sure you weren't running some sort of kiddie porn ring or something. You hear all kinds of things like that on the news, you know."

Mike reached out and took his hand, shaking it. "It's okay. I just don't want to say too much about what happened in front of the kids. I think some of them might have lost their parents in the accident and they've been through a hard enough time of it themselves."

Brad nodded. "I understand." He put his hands together. "Well, okay then. Let's get you folks to a pay phone."

There was something about Mike that reminded Brad of his older brother, Lawrence, who worked as an inspector at the Occupational Safety and Health Administration out of Augusta. It wasn't so much in his appearance but more in the way he spoke. They had similar voices.

His younger brother, Milford, worked as a part-time news anchor out of Bangor. Brad thought he'd give him a heads-up tip on a breaking news story, as soon as he got home.

It must have been *some* accident to practically wipe out an entire town.

The State Police from Machias were the first to arrive in Gotham Creek at the break of dawn. Four cruisers pulled off Route 1 and stopped just short of the town line. "The road's all broken up," Sergeant Murphy said into his radio. His car had been the first in line. "These aren't potholes, men. Imagine the San Francisco earthquake and you'll get the picture. We'll have to go in on foot."

The police left their cars and started walking into what was left of the town. Sergeant Murphy told Officer Fitzgerald, the rookie, to go back to the car and radio in for the search and rescue canine unit.

"It will be a miracle if we find anyone alive," he muttered after Fitzgerald left.

"What could have caused this kind of mass destruction?" Officer Gilpatrick asked him.

Sergeant Murphy shrugged. "It must have been an earthquake; it's the only thing I can think of. Either that or a meteor shower."

"If that were the case, wouldn't other towns have known about it? Felt the shaking or seen the meteors?"

Sergeant Murphy turned to him. "Look, there are many miles between here and the next town. Yes, it's possible someone else might have heard or felt something out of the ordinary. But it's equally possible that they didn't, too."

The police approached the first flattened building. The sign, untouched, outside read: *Gotham Creek Convenience* and underneath *Open Daily, 8-8.*

"I guess they're closed," Officer Gilpatrick remarked, earning him a humorless glance from the sergeant as he opened the roll of yellow tape. Then something caught the his eye and he turned, cursing. "Oh great, this is *just* what we need."

The other officers turned to look at the Channel 4 News van parking beside the cruisers.

The cameras were rolling before Milford Davis got out of the news van. He grabbed the mike, and looked around for a moment before speaking into it.

"Good morning, this is Milford Davis, reporting for Channel 4 News. I'm in what was once the thriving town of Gotham Creek and as you can see, it's quite literally been laid to waste. Brad Davis of Milbridge supplied the tip early this morning that something terrible had happened here. He said he learned about the accident after picking up five survivors on Route 1 late last night. But what kind of accident was it? And are there any other survivors?"

Sergeant Murphy approached the news van, frowning.

"Is that Murphy?" Milford whispered to his cameraman, covering the mike with his hand.

"Sure is," he whispered back.

Milford stepped forward, holding the mike out to Sergeant Murphy. "Perhaps Sergeant Murphy of the Maine State Police has a statement for us? Can you tell us what happened here, Sergeant?"

Sergeant Murphy held up his palms. "We have no word on anything yet. Right now, we're just looking for survivors."

"Have you located any so far?"

"Yes, there are a few that came into headquarters last night, but I can't give you the details until we notify family members. We've just begun our search here, so if you'll excuse me, I've got to get back to work."

"You'll keep us updated, I hope."

"You betcha." Sergeant Murphy gave a wave of his hand and turned away.

"Well, there you have it. We'll continue to keep our viewers informed of what's going on in Gotham Creek as the story develops. And now for your morning news…"

"Cut, that's a wrap," the cameraman said to the sound mixer. He removed the camera from his shoulder and shook his head. "I've seen a bunch of bad shit, but never anything like this. It looks like the town got bombed."

"Great story, isn't it?" Milford asked, slapping him on the back. A gem like this could mean a move up from part-time to fulltime anchorman.

Maisie covered her mouth with her hand and stared at the television screen. "Oh my God! Oh my God!" she kept saying. She glanced over at Eddie, who was sound asleep in his hospital bed. She picked up the telephone.

She dialed home but the phone kept ringing.

Ned and Kate made it out before the accident happened, she assured herself. But if that was so, why hadn't they arrived or called to let her know?

She put down the phone, picked it back up, and dialed the operator. She kept her voice low, so she wouldn't wake up Eddie. "Yes, yellow pages. Please give me the number of a taxi service in Machias," she said.

Kate Speers awoke at 5:30 a.m. and for a brief moment, she didn't know where she was. The previous night had been a blur of questions and statements, interviews and reports with the State Police. Another handful of survivors had come in: Mike Elwin, Jess Brown, Megan Kingsley, Amy Sands and Barbie Kelwick. Kindly, they'd found accommodations for her and the other Gotham Creek survivors at a hotel for the night.

She sat up, rubbing her eyes. In the bed next to hers, sisters Missy and Amy slept, their arms around one another. Megan and

Barbie were in the room across the hall, and further down, Jess and the men each had their own rooms.

I have to get to the hospital, she thought. *I have to tell Mom what happened and check on Eddie. How do I break the news to Mom? How can I tell her I think Daddy was killed?*

She swiped at a tear that rolled down her cheek. *Gotham Creek is dead and we ten are probably all that remain.*

She owed her life to Hap Kingsley. If he hadn't stopped to pick her up, those horrible things coming up out of the ground would have gotten her. She'd seen what some of them were doing to people. Squeezing, whipping and smashing them against things. If Hap had tried to turn around and take Route 1 to Machias, Kate knew they might not have made it back through town. Route 9 was the long way, taking five times as long to get there, but it was safer.

The destruction seemed contained within Gotham Creek. The neighboring towns of Columbia Falls, Addison, Jonesboro and Princeton remained unscathed, as was Woodland and all the smaller towns along the way.

She swung her feet over the side of the bed and stood up. At that moment, Missy rolled over and opened her eyes.

"Hi," she said in a sad voice.

Kate nodded, "Hey."

"What are you doing up so early?" Missy asked, glancing over at the clock on the nightstand.

"I've got to go see Mom and Eddie. Eddie's in the hospital. Dad said he was in a coma and Mom's with him."

"I hope he'll be all right."

"Yeah, me, too."

"How are you going to get there?"

Kate shrugged. "I'm going to walk. It's only a mile or so."

Missy looked down at her sister, lying beside her, still sound asleep. "We were so lucky to get out. At least we've got part of our families. Hap's got Megan, I've got Amy and you've got your Mom and Eddie. It's more than a coincidence, don't you think?"

"I don't know." Kate picked up her shoes and socks and sat back down on the side of the bed to put them on. "To be honest, I'm not sure I know much of anything anymore. You know, it's ironic. We think we have everything all figured out. We make our plans and follow them through, then something—fate, nature, I don't know—throws a monkey wrench into the whole works and our lives are changed overnight."

Missy leaned up on an elbow and whispered, "So what do you think it was back in Gotham Creek? What made the trees do that?"

Kate shook her head as she tied the laces on her shoes. "I don't know."

"Aren't you even curious?"

"Yeah. But don't ask me how it happened because I really don't know."

"Think you'll ever go back there?"

Kate stood up. "God, I hope not."

"Give Eddie our bests, okay?" she softly called out as Kate went to the door.

"I will, thanks. You and the others do what you can to help Barbie. I think she's having a really hard time with all of this."

Seeing Missy's nod, Kate left.

David Hardecastle shook his head as he rubbed his temples. *Harvesting the forest at Gotham Creek was a goddamned boondoggle. How many machines had he lost? How many men?*

Those who'd made it out returned to the mill with a strange story of trees that came to life. Killer trees. A flesh-eating forest. It made absolutely no sense whatsoever but the proof was in the losses. *Something* had happened there, exactly what, he wasn't sure. It was bad enough that Bert Colby had the ill fortune of falling down some hole in the woods and was still in the hospital collecting unemployment.

And it was unfortunate that several of the company machines had been left behind at Gotham Creek, abandoned by their operators.

"I'll have to send a crew to recover them," he muttered, pinching the bridge of his nose with his fingers. Rumors about what had happened there were already spreading throughout the mill, re-fueled by the morning's news on Channel Four.

Why'd I leave right after the meeting at the town office? Had anything really been so pressing that I couldn't stay to make sure the operation went smoothly?

It was because of that woman, wasn't it? That pissy bitch didn't want us there. Who the hell did she think she was, disrupting the meeting like that?

She'd reminded him too much of his ex-wife and seeing her, listening to what she'd said, made his head hurt. David knew he had to get away from her or he was going to end up killing her just to shut her up.

I should have stayed longer, he decided, reaching for the aspirin bottle on his desk. *If I'd been there maybe none of this would have happened.*

He sighed, knowing he'd have to return to Gotham Creek on a recovery mission.

Maisie Speers looked out the window of the taxi as it sped along Route 1. It was a sunny autumn morning, clear and crisp, and in all the little towns they passed through, everyone seemed to be going about their normal business. She saw children with backpacks waiting at the ends of their driveways for school buses to arrive, men and women getting into their cars to head for work. Stores were opening up, flags were being raised outside of post offices. Everything was normal except for the way she felt.

She hadn't heard from Ned or Kate, and that had her so worried she wasn't even aware that she was rubbing her hands together.

"I saw what happened to Gotham Creek on the news this morning," the driver was saying. "Couldn't believe it, either." He looked over at her. "Ma'am, I don't usually offer this—it's against company rules—but I'll make an exception in this case. Would you like a smoke? It might help calm your nerves."

He was a dark-haired man with blue eyes and a friendly sort of face. A bit too angular to be considered really handsome but his personality more than made up for it. For this reason, she felt she could trust him. He seemed just a few years older than her daugher.

Maisie, who'd never so much as experimented with smoking, glanced over at him and nodded. She watched as he pulled a pack of Marlboros from his shirt pocket, shaking it once so one popped up from the pack. He held it out to her and she took it.

He took one himself and slid the pack back into his pocket. Then he reached into his jeans and pulled out a lighter, offering it to her.

Her hands shook as she lit the cigarette, then she returned his lighter.

"You've got family in Gotham Creek, don't you?" he asked, lighting up.

"Yes, my husband and daughter."

"I'm real sorry to hear that."

"Thanks." She inhaled, coughed a little and rolled down her window just a crack, then exhaled, watching the smoke drift out the window.

"Were they rescued and hospitalized?"

"No. That's my son in the hospital. He was in a coma." The driver looked at her with sadness in his eyes. "Sorry. Will he be okay?"

She nodded. "I think so. Nobody seems to know what's wrong with him, but I think he'll be all right. He's *got* to be all right. He may be the only family I have left."

The driver nodded. "I'm sure he'll be just fine. Machias is a good hospital. My name's Scott West, by the way. I was born and raised here." He tapped his cigarette so the ashes went out his window.

"I'm Maisie Speers." The cigarette he'd given her was making her a little dizzy. She sat there and looked at it in her shaking fingers.

"You don't smoke, do you?" he asked.

She shook her head.

"Here, give me that butt." When she passed it to him, he pinched it off and slid the remainder of the cigarette back into his pack. Thrifty man.

"Maybe your husband and daughter are among the survivors," he suggested, trying to sound hopeful. "They did say there were some people who made it out alive."

"I hope you're right."

"You'll have to tell me where Gotham Creek is," he said. "I've heard of it but I've never been there myself."

She nodded. Her mouth tasted the way an ashtray smelled and she couldn't keep her hands from trembling. She pointed a shaky finger. "The turn-off is just up ahead on the right."

They'd only traveled a little ways when they saw the State Patrol cruisers and the Channel Four News van parked off to the side of the road at the townline. Someone had put a row of orange cones across the way, making entry impossible except on foot.

Scott stopped the taxi and turned to Maisie. "Do you want me to wait for you? I will, if you want, and it won't cost you a dime."

She pressed her lips together, thinking. "I don't know how long I'll be. It could be hours before I find Ned and Kate."

"It's all right. I'll wait here if you want."

Maisie nodded. "Okay. That would be real nice, thank you."

She started to open the door but he reached over and squeezed her hand. "Hey, good luck. I hope you find them."

Her eyes filled with tears for all his unexpected kindness. "I sure hope so."

Eddie woke up as Kate walked into the room and went to his bed. "Hi," he said, smiling slightly. "I knew I shouldn't have listened to you when you said I had to tell Mom and Dad about my ears. Look where I've ended up."

"Oh, Eddie." Kate's voice caught in her throat. "I thought you were in a coma. Dad said..."

"Well, I'm awake now. Hey, what's wrong—I was only kidding about my ears."

"It isn't that. Oh my God, you don't know, do you?"

"Know what? Kate, what's wrong?"

It took a great deal of strength to keep from breaking down, sobbing, as she went around to the side of the bed and sat in a chair, pulling up close to him.

"Something terrible happened last night in Gotham Creek," she said. "It was awful. Tree roots were coming up out of the ground and people were getting killed. I'm so glad you and Mom weren't there when it happened."

Eddie's eyes widened. "Where's Dad? He's with you, isn't he?"

"Oh, Eddie..." She put a hand over her mouth to keep from crying out.

"What? Tell me what's going on."

She could no longer keep herself from weeping and found it difficult to speak. "I tried to save him, I really did. But those roots came up through the living room floor and grabbed him. I couldn't hang on, Eddie. I just couldn't."

He reached up and touched her arm. Boys weren't supposed to cry unless they were sissies, but he couldn't help himself. It had all seemed so real when his dad was with him on the meteor and the news of his death was just too much for him to hold inside.

It hurt more than he thought it was possible to hurt and still be alive.

She looked up with red-rimmed eyes. "Where's Mom?"

"I don't know."

"I thought she was here with you."

"Well, she was, but I haven't seen her this morning."

She got up, wiping at her face with the back of her hand. "Maybe the nurses know where she went? I'll go ask and I'll come right back. Are you going to be okay?"

Eddie shrugged, still crying.

She hated leaving him like that, but she had to find their mom. At the nurses' station down the hall, she asked if anyone knew where Maisie was. No one did, but an orderly spoke up and said that on his way in, he'd seen her getting into a taxi.

She thanked him and hurried back to Eddie's room.

"I bet Mom's gone back to Gotham Creek to find Dad," she told him.

Eddie sat up and swung his legs over the side of the bed.

"What are you doing?"

"Well, we've got to get out of here. We have to find Mom."

"What do you mean *we*? You're supposed to stay in bed, aren't you?"

Eddie's jaw tightened. "Screw all this," he said with a nod at the machines. He looked down at the I.V. tube going into his arm and started to unwrap the white tape that held it in place.

"Hey, I don't think that's such a great idea," she said.

He winced as he pulled the needle from his arm. "I'll be fine."

She crossed her arms and looked away as he began to pull on his clothes. Part of her wanted to yell for the nurses, to make them come and force him back into bed, but her heart told her that if she were in a similar situation, she'd probably do the same thing he was doing now.

"I don't think I can sneak you past the nurses' station," she told him, nervously biting her bottom lip.

"You won't need to," he said. "This room's on the ground floor. We'll just climb out the window."

"Mom's going to pitch a cow because I let you do this; you know that don't you?"

"Hey, if she's mad, she's still alive, right?"

Kate cranked the window open and climbed out first, then reached up to help Eddie.

"I bet I can get us a ride to Gotham Creek at the hotel," she said.

"Who else made it out of town alive?" Eddie had to know.

"Jess, Mike Elwin, Megan, Amy, Barbie, Missy, Jim Digby and Constable Hap."

He almost smiled for the first time this morning because his best friend Jess was among the survivors. "Let's hurry," he said, breaking into a trot.

Kate reached out and grabbed him by the arm. "Slow down! Remember, you've been in a coma, so take it easy. The hotel's not that far and we'll be there in no time."

Maisie stepped around the orange cones and gasped as she looked down the hill toward town. All the buildings had been leveled, smashed to the ground, and there was debris scattered everywhere. *Ned, Kate, I have to find you!* she thought, bewildered at where to start looking for them.

She started walking, wishing she'd asked Scott the taxi driver for another cigarette; she could really use one now.

"Hey!" a man yelled at her. "You're not supposed to be here."

"Like hell I'm not!" she called back.

The man was stepping around the edge of a crumbled building and another man was following closely behind, carrying something on his shoulder. A video camera. Maisie tried to ignore them as she stopped and looked around, trying to decide which was the easiest path to the place where her house once stood.

"We're going to have to ask you to leave, ma'am," the man in front was saying. She turned toward him and in an instant she knew who he was. She'd seen him on the news on television.

She crossed her arms and frowned. "I'm not going anywhere until I find my husband and daughter."

He stopped and looked confused. "You're a resident here?"

Maisie looked around, obviously annoyed. "I was."

"Look, ma'am, this isn't really any place for a lady like yourself. Not right now. They're searching for bodies and, well, it's not very pleasant."

She dismissed him with a wave of her hand. "Just leave me alone, young man. And you'd better not be taping this because if you are, I'll sue the pants right off you."

He turned and made a signal with his thumb across his neck and the other man lowered the video camera. "Ah, good, here comes the sergeant. He'll escort you out of here," he told her.

"What's going on?" Sergeant Murphy asked the cameraman, who managed an innocent-looking shrug. Then he looked at Maisie. "And who are you?"

"Maisie Speers. I live...*lived* here. I need to find my husband and daughter."

He offered her his hand and as she shook it, he said. "Sergeant Murphy, State Patrol." He glared at the newsmen. "Back off and give this lady some room." He looked back at her with a frown and shook his head. "Media, sheez."

"Have you found anyone yet?"

Sergeant Murphy rubbed his nose with his fingers. "Not exactly. I'll tell you straight; we've only located parts and pieces of remains so far. Nothing readily identifiable."

Maisie cupped her hand over her mouth in shock.

"Are you going to be all right, ma'am? I don't mean to upset you—I think you've been through enough already. But I have to warn you, the search is getting gruesome."

She lowered her hand and steeled herself. "I need to find Ned and Kate."

He nodded. "I understand. I'll help you look. Do you know the general area where your house was?"

Maisie nodded and pointed her finger. "Yes, it's on the road just past the school."

"Well, let's head over that way. Watch your step."

Behind them, the newsmen followed but they kept their distance.

"What do you mean you want me to drive you back to Gotham Creek?" Hap asked, looking at Kate and then at Eddie, as if the two of them had lost their minds. "We were lucky enough to make it out alive—and now you want to go back? That's nuts."

"Mom's gone there to look for me and Dad," she told him. "She must think we're both dead. We have to be with her—she's going to take the news about Dad real bad, Hap. Look, if you don't take us, we'll hitchhike. Either way, we're going."

Hap sighed in defeat and held up his palms. "Fine, I'll take you. But we're just staying long enough to pick Maisie up. Then we're all coming back to Machias. Understand?"

Kate nodded.

"Can Jess come, too?" Eddie asked.

Hap just shook his head. "Yeah, why not. Let's just make a picnic out of it."

The three followed him out to the cruiser in the parking lot.

"Did you say your daughter's name is Kate Speers?" Sergeant Murphy asked Maisie as they picked their way through the rubble on their way to where her house once stood.

"Yes. Why?"

"Well, Mrs. Speers, I have some good news for you. Kate came in last night with your constable, Hap Kingsley and a couple others. She's safe. We put up all of them in a hotel for the night and—"

"She's alive!" Maisie almost hugged him. "Oh my God, that's such a relief!" *If Kate survived, that meant Ned had a chance, too.*

"I should have told you before, when you mentioned her name, I just didn't put the two together." He offered a gentle smile. "It hasn't been the best of mornings, you know,"

Maisie nodded. She knew.

19

Norris stayed awake the entire night Gotham Creek had been destroyed. Although he had no way of knowing *exactly* what was happening there, he had a strong sense of the violence and agony—and death. Lots of it.

How this knowledge came to him was a mystery, perhaps a secret of nature, information passed along a network of underground roots. He could almost hear the screams of terrified people and the sounds of buildings crashing down around them.

Clutching the seedling he'd taken from Doc's body, he burrowed down into the piles of needles under the old tree and waited out the storm, tempering his feelings of hopeless fear with thoughts of beer, cigarettes and sex.

Sometime in the middle of the night, he'd crawled out from under the tree to piss. He watched in awe as the stream came out of him, neon-green in color. Even the steam rising up from it had taken on a glowing hue.

And it smelled strange, too, kind of like Prestone Anti-Freeze, almost sickly-sweet in its bouquet.

He scratched his head with his free hand, thinking *the green*, as he called it, was all through him now. And he wondered why he wasn't sick from it, the way Doc had been sick just before he died.

The rain was coming down harder, cold and sharp, so he zipped his pants and burrowed back under the tree. Holding the seedling close to him afforded some comfort but he knew if it was going to live, he'd have to plant it soon.

When dawn finally broke, the rain was done and the sun was shining, golden and bright. He crawled out from under the tree and shook himself off. He felt hungry, not starving, but had a keen hankering for liver and onions fried in butter, washed down by a couple of icy-cold Colts. With this thought in mind, he walked, not knowing or even caring where he was going, as long as it wasn't back to Gotham Creek.

Two hours later, he found a small, abandoned camp deep in the woods, a shack probably built by a hunter. It was constructed of old planks and boards held together with rusting nails and topped with a peeling, tarred-paper roof. Norris crept up to it and peeked in through the single broken window.

From the looks of it, nobody had been inside for years, maybe even decades. He went around to the front and tried to open the door but it was stuck. When he twisted the knob, it fell off in his hand and he could see the inner workings were badly rusted. He set his seedling down a safe distance from the door and went back around to the broken window. Yes, it was large enough that he could fit himself through without too much trouble, so he pulled the jagged pieces of glass from the frame and climbed in.

The single room was dark and quite musty. He went to the door and leaned his weight against it and with a groan of its rusty hinges it finally yielded, opening up. Morning light spilled inside and he looked around, frowning.

The camp was dingy, crawling with wood lice and silverfish, but this place was perfect, hidden far enough away from people so no one would ever bother him here. It did need a serious cleaning, though, but first he went to the closet in the corner to see if there was any food.

He was in luck but it wasn't good.

There was an old can of Spam with a mottled label and a box of Saltine crackers that mice had long since chewed open and made a home in. They'd abandoned it, leaving nothing but a mound of paper bits. He shut the closet door and looked around.

A single sorry mattress on the floor sat surrounded by piles of grey stuffing that had probably been pulled out by squirrels and mice. That would be the first thing to go. He went over and turned it up on its side. Underneath was a 1977 issue of *Playboy Magazine* with a model on the cover who looked a lot like Deidre and he stooped down to pick it up.

It wasn't Deidre, of course, but sultry actress Susan Kiger, sporting a tank top so sheer her nipples showed through its white fabric. Noticing the beer in her hand, he ran his tongue over his lips. The featured articles about Billy Carter and college basketball forecasts didn't interest him much, but the photos in "Sex In Cinema" and "Bunnies '77" could do something for him, as well as the centerfold of November Playmate, Rita Lee. He flipped the magazine open to the centerfold. Yep, Rita could definitely work for him, and even though the picture wasn't as graphic as those in his Hustler collection back home, it was enough.

He rolled up the *Playboy* and jammed it into his back pocket, then proceeded to drag the old mattress outside. It wasn't just ruined; it reeked of stale sweat and mildew and was heavier than he'd thought possible. He pulled it out through the door and a good distance away from the camp. On his way back, he stopped to break a branch from a nearby fir. This would serve as a broom; it was the best thing he could think of to use.

Before he swept, however, he went over to the woodstove in the corner. It was a homemade contraption, a twenty-pound propane tank. Someone with ingenuity had sawn a hole for a door in the front and another hole in the top, fitted on a rusty stovepipe and ran the pipe out through the wall. Norris opened the door and found it not only full of ashes but there was a dead mouse in there, too. A bent serving spoon leaned against the wall behind the stove and beside it sat an old coffee can.

Using these, he cleaned out the stove. His efforts were clumsy and he spilled some ashes on the floor. The mouse was petrified, as stiff as a cracker, and it wouldn't stay on the spoon, so he had to remove it by hand.

He took the can of ashes and dead mouse out and dumped it, then brought it back inside. There were large gaps in the wooden walls, so he chinked them with some of the stuffing that had fallen out of the mattress before sweeping the whole mess through the door with his makeshift broom.

A calendar had been tacked to the wall over where the mattress had been, a First National Bank freebie, dated 1978. All the months except November and December were missing. Norris pulled it down and put it in the stove for kindling but he pocketed the tacks.

He'd use them later for pinning up Miss November.

Back outside, he took a stick and dug a small hole in the middle of the clearing in front of the camp. The soil under the dead grass was black and moist from last night's rain and as he set the seedling down into it, he smiled, trusting that this part of Doc would live on.

It will do just fine here, he thought, patting dirt around its base.

David Hardecastle drove up to where the cars were parked at the Gotham Creek town line. He saw State Police cruisers, a news van and a taxi. The taxi driver gave him a wave, which he ignored as he pulled in behind.

And right behind him, another police cruiser drove up and parked.

What is this? he thought with a grimace. *Grand Central Station?*

Three kids got out of the cruiser and the oldest, a pretty girl wearing jeans and a sweater, stopped and looked at the company logo on the side of his car. The boys stopped behind her and stared back at him. A policeman got out, too, his face grim as he approached.

"You're from Piston Paper, right?" he asked.

David nodded.

"Well, I hope you've come to finish cutting Old Woods."

He frowned. "Actually, I'm here to see if I can retrieve my equipment."

"You're not going to stay and finish the job?" Kate asked.

He shot her a look of contempt. "Not on your life."

That's when the taller boy spoke up. "But you have to. You said you would and we're depending on you to get the job done."

"At what expense? This has already cost a mint in equipment and lives—and I'm not willing to lose anymore."

The girl pushed a long, dark strand of hair away from her face as she addressed him. "What if you were given the woodlot, free and clear? Would you do it then?"

David bit his lip, thinking. "I might consider it."

The policeman gave him a hard look. "We'll see what we can do about that, okay?"

He gave him a curt nod and they walked away. After a moment passed, he got out of the car, dreading to go down the hill to see what kind of shape his machines were in. Why were they so willing to give him the woodlot? What was the catch? He smelled a rat, but being a rat himself, he'd leave the bridges behind him open rather than burning them.

"You kids shouldn't be here," a young policeman called out as Kate, Eddie and Jess made their way down the hill. He jogged over to them, skirting debris. "This place is just too dangerous right now. I'm going to have to ask you to please go back home."

"This *is* our home," Kate told him, looking around at the destruction. "Well, it *was* until yesterday."

He peered into her eyes. "I'm real sorry about that," he said. "But you can see for yourselves there's nothing here for you now."

Hap made his way around a pile of debris and spoke up. "Officer, we have reason to believe these children's mother is here."

Seeing a fellow lawman, he changed his tune. "These people are with you?" he asked him.

Hap nodded and Kate added, "Maybe you've seen our mom? Short, brown-haired lady?"

The officer nodded. "She's here. Follow me and don't touch anything, okay?"

Her eyes were hopeful as they picked their way through the debris that had been Gotham Creek. She glanced over her shoulder at Eddie and Jess. They were stunned as well, looking around in shock. Hap said he was going to check his house or what was left of it. He followed them for a while, then walked on toward Old Woods Road.

It took them half an hour to walk to where the school had been and from there, they spotted Maisie and another officer sifting through the wreckage that had been their home. She looked up when Kate yelled to her.

"Thank goodness, you're safe," she shouted, running over to hug her children. She took Eddie's chin in her hand and added, "What are you doing out of the hospital?"

Eddie hugged her. "Don't worry, Mom, I'm fine. I had to come."

She looked over at Jess and swallowed a sob as she put her arms around him. "I'm glad you're safe, too."

Kate cleared her throat. "Mom, about Dad—"

"We're looking for him now, honey. You and the boys can give us a hand."

"No, Mom. It's too late. I was with him when it happened, and I tried to save him, but I couldn't." At this, Kate broke into fresh tears.

Maisie shook her head. "No, Ned's in there somewhere; I just know he is. We could use your help getting him out."

Kate glanced over at the boys, knowing there was no possible way Ned could be alive but she didn't want to argue with her mother. "All right, Mom," she said. "We'll help. I think we might find Dad in the basement."

They walked over to the heap of broken wood and glass, and Maisie introduced them to Sergeant Murphy. Just then, a voice came over his two-way radio announcing that the canine search and rescue team had arrived.

"Send them down here, first," he ordered, then he glanced back at the family. "I can't promise they'll find anything," he said to Maisie, "and even if they do, it might not be good news. I just want you to be prepared."

Maisie pressed her lips together and nodded.

"Why don't you have a seat in that car over there while we wait for them to arrive?" he asked, pointing to Kate's Honda, which had been left virtually untouched. Kate put her arm around her mother and walked with her to the car. Eddie started to follow but stopped when he realized Jess wasn't coming with them. He turned around. His best friend was staring across the yard, at the place where his house had been.

"Has anyone seen my parents?" Jess was asking Sergeant Murphy.

"I'm afraid not, son. Not yet."

Eddie went up to him. "If we can't find your folks, then you can stay with us, okay?"

Jess nodded and as Eddie released him, he saw the look in his eyes. It was as if he'd instantly aged ten years, no longer a boy but a man. A young man who was trying his best to keep it all together and doing a courageous job of it.

Eddie walked with him back to the car.

Twenty minutes later, the canine unit arrived. Two officers flanked a couple of large German Shepherds they held on leashes. They went over to Sergeant Murphy and talked while everyone got out of Kate's car.

Eddie held out his hand as he approached one of the dogs, letting the animal sniff it. "Good boy," he said, patting the dog's head.

Sergeant Murphy held up a hand. "Okay, everyone, you'll need to step back to give the dogs some room to work." As they backed away, he pulled Maisie aside.

"You might not want the kids to watch this," he warned.

She sighed, dragging a hand through her hair. "Okay. I'll take them back to the car. Just promise me the second you find him, you'll let me know."

"You'll know," he said.

The dogs began their work as the family once again got into the car. Everyone watched out the windows as the officers unleashed the animals and immediately, they started digging their way into the debris.

Minutes passed, turning into an hour.

One of the dogs began to bark, joined in chorus by the others. Maisie opened the door and jumped out of the car, telling the kids to stay put.

Sergeant Murphy and the other officers were meeting the dogs as they crawled their way up out of the debris and Maisie saw him take something from one of the dogs and slip it into a dark-colored bag.

"What is it? What did they find?" she called out as she jogged over.

Sergeant Murphy turned to face her, his expression grim. He pressed something into her hand and when she looked down, she recognized it instantly. Ned's wedding ring.

"Where'd they find it?" she asked, still hopeful.

"It was on his hand, ma'am." He reached out and held her by the shoulders. "One hand is all they've found and it's in that bag over there. We have to assume your husband is deceased. I'm very sorry but we're going to have to ask you and the children to leave now so we can continue searching for others who might still be alive."

Maisie clutched Ned's ring to her breast and sank to her knees in the grass. "No, oh no," she sobbed.

Hap jammed his hands into his pockets and sighed. His house was gone, reduced to rubble. All his earthly belongings, save the clothes on his back, lay in the damaged heap that had been his home.

Felicity was nowhere to be found and although he'd loved her, his eyes remained dry. He knew she was probably dead; there was no possible way anyone could have been inside the house when it collapsed and live through it. The time for mourning his losses would come later and probably late at night, when he had nothing to do but think.

And remember.

Sadly, no survivors were found and later, while the bulldozers and dump trucks worked to clear the debris human remains continued to turn up. Hands and feet, mostly, and the occasional leg or arm.

The handful of survivors decided they could no longer live in Gotham Creek. It was just too painful; the memories of their lives there were too tainted by their shattered hopes and dreams.

On November 6, 1996, a Quit Claim Deed was signed by the former residents signing all rights to the woodlot over to Piston Paper.

David Hardecastle was pleased. He hadn't lost much in the way of machinery. Several of his workers were still missing and presumed dead, but those he could replace. He quickly re-made plans to harvest.

20

The nearest house was roughly ten miles away, as best Norris Hymes could determine. It was a small log home at the end of a long dirt driveway and a woman lived there with her son, a boy of about seven.

She was one of those back-to-the-earth types. He'd hidden out of sight, watching her putting the leaves she'd raked up into a compost bin in the backyard. She was a pleasant-looking woman, although a bit too muscular for his tastes.

Part of him wanted to call out a friendly hello but he knew if he did, his appearance would frighten her and he didn't want to do that. All he wanted was some food.

While she worked on her backyard, he crept around to the front of the house and tried the door. It was unlocked and he let himself in, easy as pie. He went straight to the kitchen and made a beeline for the refrigerator.

His eyes grew wide when he saw what was inside.

There was half of a small ham, wrapped in cellophane, a tub of butter, a carton of whole milk, pickles, eggs, cheese, the list went on. Norris hunkered down and tore open the package of cheese. It was cheddar and it tasted heavenly.

He shoved food into his pockets as he devoured the cheese. Not wanting to take too much, he shut the refrigerator door and began rummaging through a nearby cupboard. There were cans of milk and soup, boxes of cereal. Sugary kids' stuff, mostly, and healthy snack foods. He pocketed a couple cans of soup and a bag of Mr. Crisper pork rinds and was about to reach for the cereal when a child's voice called out:

"Hey, Mom!"

He stood up in alarm at the sound of the boy's footsteps coming down the stairs, then bolted for the front door. He'd just reached it when the back door opened, then shut.

Creeping away from the house, he could hear the voices inside of mother and son talking. They didn't sound panicked or frightened and that was good.

He jogged back into the woods with his loot, looking forward to a hot supper.

"Billy? Billy, where are you?"

The woman's voice drifted down through the trees and Norris heard it. He was on his way back to the camp, this time carrying some clothes he'd snagged from another neighbor's clothesline and a six-pack of beer he'd lifted from a cooler in their garage.

He stopped dead in his tracks.

The woman was closer now; he could hear her soft footfalls crunching on the forest floor. He could hear her muttering, too. "How many times have I told him not to run off? A hundred? A thousand? The woods are dangerous—there's bears here for crying out loud." She yelled again, "Billy? William Lewis McCabe!"

Not wanting to be seen, Norris began to run. He estimated that his camp was still six or seven miles away so he headed in that general direction.

He'd just come up over a hill when he spied the boy, wandering through the trees, humming to himself. Again, Norris stopped. Now he was between mother and son, and no matter which way he went he was going to be spotted by one of them.

He took his chances with the kid.

"Hey," he called out as softly as he could. "Are you lost?"

The boy looked up and his eyes widened. "Wow, mister! You're green. Are you a Martian or something?"

Norris chuckled as he walked closer to the child. "Yeah, I guess I am."

"So what happened? Did your U.F.O. crash or something?"

"You might say that." He pointed westward. "You know your mom is over there looking for you? She sounds pretty worried."

The boy looked down at his sneakers. "Yeah, I know. She gets upset when I go hunting."

"Hunting?" He didn't see that the child had a gun, then the boy grinned and pulled a slingshot from his back pocket. Norris laughed in relief.

"Hey, that's quite a slingshot! Where'd you get it?"

"My dad gave it to me. I've got a ton of them." He held the slingshot toward Norris. "You can have this one, if you want."

He beamed as he took the gift. "Thank you. Say, I really think you'd better go see your mom now," he said. "She's on the other side of that hill over there."

"Okay, mister. Thanks."

He watched Billy scamper up the hill through the trees. *That was a close call,* he thought with a sigh. *At least it had been a kid. If he tells anyone about meeting a Martian in the woods, nobody's going to believe him.*

Norris made his way through the woods toward his camp, looking forward to opening that sixpack.

The harvest of Old Woods began anew. David Hardecastle had a difficult time talking some of the men into going back there and finding new ones to hire that didn't believe the story about the trees coming to life and turning violent.

He'd had the road going into Gotham Creek rebuilt and as soon as that was finished, the first of the crew arrived. With cranes, they picked the machines up from their sides and set them back down on their tires. So far, only one piece of equipment, a feller buncher, had been ruined and was deemed unusable.

David stayed in the woods with his crew to make sure nothing out of the ordinary occurred.

And it didn't.

He was doing exactly as he had promised. Planning to level Old Woods to the ground, he wouldn't allow one sapling left behind. Come spring, Piston Paper would come back and replant the lot with a variety of soft and hard wood saplings.

At Billy's insistence, Shirley McCabe began leaving food outside for the Martian. At first she didn't believe her son's story; but the food was gone every morning and he was delighted, confident that the Martian had eaten it. She was sure it was raccoons or squirrels, which were no doubt thrilled by these little feasts.

Late one afternoon, however, while taking her laundry in from the line, on her way back to the house, she dropped a clothespin on the ground. When she turned around to pick it up, something from the edge of the backyard caught her eye.

It was a man, or what appeared to be a man, standing in the bushes. And his skin was bright green. She forced her eyes away and picked up the clothespin. Then she carried the basket back to the house.

She looked for him as she shut the door but he was gone.

She was never quite sure if she'd really seen him or just imagined that she had, but that night, in addition to the food, she left out a warm, wool blanket.

It, too, was gone by morning, and in its place, was a pair of rabbits, freshly killed and cleaned.

She'd reached down and picked them up. *That's some Martian,* she'd thought with a smile.

21

Henry Jenkins leaned near the window as he shifted position on the yoke and rudder causing his plane to take a graceful left bank. A thousand feet above the earth, he circled the sky over Gotham Creek. What had once been a Rockwell-picture-perfect town of tidy streets and well-groomed lawns with pretty houses in neat rows now lie demolished and deserted. The woods toward the northeast were gone, the forest leveled.

Henry gazed down into what appeared to be a huge crater in the place where the woods once stood. It looked like a bowl cut into the earth, stripped bare. Raped.

The news reports had been right on target. Gotham Creek was gone and so were the giant oaks that had been her pride. No one could see this from Route 1 and the road that had been Main Street was closed to traffic.

His eyes welled up with guilty tears. *Dammit, it's all my fault,* he reasoned. *If only I had minded my own business and hadn't called the National Forest Service.*

'If' is a nasty little word, he thought, allowing the plane to continue on a low left bank. *Everything boils down to 'if', doesn't it? 'If' you do this, something will happen and 'if' you don't do this, something else will happen. And sometimes, you're damned 'if' you do and you're damned 'if' you don't.*

This time was different than the last time he'd flown over. The compass didn't spin. Nothing was out of the ordinary, except for the destroyed town and forest below, and the red light flashing on the gas gauge. Gradually, the left engine sputtered, then stopped, and then the right engine did the same. For what seemed like an eternity, Henry glided in the air, passing one last time over Gotham Creek and then south toward Route 1.

Then the nose dipped and the ground came up fast.

Kate glanced over at her mother in the passenger's seat. Maisie still clutched Ned's wedding ring in her hand but she was going to be fine. It would take them all a long time to get over what had happened at Gotham Creek, if they ever could. But at least they were all together.

Maybe, she thought, *just maybe, it's not entirely bad or wrong. We've been given a fresh start without the restrictions of a false religion that took away more than it could give. It's not going to be easy finding a way to live but we're no longer on the 'outside' anymore. We're just the same as everyone else.*

She smiled at her brother's reflection in the rearview mirror. He looked so much like Ned, it almost hurt. It had been his idea to call Cousin Mark and when he'd offered them a place to stay until they got back on their feet, she'd readily agreed. Mark had made it, living outside Gotham Creek, and there was no reason why they couldn't do the same.

Beside Eddie, Jess had fallen asleep. *Poor kid*, Kate thought. *He'd been through so much, losing both parents, but we'll help him make it through...*

"Hey, look at that plane!" Eddie blurted out, interrupting her thoughts. "I think it's going to crash."

"Where? Where is it?" Kate looked around but she couldn't see it and keep her eyes on the road at the same time. She heard a loud boom, felt the vibrations of it through the steering wheel.

"Over there!" Eddie was pointing out the window. Jess woke up and leaned over to see what Eddie was talking about. That's when Maisie covered her mouth with her hand and gasped.

Kate slowed down and pulled the car over to the side of the highway. She could see the plane now, with its crumpled nose half buried in a field, its tail bent and wings broken. Eddie was first out of the car. She stared at it in shock, not quite believing what she was seeing.

"Come on! We've got to help the pilot." Eddie began running toward the plane.

Kate opened her door and got out. "Wait!" she yelled at him. "Stay back in case it explodes."

But the plane wasn't on fire and her brother wasn't listening.

She ran after him and Jess followed while Maisie sat in the car, clutching Ned's ring, looking on in apprehension.

The pilot was barely alive. The steering column was buried deep in his chest and there was no way they could get him out without help. Kate looked over at the boys. "You guys stay with him," she said, "while I find a phone and call an ambulance."

Eddie watched her run back to the car and drive away, then he turned back to the pilot. "You're doing good," he told the man. "Hang on, you're going to be just fine."

But the pilot shook his head and a trickle of blood ran out of his mouth. "Stop lying, kid. I'm dying and I know it. It was all my...fault."

"What? What was your fault?" Eddie asked.

"The woods. What they did to them."

Eddie looked perplexed. "You mean the Old Woods?"

The pilot nodded with a grimace. "Yeah. I'm the one who called and got the government involved...I thought I was doing a good thing, saving the forest. So much for being a hero, huh?"

"It wasn't your fault," Eddie told him. "Please don't think that it was. There was a lot more going on in Gotham Creek than you could imagine and a good deal of it was bad. I think you did the right thing."

The pilot raised his bloodshot eyes. "How would you know?"

"I lived there." Eddie looked over at Jess. "*We* lived there." He thought he saw the pilot try to smile, then his head dropped. Blood ran from his nose as well as his mouth.

Jess stepped back but Eddie reached in and felt the pilot's throat. He couldn't feel a pulse.

"I think he's dead," he told Jess.

Jess shook his head. "No one could have lived through that."

The boys looked up as Kate returned. Both she and Maisie got out of the car and began walking across the meadow.

"It's too late, I think," Eddie called out. "He hasn't got a pulse."

Kate looked down. "The ambulance is on their way. Maybe they can revive him."

"He thought it was his fault," Jess said. "Can you believe it? He thought he'd caused everything that happened in Gotham Creek because he'd called the National Forest Service about the trees."

"The poor man," Maisie said. She walked closer to the plane and peered at the pilot, which was easy enough to do because the door had come off in the crash. She looked into his bloodied face and reached over, taking his hand in hers.

She knew him.

This was the boy who'd been kind to her in high school, who'd always taken the time to talk to her, who always had a smile. He'd grown up to be exactly what he'd wanted to be, making his dreams come true.

Well, maybe not all of them.

The kids didn't know any of this; it was to be her secret. She pushed Ned's ring onto his finger, and closed her hands around his. It was a perfect fit. His hand was still warm, but she could feel his life force slipping softly away.

"You did the right thing, Henry," she whispered, with a sob catching in her throat.

It was time for a fresh start on the *inside* as well as on the outside.

When the logs with the white marks arrived from Gotham Creek at Piston Paper in Portland, they were put into deep vats of water to soak, then tumbled into drums to remove the bark.

The chipper operator noticed that some of the chips coming from the debarked logs were quite red and he thought it strange enough to shut down his machine.

He picked up some of the red chips and examined them, then called for David Hardecastle.

"I don't care if they're purple with pink freaking polka dots," his boss barked. "Chip them up and send them to the digester."

"But I'm not sure the bleaching will get the red out," he maintained.

"We'll worry about that when the time comes," David told him. "I've got a distributor who's depending on this lot being done as soon as possible, so get on with it." And with that, he hung up.

The chipper operator watched the reddish chips being loaded onto the conveyor belt, headed for the digester and he shook his head.

"Looks like there's raw hamburger mixed in with them," he noted, watching them go.

The digesting process removed "lignin", the wood's natural glue, from the chips. They were belt-fed into the top of the digesting vat and mixed with sodium sulfate and sodium hydroxide to be cooked into a "white liquor".

Pulp came out of the bottom of the digester as pure cellulose fibers. But these fibers weren't exactly pure. The digester operators gathered around and examined the strange-looking reddish stuff mixed in with the pulp.

"What do you think it is?" a woman asked.

"I've no idea. We've seen red fibers before but nothing like this. And look at those little bits in there. I know it's impossible, but they sort of look like chips of tooth…or bone," the man beside her said.

"Eww. Now that you mention it, I do see them. Think we should notify Hardecastle?"

The man shook his head. "Not unless the building's on fire and I'd think twice about it even then." He gave her a reassuring smile. "But don't worry, I really do think the bleachers will take care of it."

There were several stages of the bleaching process and as the fiber pulp ran through, it became clear that the red parts were coming out as pink at best. As a last resort, the foreman in charge of the bleachers mixed them in with clean pulp, hoping to diffuse the pink fibers so it would be less detectable.

From the bleachers, the pulp was sent to the refiners to be beaten. Because this was oak pulp, the fibers required a longer beating time than softer woods. By the time it was done, it was flat and frayed, ready for bonding. It still didn't look quite right, but David Hardecastle was adamant that it go through the process.

Further down the line, it was rinsed and the fillers were applied. In this case, talc was used, mixed with water and pulp and pumped into the head box of the paper machine. From here the pulp, now known as 'furnish' was poured onto a conveyor belt of plastic mesh. Water dripped away, causing the pulp on the belt to form a paper web and from there it went to the felt in the press section. This was where cloth belts rolled, squeezing out even more water from the paper web. Everyone grimaced when they saw the pinkish splotches going by, but by now it was too late to ever get them out.

It went to the driers without another call to Hardecastle.

At the driers, workers tried to 'tame' the red splotches with pigment but when it came out of the "calendars", those metal rollers which pressed it smooth, it was still full of imperfections. One of the workers whispered "Good riddance!" when it was finally collected on a take-up roll and on its way to the cutters.

The inspectors at the cutters gave it a final nod. The pinkish splotches were noticeable but not terribly so, thus the paper was cut for paperback novels just like the one you're reading now.

News clippings from Eddie Speer's scrapbook:

The Washington County Journal

Gotham Creek Destroyed—The Washington County town of Gotham Creek is gone, according to former town manager and long-time resident Jim Digby. While he declined giving reasons why, he's said in an interview this morning, "...the roads will be closed until further notice, available only to the logging machines of Piston Paper. A detour is being constructed for motorists who wish to reach Route 9 via Route 1..." and he apologized for the inconvenience.

Several former Gotham Creek residents have located to nearby towns and have already encountered problems concerning proof of birth certification as well as social security numbers. Says Pat Nevels, who was born and raised in Gotham Creek, "I just don't understand the problem. Looks like Augusta's filing system is flawed. I'm here, isn't that proof enough?" Gotham Creek's former Constable Hap Kingsley, in a phone interview on Saturday declined comment.

Tunk Lake Chronicle, Nov 14, 1996

Food taken from Spring River Residences—Yesterday morning, the Jackson family of Sprague Falls awoke to find some of the food in their refridgerator missing.

"I don't know what's going on here," Randy Jackson told local constable, Terrance Wakefield. "If someone was hungry and needed the food, I'd gladly share with them. But to break into our houses and take it, now that's just not right."

Residents are warned to keep their doors locked to deter the thief or thieves.

The Columbian Falls Times 11/5/1996

Mystery Surrounds Gotham Creek—One of Maine's communities has virtually disappeared overnight, causing many to wonder what really happened in Gotham Creek, a once thriving town of 650 souls. One cannot help but imagine if this is a current-day ghost town like Roanoke, Virginia or Derry, Vermont.

Undisclosed sources have led this reporter to almost believing the rumors concerning a secret religion not unlike Druidism and possible toxins emitted from Gotham Creek's old silver mine. Something drastic happened there to cause surviving residents to move out almost overnight. But what?

The Franklin Gazetteer 11/20/1996

Reports of Alien Sightings Panic Some, Amaze Others—Shirley McCabe was taking her laundry down from the line just outside her residence when she saw what appeared to be a glowing man standing at the edge of her lawn. "He had to be an alien, an extra-terrestrial," she told reporters and neighbors. "His skin was green in hue and glowing," she added. After being asked if he had approached her or injured her in any manner, McCabe shook her head. "No, he was just standing there, watching me. Then he turned and ran off into the woods."

The FCC and Air Force officials report they have seen nothing unusual on the radar over Maine in recent years. "It sounds like a hoax," says Air National Guard General Vincent Prague. "We've investigated such things in the past and it always turns out the reports are false or exaggerated."

And at the bottom of the page, in Eddie's own handwriting:

An oak grows in the forest. Can you hear it scream?

Printed in the United States
54111LVS00001B/126